STORM OVER CORONADO

Book 1
PICS Series
(Partners in Crime Solving)

Donna Jeremiah
and
Peggy Leslie

XULON PRESS

Storm Over Coronado
by Donna Jeremiah and Peggy Leslie

Printed in the United States of America

ISBN 978-1-60791-313-9

This book is a work of fiction. With the exception of known historical personages, all characters are the product of the authors' imagination. *Storm over Coronado* is set on the island of Coronado, a suburb of San Diego, California. Most of the locales are real. A few, however, are figments of our imaginations. We hope those of you who are familiar with the beautiful island will have fun distinguishing between the two.

www.xulonpress.com

Dedicated to
DAVID AND GENE
with love and many, many thanks
for your love and support
in this project
and in our lives.

ACKNOWLEDGMENTS

"How can I say thanks for the things You have done for me?" These words begin a song that expresses our gratitude to God for guiding and enabling us through the process of writing this book. All the true glory goes to Him.

At the same time, He has used many people to help and encourage us. Without them, our story would have been incomplete. Below are a few who were most helpful.

- Our husbands and families. Thank you for your loving support.
- San Diego Christian Writers Guild, El Cajon Critique Group
- People who allowed us to use their names:
    Linda Elfmon Fleishman and husband Joel,
        Greensboro, North Carolina
    Durant Vick, Roanoke, Virginia
    Tim Volstad (also for information on Norwegian food and
        names), Anchorage, Alaska
- Hotel del Coronado staff
- Sharp Coronado Hospital staff
- Cover design: AmyWhitt
- Pre-editing: Diane Stark, April Leslie, Kate Hagen, Ann Leslie
- Xulon Press staff: Tom Freiling, President; Angelica Garnica, Author Services Manager; Angie Kiesling, Editor; Karen Kochenburger, Publishing Consultant Manager

FOREWORD

For as long as I can remember, I have loved mysteries. I was one of those kids who used to sit on the couch, with my ear next to the radio, listening to "Lights Out," "Suspense," "Mystery Theater," and, scariest of all, "The Shadow." When television came along, I upgraded to "Alfred Hitchcock Presents," and "Murder She Wrote."

It wasn't long after I met Donna that I discovered she too loved mysteries! During our forty-plus years of marriage, I'm sure she has read over one hundred mysteries. All of the Mary Higgins Clark, Mary Jane Clark, and John Grisham books, to name a few.

Somewhere along the way, I got hooked on John Grisham. I remember reading *The Firm* at three o'clock in the morning. For almost two years, I resisted the blockbuster DVD series, *Twenty-Four*, and then in a moment of weakness, I gave in. During a vacation period, we watched the entire Season Five together. "This is absolutely the last episode we're going to watch tonight," we would say. And when that was over, we would look at each other, laugh, and watch the next one.

All this to say, "We love mysteries."

So I guess I shouldn't have been surprised when Donna told me that she and her best friend, Peggy Leslie, were working on a mystery of their own. They were not far into the process before I realized they were very serious about their joint enterprise. They spent hours at our kitchen table, and at Peggy's, laughing and plotting, writing and rewriting. I found out later they actually went on location to the place where their mystery happened and researched the surroundings so that their story would be accurate in every detail.

For a whole year as Donna and Peggy worked on their mystery, I kept asking if I could read what they were writing, and they told me I would be allowed to read it when it was finished. So much for being the head of my family!

A couple of months ago, I was finally given a copy of their story. Now you have to remember that I'm married to one of the authors, but I have to confess that I read their book in less than two days. I did not know "who dunnit" until the very last pages of the book. *Storm Over Coronado* is a great story, with intriguing sub-plots and fascinating characters.

I think I should tell you this book is not a work of theology...it is a mystery...a first-class story about two-long time Christian friends who face a number of heart-wrenching struggles in their personal lives and in their faith. At times, these godly but very human women come through with flying colors; at other times, they are less successful. Still, in the midst of it all, they trust God to see them through. You will not be very far into the story before you are captivated by their struggles, their successes, their failures, and their ultimate faith in their Savior.

On the spine of the book you will see the words, "Partners in Crime Solving No. 1." Peggy's husband, Gene, and I are not sure if the partners in crime are the characters in the story or the authors. We have concluded, however, that if there is a number one in this series, there is probably going to be a number two!

David Jeremiah
San Diego, Ca
May 5, 2009

PROLOGUE

Saturday, August 16

"And now, I think—"

A clap of thunder interrupted Victor Carrington's words. Many of the two hundred guests in the Oceanfront Ballroom of the Hotel del Coronado started at the sound. A murmur of concern came from others who cast worried glances at the sky outside. A few nervously fingered diamond necklaces or tugged at gold cufflinks. Yet all seemed eager for what they knew they were about to hear.

The thunder died down, and Victor continued, "—my brother has a few words for you." He made a sweeping gesture toward the dark-haired, aristocratically handsome man to his right.

Braxton Carrington stood leisurely to warm applause. Dignified, smiling, nodding left and right, he accepted the acclamation as his due.

"Thank you. Thank you all for coming tonight." His rich baritone voice filled the room as he spread his arms and took a slow, deliberate look around. "What better place for this event? What better place than the *Hotel of the Crowned* to announce my intention to press for the honor of mayor of Coronado, the world's greatest little island, the very crown of America's Finest City? My own great-great-grandfather, William Carrington, attended the Del's grand opening in 1888. And I'm proud to say that Carringtons have been active in island civic activities ever since."

Braxton paused, letting the words sink in, subtly reminding his guests that Dominic Giovanni, his major opponent in the mayoral race, was only a second-generation Coronadan.

A ripple of good-natured laughter filled the room, and Braxton thought of how this gala had been a huge success so far. All the right people were here: most of the local elite, several San Diego and State of California officials, and a number of officers from North Island Naval Air Station, all carefully chosen. Even those who didn't particularly care for him agreed that Braxton was the man for the job. Admittedly, a few had good reason to dislike him, but he had them under control.

The laughter died down, and he continued, "Now. Let's get down to the nitty-gritty. Let's talk about where I, as your future mayor, plan to take the island of Coronado."

At that moment, a streak of lightning lit up the moonless sky beyond the huge windows facing the water.

Braxton chuckled. "The weatherman was right for a change. Looks like that storm they've been predicting has hit us."

Smiling at his beautiful wife Cami, seated next to him, he reached for his flute of pink champagne, gave it a little swirl, and took a sip.

Suddenly pain slammed his chest. His glass clattered to the table as both hands clutched the tuxedo fabric over his heart.

"Cami!" he cried out.

The pain sharpened—like someone had stabbed him. He felt himself losing control.

"Cami!" This time the word came out in a hoarse whisper.

He groped toward a white-faced Cami, who had half risen from her chair.

"Ca...."

He collapsed.

Amidst gasps from the guests, a crash of thunder shook the room, and the lights went out.

Tuesday, August 12

Chapter One
Four Days Earlier

*T*he table. I'd better check the table.

With a tug at her Italian striped silk blouse worn over jeans, Cami Carrington rushed to the sunroom of her luxurious home on Coronado, an island suburb of San Diego. Fists jammed against her hips, she surveyed her handiwork with a critical eye.

I'm glad I chose the sunroom. It's the perfect spot for an intimate dinner. That big ol' dining room is just too formal.

Not only was the atmosphere here cozy and intimate, she assured herself, its view of the ocean through the large windows lent an air of romance.

Romance. Ha. I hardly remember what the word means. But tonight... maybe tonight Braxton and I can reconnect. Maybe tonight we can get back those old, wonderful feelings. Maybe tonight he'll....

The jingling of the telephone interrupted Cami's thoughts. She hurried to the nearby kitchen and picked up the receiver.

"Hello."

"You sound a bit rattled," the Boston-accented voice on the other end told her.

"You always could read me, Kate. I never could hide a thing from you."

That was true—had been true since Cami and Kate were roommates at a small Baptist college near Raleigh, North Carolina.

"What's wrong, Cami?" The genuine concern in Kate's voice warmed Cami. "I hoped you'd be happy today."

"Oh, I am!"

"Cami."

"Why shouldn't I be happy?" Cami couldn't help her note of bitterness. "Today's my twenty-second wedding anniversary. I mean, just because I'm not even sure if my husband is going to bother to come home for the special dinner I've prepared."

"I'm so sorry, Cami. I hope my coming to visit won't complicate things."

"Not one bit. I can hardly wait to see you. It's been too long—what, two years?"

"Two years last month."

"Right." Cami smiled. Trust Kate, with her precise, methodical thinking, to know exactly how long it had been. "Anyway, I'll meet you at the San Diego airport at two."

"One fifty."

"Tomorrow afternoon. Like I said, I can hardly wait."

"So, tell me about this special dinner you've planned."

"Okay." Cami was glad to move away from the subject of her relationship with her husband. "The twins are in summer school—at Pepperdine University in Malibu—and the maid, the cook, and the gardener have the night off, so Braxton and I will be alone. And I'm cooking everything myself."

"You're one of the few millionaire's wives I know who would do that."

"Many thanks to Mama's cooking skills." Cami paused, then added, "And to the fact that I didn't grow up wealthy. Besides, this has to be *my* effort."

An uncomfortable silence resounded over the wires.

"Oh, okay. I know what you're thinking. It needs to be mine and *God's*. I may have slipped a bit spiritually over the years, but I haven't left God out of my life. I still go to church pretty regularly, you know. And I've prayed and prayed for this to be one of the most special nights of our marriage."

"I'm not judging you, Cami," Kate answered seriously. "I can see it now," she went on, now speaking lightly. "You're using the sunroom rather than the dining room. The table is set with your Sevres china and Waterford crystal. You're using your best silverware and finest linens. What else? Oh, yes. There's a bouquet of fresh flowers for a centerpiece. Roses? Calla lilies?"

"You're amazing. The flowers are mauve freesias."

"Heavenly. I can smell them all the way to Boston. Steak with mushroom sauce?"

"Chicken Cordon Bleu, ready to slip into the oven. Caesar salad already in the fridge. Raspberry tarts for dessert. We can eat in less than half an hour after Braxton gets home. You'd be proud of me for how organized everything is."

"Well, I won't keep you. But tell me, is the party for Braxton still on for Saturday night?"

The slight hint of disapproval in Kate's tone annoyed Cami a little, even though she herself felt an undeniable tightness inside whenever she thought of the party that would launch Braxton into a bid for mayor of Coronado.

"Yes, it is. And knowing Ashley, it'll be a real blowout."

"Oh, yes. Ashley."

Both women were silent for a moment thinking of the domineering wife of Braxton's younger brother Victor. Ashley owned SeaView Ventures, a business that planned major events for various organizations that took advantage of San Diego's semi-tropical scenery and temperate climate. Braxton had hired her to arrange the gala at the sprawling Victorian-style Hotel del Coronado.

"I'm kind of dreading it, to tell you the truth," said Cami. "You know what? There's a storm predicted for that night."

"In San Diego? In August?"

"Hard to believe, I know. Almost unheard of, in fact. Maybe it will be bad enough to cancel the party."

"Cami!" Kate said in mock surprise.

Cami laughed, and soon both women were giggling like the coeds they once were. Finally, Cami caught her breath and cleared her throat. "Sorry, that was mean. I'm sure the party will go on, and I'm glad you'll be here to hold me up."

"Don't know how much good I'll be." Kate laughed. "But I've already been praying the Lord will hold you up. I hope the outfit I bought will be okay. You know me, I hardly ever dress up."

Cami knew that to be true. Kate had always stuck to the classics, very rarely venturing into trendy or dressy styles. Yet she answered truthfully, "I love your style, Kate. You'll look great."

"One last thing. I guess the twins will be there. Malibu isn't that far away, is it?"

"Two and a half hours. Debra's really excited about the party. You know what a daddy's girl she is. Braxton's proud of the way she's doing so well in her classes."

"And Durant?"

"Things are pretty bad between him and Braxton—especially since he and Debra visited you in Boston two years ago."

"And he decided to give his life to Christ. How well I remember. Anyway, that's one more thing to pray about."

That remark from almost anyone else would have sounded self-righteous to Cami, but she knew Kate's deep sincerity and dedication to God, so she simply said, "Thanks, Kate." Changing the subject, she went on, "By the way, I've done a little checking. San Diego has several RV sales lots. Are you still determined to buy a motorhome and set out across country all by yourself?"

"Sure thing. Can't think of a better way to spend my sabbatical from Boston U."

"Better you than me. What about Gunther?"

"Gunnar. Volstad."

"The big, lovable Norwegian from Minnesota. I thought you two were getting serious."

"I don't know, Cami. When you've had what I had with Joel...."

"Kate, he's been gone for four years."

"Four years and five months. When he died, I never thought anyone would ever appeal to me again."

"And along comes Gunnar, who not only adores you, but is a solid Christian to boot. Oh, Kate." Cami breathed a deep sigh of sympathy. "How's he feel about being away from you for a whole year?"

"Not happy. But I've told him I need to get away and pray about the matter. It's too hard when I'm with him. Look, we'll talk about all that in—ta-da!—California!"

"Can't wait. See you tomorrow afternoon at 1:50!"

Chapter Two

Kate Elfmon stared long and thoughtfully at the telephone she held. Shaking her head to clear thoughts of Cami Carrington's marriage woes, she returned the receiver to its cradle. She had too much to do to prepare for her flight to San Diego tomorrow to waste one minute of her time.

The Lord's voice was unmistakable. ***Waste your time, Kate? Is that what you call feeling concern for your friend?***

Instantly chagrined, Kate closed her eyes. *I'm sorry, Lord. If You'll tell me how to pray for Cami, I'll do it.* She paused and looked sheepishly upward. *Is it okay if I finish packing while I'm at it?*

Kate folded a pair of dark blue pants as her mind wandered back to the first time she heard of Cami.

Kate was enrolled as a freshman at Compton College, a small Baptist girls' school near Raleigh, North Carolina. She was supposed to room with another New Englander, a girl from Connecticut. That suited Kate perfectly. A serious student, she didn't want to get saddled with some fluffy Southerner more interested in the social scene than in education.

However, the day she arrived at her dorm room, she saw a willowy, spiral-permed blond taking a pink ruffled blouse from a purple trunk and transferring it to a chest already scattered with perfume bottles and makeup. Surely this wasn't—

The phone rang. Any fleeting hope Kate had entertained that this girl was from Connecticut flitted away at the sound of the pronounced drawl that answered, "Hello. Yes ma'am, this is Camilla Leigh Stewart."

Her back to Kate, she continued, "No ma'am, she hasn't arrived yet. I'll let her know. Bye now."

"Let me know what?" Kate heard how her clipped speech contrasted with this Camilla Leigh Stewart's drawl.

"Oh!" The other girl spun around, her smoky blue eyes wide with surprise. "You must be Katherine Kelly." She smiled widely and extended one pink-nailed hand. "I'm Cami Stewart. That girl from Connecticut—lucky dog—got married. I'm your roommate."

Kate felt like heading back to Boston.

No two people could have been—and still are—more opposite, Kate thought now as she placed a conservative beige outfit in her suitcase.

She pictured the two of them in those days: tall, beautiful, blond Cami and petite, dark-haired, brown-eyed Kate. But the contrast went far beyond physical differences. Cami came from a loving, religious home with two older brothers. Kate was the only child of an agnostic couple whose existence revolved around politics and university life. Kate had arrived long after they expected to start a family. Though they treated her kindly, Kate came to realize she was an intrusion in their well-ordered lives.

One reason Kate had chosen a girls' school was to eliminate the distraction of male students. However, their absence on campus did nothing to limit Cami's social life. Soon Kate was gritting her teeth at the unending phone calls and Cami's Southern purr.

"Hey there, Beau." (Did every Southern family have a Beau or Bubba or Buddy?) *"This weekend? You're drivin' up to see me? All the way from Atlanta? I can't wait!"*

"Oh, Winston, I'd love to go to a Wolfpack game with you."

"Robert, I got a part in the play the Drama Club's doing! You've got to promise me you'll come and see it."

Kate joined the Debate Club.

To the amazement of both girls, little by little their very differences drew them together. Before long, Kate learned that Cami was not the airhead she appeared to be. Behind that pretty face was an intelligent mind and a sensitive spirit. And Cami managed to delve into Kate's no-nonsense approach and methodical mindset to find a heart more caring and tender than Kate had ever revealed to anyone else. By the end of the first semester they had formed a friendship that was a source of deep joy to both of them.

A joy that remains to this day. Kate smiled, looking down at the Bible she was about to pack. She ran her fingertips over its worn leather before placing it on top of the pile of clothing.

Near the end of their freshman year Cami handed Kate a printed flyer.

"What's this?" Kate asked.

Cami looked a little uncomfortable. "It's, um, about that speaker I mentioned to you."

"That religious speaker, you mean." Kate had actually curled her lip as she spoke.

"I don't understand you, Kate." Cami threw up her hands in exasperation. "Why did you bother coming to a Christian school if you're against anything that's the teeniest bit religious?"

"Because of the school's excellent educational reputation," Kate replied, knowing she sounded pompous and feeling a little surprised at Cami. The girl was so easy-going and amenable that she rarely put forth arguments. "And I wanted to get away from Boston." *And my parents,* she didn't add. "Anyway, I thought we'd agreed you wouldn't try to drag me along to your little meetings."

"And I think I've done pretty good."

Kate had to agree. Cami had never tried to force her faith on her. Actually, Kate thought she treated it rather lightly despite her involvement with a campus Bible study.

"Anyway," Cami said, "I've heard that this woman comes at it from a really intellectual point of view. I think you'd like it."

In the end Kate reluctantly accepted Cami's invitation, never suspecting that before the last amen, she would give her heart and soul unreservedly to Jesus Christ. Never would she have believed how that one act could so fill her life, influencing her every thought, word, and deed. And the love she felt, both received from and given to her new Lord! Never had she experienced such joy—certainly not in a home where open expressions of affection were frowned upon. How, she often wondered, *how* could Cami maintain such a casual attitude toward her salvation?

That attitude hasn't improved in her twenty-two years of marriage to Braxton Carrington, has it, Lord? Kate frowned and closed her suit-case with unnecessary force. *Is that what You want me to pray about, Father—Cami's spiritual condition? Or maybe the state of her marriage?*

Both, Kate. Both.

Kate set aside the compulsion to put her second suitcase in order and fell to her knees to pray for her dearest friend. About the time she arose, her doorbell rang. She rushed to answer it, knowing whose face she would see and trying to deny a delicious surge of excitement.

Chapter Three

"She's lost her mind!" Gunnar Volstad muttered to Boston's warm summer evening air.

He shifted his large frame from side to side on the front stoop of Kate Elfmon's house. Usually, as he waited for her to answer the bell, he allowed himself a moment to appreciate the tall, narrow two-hundred-year-old brick home Kate had grown up in. In this city famous for its history and intellectualism, it suited her.

Tonight he was too agitated to notice, his normally easygoing temperament on edge.

He kept muttering. "Okay. Okay. So she's lost her mind. But don't say that to her, Volstad." *Not if you don't want to see the sparks fly. Kate may be a dedicated Christian woman, but she's not half Irish for nothing.*

Gunnar had met Kate a year ago at a prophecy conference sponsored by their church. He was immediately drawn to the serene glow in her eyes and later to her dry wit tempered by compassion. True, her driving perfectionism sometimes set his teeth on edge; on the other hand, it was a balance for his own laid-back personality.

By their third date Gunnar knew Kate could be the answer to the deep loneliness he had felt since the death of his wife Brita several years earlier. Besides everything else, Kate displayed the deep, genuine faith Gunnar sincerely desired in a life partner. Such faith, he knew, was rare in a person of her intellect.

But that's not all, he thought, grinning, shaking his head and thinking of how Kate stirred his blood and quickened his pulse. *No wonder I'm in love with that maddening creature.*

During these past six months, Gunnar thought things were progressing nicely. He was sure he'd seen a lessening in her obsessive clinging to the memory of her late husband Joel. Then, a couple of weeks ago, Kate up and announced she was going to take a yearlong sabbatical from her position as a professor of Political Science and—he could hardly fathom the idea—travel the U.S. in a motorhome! No doubt about it. She'd lost her mind.

"Don't say that to her, Volstad," he told himself again. He'd seen her eyes flare with anger or indignation a few times and didn't want to be on the wrong side of her.

When he'd begun to think Kate would never answer, he heard the lock turn. She cracked the door to the end of the safety chain and peeked through.

"When did you start talking to yourself?" she quipped as she fiddled with the chain.

"You know what they say."

"What do they say?"

"When you talk to yourself, you always know somebody's listening."

"And you always get the answer you want," she said, releasing the chain.

Suddenly, Gunnar felt hesitant, a little shy, an unfamiliar and uncomfortable sensation for him. Still standing on the stoop, he drank in the sight of her, from the dark hair falling in a soft chin-length bob, to the high cheekbones that bespoke a spec of Native American blood, to those amazing chocolate brown eyes.

Kate gave him her brilliant smile—the one that spread slowly from her lips to her eyes to her whole face and transformed her attractive countenance into a thing of beauty. He opened his arms and she walked into them and laid her head on his broad chest.

"Kate, my Kate," he whispered, pulling her closer to him. He lowered his head and gave her sweet lips a lingering kiss.

She leaned into his embrace for a few seconds before giving him a gentle shove away. "Mr. Volstad, how you distract me." Her teasing voice was a little shaky. She took his hand and pulled him inside.

"Don't expect me to apologize. One of my greatest desires is to totally distract you."

"For shame! What if your Bible study class heard you?"

"They'd think, 'Maybe ol' Gunnar's finally about to rejoin the ranks of respectable married people.' They'd throw a party!"

Gunnar almost groaned out loud. *How could I be so stupid? Hardly in the house and making remarks that put her on her guard. Slow down, Volstad, slow down.*

Kate's smile faltered and she released his hand. By now she had led him past the semi-formal living room and dining room to her bright but cozy kitchen.

"Look." She gestured toward a small round oak table that had, like many pieces in the house, been in Kate's family for several generations. He appreciated how she felt free to mix cherished antique pieces with more contemporary ones. The combination made for a charming, homey atmosphere.

After pulling out a sturdy carved-back chair for Kate, he lowered himself into the one across from her.

"Vell," he said, putting on his best Norwegian accent and indicating the plate in the middle of the table, "vat haf ve here?"

"Ve haf *kringlaf.*" Her own mocking Norwegian accent was not half bad as she pointed to a figure-eight-shaped coffeecake sprinkled with almonds.

"*Kringlaf?* The assistant head professor of Political Science at one of the country's most prestigious universities made *kringlaf?*"

"You've got to be kidding. Fresh from the oven at Olsen's Bakery this very morning. You should know by now that I'm the world's worst cook."

Having grown up in a small Norwegian community in Minnesota where arrays of mouthwatering delicacies were everyday delights, and having tasted some of Kate's culinary efforts, Gunnar couldn't refute her words. He chuckled and held out his plate.

As they consumed the delicious, not-too-sweet dessert, they talked casually about the weather, Gunnar's work at Hub Digital Corporation, mutual friends at church—everything except the subject Gunnar knew was uppermost in both their minds. When he couldn't bear to avoid the issue another minute, he eased into it by referring to the first part of her trip.

"Have you talked with Cami today?"

Kate tensed a little, clearly aware of where this conversation was going. "About an hour ago."

"I'm sure she's looking forward to your visit," he said, cutting himself another piece of *kringlaf.*

"She is. But she was a little preoccupied, so we didn't talk long."

"Mmmm. I'd have thought 'Miss Bubbly' would be too excited to be preoccupied."

Kate frowned. "Cami may be a very outgoing, enthusiastic person, but empty-headed 'Miss Bubbly' she is not. Her preoccupation had nothing to do with me."

Gunnar waited for Kate to explain.

"Today is her and Braxton's twenty-second wedding anniversary, and she was in the midst of preparing a special meal. I've told you before she's an excellent cook. " She smiled ruefully. "Not at all like yours truly."

Something in Kate's voice made Gunnar ask, "Trouble in Paradise?"

Kate pushed around the crumbs on her plate. When she answered, she sounded sad but not surprised. "Yes."

"You don't like Braxton much, do you?"

"I've never liked him from the day I first laid eyes on him when Cami and I were in college. I didn't trust him then, and I don't trust him now. I tried to warn Cami about him, but she was so completely mesmerized she hardly even heard me."

"Why do you dislike him so much?"

"Besides the fact that he's arrogant, patronizing, and controlling? I can hardly bear the thought of his running for political office."

It surprised Gunnar to hear Kate make such critical remarks. "Doesn't the poor fella have *any* good qualities?"

"Poor fellow? One of the richest men in Southern California? Sorry. That was judgmental. Well, let me see. Braxton is an astute businessman. He gives generously to several charities. But that may be for tax purposes. Besides, it looks good for a political aspirant. There I go, being judgmental again." Kate put one finger to her forehead. "Let me think. Braxton's good qualities. He's extremely good-looking. And, oh yes, he adores his daughter, Debra."

"What about the other twin—the son? The one you led to the Lord?"

"Durant? Let's just say that Braxton and Durant rarely see eye to eye."

"Hmmm. And as a husband? Is Braxton good to Cami?"

"If you call playing big daddy to a helpless little girl being good, I guess so. He certainly provides her with anything her heart desires, as long as she accounts for it," Kate said. "Now. Let's think of something more pleasant to talk about."

Gunnar leaned the chair back on two legs, seriously testing its stability. He crossed his big arms over his chest. His eyes searched hers for several seconds before he let the chair down with a bang. He could feel his expression go stony when he said, "The only subject on my mind is not one you'd call pleasant."

"Please, Gunnar. We've gone over all this before. I *am* going to visit Cami for several days, then fly up to Oregon to teach a class at Portland University for a month. While I'm in San Diego I *am* going to buy a small motorhome. And when I get back there, I *am* going to travel around in it for several months, maybe the rest of my sabbatical."

"And you've prayed about it, you say." Gunnar could hear a sarcastic edge in his words.

"You know I have," she shot back.

Gunnar stood abruptly and said exactly what he'd cautioned himself not to. "You have lost your mind!" He winced, wishing instantly that he could call back his words.

Kate sprang to her feet. "I have *not* lost my mind! I know exactly what I'm doing."

"Tell me this, then. Have you ever even driven a motorhome?"

"No. So what?"

"I'll let that pass. Do you have any idea what's involved with setting it up when you find an RV park?"

"I've researched it all quite thoroughly."

"You would."

"When I buy a motorhome, they'll teach me what I need to know. Besides," Kate went on in an exasperated tone, "if I managed to get a Doctorate in Poly-Sci, I think I can figure out how to park a small RV."

"Why do you want to be away for nearly a year? I love you. I want to marry you. It cuts me to the core that you're willing to be gone from me so long with no regrets."

Kate turned her back on him. "Who said it was with no regrets?"

Gunnar seized her arm and turned her to face him again. "Then why? Tell me why!"

"You're hurting me. Let me go." He dropped his arms to his sides. "I'm confused, Gunnar. That's why."

She began to pace the floor. "I never thought I'd marry at all. I thought the Lord simply wanted me to get my education and teach, trying to be a Christian influence on my students. I was perfectly content doing those things—until a few days after my thirty-third birthday. That's when I met Joel Elfmon. In no time he changed my mind completely." She paused, seemingly lost in a sweet remembrance that shut Gunnar out. "Joel and I had five wonderful years together. After he died, I knew I'd never marry again. It wasn't something I decided. I just knew. Now you come along and…and… Oh, I don't know. I just don't know!"

"Don't know what?" Gunnar asked quietly. "If you love me or not? If you don't, I'll try to accept that and let you alone."

Kate looked down and didn't reply at first. After a few moments that seemed like hours to Gunnar, she said in a whisper so low he could barely hear her, "No, that's not it. I do…care for you…deeply. But—"

The term "care deeply" rather than "love" wasn't lost on Gunnar.

"But you're still tied to Joel." His words were a firm statement. When she didn't answer, he pushed on. "That's it, isn't it?"

When Kate looked up, tears were cascading down her face. She nodded. Gunnar felt like she'd kicked him.

"Four years later, and you're still married to a memory. I'm sorry, Kate, I would fight a living man for you, but I can't fight a memory." His voice full of regret, he said, "I'll go now and pray that God will keep you safe. Good night."

He strode away from Kate.

"Wait! Don't go, Gunnar. Don't go!"

"There seems to be nothing for me to stay for." He slammed the door and went outside.

On the stoop, he paused. If she beckoned him back, he would go. He waited. Soon he heard the lock click, the chain rattle. He took the steps two at a time down to the street to his car. In seconds he was speeding away from Kate's house.

***

Inside, Kate slid to the floor, leaned her head against the wall, and sobbed.

Chapter Four

Victor Carrington pushed his way through the plate-glass revolving door of the Carrington Building in downtown San Diego. With a curt nod to the pretty receptionist, he headed for the private elevator that led to the penthouse suite and his brother Braxton's office. Victor's own two-room office suite was on the *second* to the top floor.

As befits the second in command, he thought bitterly.

A minute later he quietly entered a thick-carpeted, mahogany-paneled reception room. Braxton's administrative assistant, Rosita DeLuca, was bent over, evidently picking up something from the floor. Good. He could slip past her. He didn't want to deal with her today.

Too late. In a blink of her humorless brown eyes, Rosita jumped up and blocked his way.

"You move fast, Rosie," said Victor, his voice a deliberate sensual drawl that he knew irritated her as much as being called Rosie. He leaned his lanky frame toward her and placed his hand over her head against the door.

Rosita stiffened still more. "May I help you, Mr. Carrington?"

Her voice held a hint of her Mexican ancestry and could have been charming if she'd only let it, Victor thought. He took in her tailored charcoal suit, slit-like rimless glasses, and black hair pulled back into a severe bun and tried to imagine her with a little more makeup and more feminine clothing. The image wouldn't gel.

He lowered his arm, stepped back, and made a formal bow. "Ms. DeLuca, would you please buzz Mr. Braxton Carrington and tell him Mr. Victor Carrington would very much like to converse with him?"

At the same time, he thought, *One of these days I'm going to tell her I've known for years she's in love with my brother.*

"If you'll take a seat." She motioned to the thick leather chairs on the other side of the reception area.

Victor threw up both hands in mock defeat and moved away. Eyeing him suspiciously, Rosita returned to her desk and buzzed Braxton.

Rather than sit down, Victor paused before a large original LeRoy Neiman oil of several horses rounding a curve similar to the one at San Diego's famous Del Mar Racetrack. Admiring the exploding colors in the painting, he thought of how an appreciation for horse-racing was one of the few things he and his brother had in common.

He moved away from the painting. It reminded him too much of the reason he was about to humble himself before the older brother he both adored and hated and in whose shadow he'd lived his entire forty-three years.

Chapter Five

Though Rosita DeLuca appeared engrossed at her computer, she was aware of Victor's every move. She saw the pacing, the tense jaw, the repeated glancing at his watch. As she watched from the corner of her eye, she wondered how three men—Victor, his brother Braxton, and Braxton's son Durant—could look so much alike, but be so different.

Durant was nearly as tall as his father and had the same broad shoulders and tapering waist. As for Braxton—as she always addressed her employer in her private thoughts—his physique was more mature, but only a little less lean. Victor, four years younger than Braxton, was the tallest of the three, but thinner. Father and son both had strong faces with high cheekbones, square jaws, and what Rosita had heard Cami Carrington call "noble noses." Victor was good-looking, too, but his less forceful character seemed to have implanted itself on his features.

All three men had very dark straight hair above deep blue eyes.

Los ojos, Rosita thought. *The eyes. That's the difference. Yes, they are the same color, but Durant's—they are* dulce—*sweet—and gentle. But Victor's look shifty. Braxton's, on the other hand....*

A small shiver swept through her. Braxton's piercing blue eyes could boost her confidence one minute, reduce her to near tears the next, and melt her insides the next—all emotions she was careful not to display to her employer. She'd never tried to fool herself. She was in love with the man. Had been from the first day she walked into Carrington Investments to interview for a file clerk position.

That was twenty-four years ago, two years before Braxton married that ultra-feminine Southerner, Cami Stewart. As twenty-year-old Rosita had entered the building's reception area with its soaring ceiling and marble floor, a tall man hurried in her direction. His navy blue suit emphasized his black hair and good looks. As he neared her, he bent his head over a thick document.

She stepped to one side. He moved in the same direction. And ran right into her. The document fell and scattered across the floor.

"Oh sir! I am sorry. I am so sorry," Rosita wailed, while Braxton let out a curse.

Rosita dropped to her knees and scrambled to gather the pages, quickly putting them in numerical order as she went along. Cursing again, Braxton joined her.

Finally Rosita tapped the stack against the floor and quickly rose to her feet. The man rose at the same time, and their heads banged together.

Rosita jumped back and looked up—into the most intense blue eyes in the handsomest face she'd ever seen. A thrill of exhilaration danced up her arms. But immediately the exhilaration became horror. What had she done? Bumping into an influential-looking man the very day she was applying for a job!

"I am so sorry!" she repeated, thinking she could kiss this job goodbye. Without another word, she thrust the papers into the man's hands, intending to flee.

His deep voice stopped her. "My fault," he said. "I should have been paying attention to where I was going." He studied her face for a moment. "You are...."

"Rosita DeLuca." She could hardly get the words out.

"What department do you work in?" His face was serious. Stern. Was he planning to report her?

"I do not work here, sir. I-I have come to apply for a job."

The man took her arm and led her, almost stumbling, to the receptionist's desk. As they neared it, he asked Rosita, "Who is interviewing you?"

"Miss Godwin." Oh no, he was going to tell the receptionist to cancel the interview. And she needed this job desperately.

He let go of Rosita's arm and pulled a pen and small pad from his pocket. He scribbled a few words, folded the paper over and handed it to Rosita.

"Miss Lockamy," he said tersely to the receptionist, "ring Miss Godwin and tell her that Miss…."

"DeLuca." *He's already forgotten my name. Maybe that is good.*

"Miss DeLuca is coming right up with a note from me."

"But, sir," the receptionist said, eyeing Rosita. "Miss Godwin is interviewing someone else right now. And several other applicants are waiting."

The man gave Miss Lockamy a look that clearly asked, *Are you questioning me?* "Tell her to wind up that interview immediately and to see Miss DeLuca next." He gave Rosita a brief nod and left, striding to an area beyond the reception desk.

Confused, Rosita stood frozen to her spot. Melinda Lockamy's sarcastic words brought her out of her daze. "Well, you certainly know your way around, don't you?"

"I don't know what you mean." Rosita's chin went up.

"Accidentally bumping into Braxton Carrington? Good job, honey. It worked." Her disdainful look took in Rosita's plain features, simple hairdo, and nondescript dress that did nothing for her feminine curves.

Rosita drew in a sharp breath. "That was Mr. Carrington? I thought he was much older."

"Drop the act, *Miss* DeLuca. I'm sure you're perfectly aware that was *Braxton* Carrington, Arthur Carrington's oldest son—and heir to the throne."

"I did not know!" Rosita said. She started to protest further, but stopped. Words her immigrant grandfather had often spoken came to her. *Do not let anyone make you feel small, mí Rosita,* he would say. *God made you as good as anyone else in this wonderful country.*

Rosita straightened and gave the receptionist a level stare. "I will go up and see Miss Godwin now. Please let her know I am on my way." Clutching the slip of paper Braxton had given her, she looked back as she walked away and smiled to see the receptionist's mouth hanging open.

Braxton had written three words on the note to Miss Godwin: "Hire this woman."

Rosita got the file clerk job. A quick learner, she soon moved to the secretarial pool, where she immediately caught on to the recently installed computer system. At that time, fewer people had mastered computer skills.

Rosita never dreamed she'd ever have another conversation—if you could call that brief meeting a conversation—with the devastatingly good-looking man who was groomed to take over his father's business one day. Then, several months later, Braxton fired his administrative assistant (the third in a year). The very next day he called Rosita into his office.

She had used every ounce of willpower to appear outwardly calm that day, though her insides felt like a mass of guava jelly. How many times had she dreamed of being near Braxton Carrington? Over the months, a dozen scenarios had floated through her dreams. But none had included his calling her to his office. Seated across from his massive desk, she forced herself to hold her hands lightly, not clutched, in her lap.

Braxton leaned back in his chair and didn't speak for a few seconds. His blue eyes seemed to pierce right through her. She wondered if her lipstick were smeared or her hair out of place. No. She'd checked the mirror before coming to his office. Then maybe she looked too plain in her simple brown dress.

"Relax, Ms. DeLuca," Braxton said abruptly. "I've never bitten an interviewee yet."

Fired a few, though, Rosita thought, but simply said, "Yes, sir."

"You're wondering why I sent for you."

"Yes, sir."

"I'm going to tell you something my competitors would be wise to learn."

"Sir?"

"It's not a good thing to underestimate my powers of observation."

"I'm not sure I understand, sir."

"Do you remember the day we literally bumped into each other?"

Oh no! "Yes, I do. And I will always be grateful for your recommendation to—"

"And the pages of my document went flying to the floor?"

"I remember." *How could I forget?*

"Do you remember what you did?"

Rosita shrugged. "I picked them up and handed them back to you."

"You did. But first you automatically put the pages in order and stacked them neatly as you gathered them up."

Rosita gave Braxton a blank look. "Isn't that what anyone would do?"

"No. You were flustered and embarrassed, but your natural sense of order took over." He gave Rosita a few moments to digest his words. "When I left you, rather than immediately leave the building, I stood out of sight and observed your exchange with Melinda Lockamy. She was offensive and patronizing, but you didn't let her get the better of you. Maybe you know, by the way, that Miss Lockamy is no longer employed by Carrington Investments."

"I knew I hadn't seen her around, but—"

"Over the months since you were hired, I've kept track of your work record and observed your demeanor."

"I hardly know what to say, sir."

"You can say that you'll consider stepping in as my new administrative assistant."

Rosita opened her mouth to speak but was glad Braxton again interrupted, as she had no idea what words would come out.

"The pay will be a substantial increase. But you'll earn every cent. I'm the ultimate perfectionist."

He fell silent, and two thoughts jetted through Rosita's brain. First, she knew her employer would think of her in much the same way as a valuable and functional piece of office equipment that would be replaced as soon as it malfunctioned or became outdated. Second, she was irrevocably attracted to Braxton Carrington, and the only future she would ever have with him would be as his employee.

She lifted her chin and put on the most confident expression she could muster.

"Perfectionism is not a deterrent for me, Mr. Carrington."

He grinned slightly. "I'll take that as a yes, Ms. DeLuca." He looked at his desk calendar. "Today is Wednesday. I'll expect you here first thing Monday morning."

"I'll be here, sir."

"That'll be all, then." He bent his head to some papers on his desk. As Rosita rose to leave, he looked up again, his gaze running up and down the plain brown dress. "By the way, you're not to come to work tomorrow or Friday. I expect you to spend the next few days acquiring a wardrobe suitable for this position. Please close the door on your way out." He went back to his paperwork.

From that day on, Rosita made it her life goal to make herself indispensable to Braxton Carrington. She came to know everything about him from the way he liked his business letters worded, to which visitors to let in immediately and which to keep waiting, to how much sugar he liked in his coffee. Her last thought every night was a prayer that he would never find reason to fire her.

For twenty-four years that prayer had been answered. But recently she had noticed the gleam in Braxton's eyes whenever Victor's stunning blond secretary came into view. Rosita was accustomed to Braxton's appreciation of feminine beauty, but somehow she sensed something different this time. Scarlett Starling was a shapely former Miss California who capably combined beauty with efficiency. And she was only twenty-five years old.

Click. The sound interrupted her musings. While she was daydreaming, Victor had slipped past her! She sprang to her feet.

Victor grinned in her direction before entering Braxton's office. "You're slipping, Rosie."

Chapter Six

Braxton, sitting at the huge desk in his elegant office, deliberately spent a minute pretending to make notes on a document before looking up when Victor came in.

"Come off it, Brax," Victor said, dropping into a chair. "Don't try your tricks on me."

Amused, Braxton laid down his pen. "And what tricks are those, little brother?" Anyone else would have squirmed at the diminutive nickname, but Victor was one of those people who lived life for the moment, rarely letting anything rattle him. Braxton hated to admit that he sometimes envied Victor his cavalier attitude, despite the exasperation and trouble—not to mention the money—it so often cost.

"What tricks?" Victor responded, looking equally amused. "The tricks you taught me yourself. You know—when someone enters your office, put on an air of indifference for a few moments. That rarely fails to inject a measure of nervousness and uncertainty in the other person, thus giving you a corresponding measure of power." He spoke as though reciting a lesson from a textbook. "Also, cause the guest further intimidation by not offering him a seat." Victor patted the arm of his chair.

"You learn well," Braxton said, making a tent of his fingertips. "What's up?"

Playing for time, Victor said, "Are you ready for your little coming out party Saturday night?"

"I'm sure you didn't pay me the honor of a visit to chat about the party. But since you brought it up, how are the plans going?"

"Perfectly. Every detail down to the last flower petal and lighted ice cube will have to meet Ashley's personal approval." A small twitch touched Victor's mouth before he went on. "By the time the evening's over, every guest will be vying to write the largest donation check to ensure Braxton Carrington becomes the next mayor of Coronado. Dominic Giovanni doesn't stand a chance."

Braxton called Giovanni a rude name. "If we let him in, he'll destroy Coronado's island atmosphere. Do you know he wants to tear down several historic structures and build a monstrosity of a hotel?" Seeing Victor's mouth quirk in amusement, Braxton relaxed a little. "Yes, I guess you do know. Nobody's heard my tirades more often than you. I repeat, what's up?"

Victor languidly crossed one long leg over the other. Without preamble, he said, "I need money."

"I wonder why that doesn't surprise me." The brotherly bantering over, Braxton pushed back his own deep leather chair and resorted to another of his favorite tricks: standing tall, forcing the other person to look up at him.

He half expected Victor, who knew that ruse well and often employed it himself, to stand, too. Instead, the younger man settled more deeply into his chair and fixed his attention on another LeRoy Neiman painting. This one was smaller than the one in the reception area, but equally as vibrant. His voice held an edge when he said, "Nothing surprises you, does it, Brax?"

"Not much when it comes to you and money." Braxton waited for Victor to continue.

Still contemplating the painting, Victor replied, "I need fifty thousand dollars."

"Fifty thousand dollars! *Fifty* thousand?"

Victor tapped his mouth in a mock yawn. "Fifty thou is a drop in the till to you."

"With what you get, it should be to you, too."

"You mean with what you dole out to me?" Victor dropped his languid pose and sprang to life. "Here I am, forty-three years old and still getting an 'allowance' from my big brother."

"Look. That's how Dad set up his will. The point is, if he hadn't put you on an allowance, I hate to think what state the business would

be in. All the same, you get more than enough to toss after your...
pursuits." Braxton took a deep breath. "What's it for this time?"

Without replying, Victor rose, stepped around his brother, and
stood before the Neiman painting.

Braxton thought he understood the move. "You've borrowed money
to bet on the horses—again! I should be used to that by now."

"Don't sound so righteous. I've seen you lay out what some people
would consider a small fortune on your favorite filly."

"Money I knew I could afford to lose and only after a great deal of
research. Don't forget, I seldom miss."

"Ooh, no. Perfect big brother never misses, on anything. It's not for
the horses. But I did first meet my 'creditor' at Del Mar during a race.
And he's breathing down my neck now."

Braxton's eyes narrowed. "If it's not for the races, what is it for?"

"Viejas."

Braxton didn't need Viejas explained to him. Nestled in a desert
valley and surrounded by imported palms, Viejas was a gambling
casino on an Indian reservation by the same name. It was only about
a forty-five-minute drive from San Diego, down Interstate 8. Though
Braxton rarely gambled and Camilla (whom he refused to call by the
cutesy "Cami" that everyone else used) considered it sinful, the two
sometimes had a meal at the casino's excellent restaurant.

Braxton exploded and spent the next couple of minutes loudly
cursing Victor and berating him for his stupidity, finally ending by
spitting out, "You're not getting another penny out of me for one of
your gambling debts!"

Victor said little during his brother's tirade, but his face grew darker
with each shouted insult. Finally, he cut Braxton off in the middle of a
particularly scathing remark. "Forget it! I can see you don't care if they
find me in an alley with my throat slit!"

"Don't be dramatic, Vic. It doesn't become you."

Victor spun around, stopped, and spun back. "You may not be so
unfeeling if a newspaper gets hold of the story that the great Braxton
Carrington's brother is nothing but a lowly gambler. What would that
do for your precious political dreams?" He stomped to the door, flung
it open, and banged it closed.

"Wait!" Braxton called out, taken by surprise for a change. He had immediately thought of the political implications and was already planning to advance the money to Victor. But he thought his brother needed to beg a little first.

He rushed out of the room to his reception area. Victor was already gone. Braxton heard the phone ring as he sped past Rosita's desk.

"Mr. Carrington!" Rosita called out. "Senator Fremont is on the line."

Braxton stopped. Fremont was one of his most enthusiastic backers in the mayoral bid. Reluctantly, he headed back to his office.

"I'll take it," he told Rosita.

He'd settle with Victor later.

Chapter Seven

Rosita wondered only briefly what this latest confrontation between the Carrington brothers was about. Before the week was over she'd know exactly what had happened. A few years ago she'd gone to Radio Shack and bought two tiny battery-operated, voice-activated tape recorders, along with a box of tapes. She installed one recorder to the underside of Braxton's desk; the other she kept at home. Most days she was able to retrieve the tape and take it home. Every Friday she would listen to tapes from the past week. Usually the results were dull, and Rosita would rewind and reuse the tape.

Occasionally, however, the conversations revealed secrets that Braxton's visitors—almost all important people in the city and state—would be deeply embarrassed to have known. These tapes she kept in a shoebox in a file cabinet in her bedroom. She wasn't sure why, except that possessing them gave her a sense of power and even superiority over people who looked right through her as though she were a piece of glass.

For the second time in less than an hour, a figure burst into the reception room, this time, Scarlett Starling.

"Ms. DeLuca, I need to see Mr. Carrington right away."

In a glance Rosita took in Scarlett's white-blond hair and a figure that looked shapely even in the conservative tan pant suit.

Who does she think she is, bursting in here and demanding to see Braxton? Rosita thought, but her voice was emotionless when she said, "He's very busy, Ms. Starling." She pointedly looked at her watch. "Perhaps if you come back in an hour."

"This can't wait an hour. I need to see him right now!"

"Well, if you insist, I'll buzz him."

Scarlett leaned down, placed both palms on the desk, and looked straight into Rosita's eyes. "I insist." She held an office memo note between two fingers of one hand.

Just then Braxton came out of his office. "Hello, Scarlett," he said affably.

Rosita cringed. Braxton never used *her* given name. It was always, "Ms. DeLuca this. Ms. DeLuca that."

"Mr. Carrington, I have to talk with you right away," Scarlett said. She looked toward Rosita, as if unsure how much more to say, then burst out, "It's about your brother."

Braxton's manner changed abruptly. "Come right in." He took Scarlett's arm and led her into his office. In his rush, he didn't close the door all the way.

Rosita's eyes glistened with glee. She didn't need to wait till Friday to hear this conversation. She stood and moved nearer, being careful to remain out of sight.

She heard Braxton ask, "What is it?"

"A couple of minutes ago I took a phone call for Mr. Carrington. I mean, for your brother."

"And? Get to the point."

"It was a man. He didn't identify himself. He said Victor—Mr. Carrington—would know who it was. He told me to write down this message word for word."

Rosita heard Scarlett rattle the paper.

"Give it to me," Braxton commanded. "*Vicky Boy,*" he read aloud. "*You have one week to get the money to me. Or else.*" He paused. "And he didn't give you a name?"

"No, sir, he didn't. He gave me that message and hung up."

"Mmm," said Braxton. "Vicky Boy. Vicky Boy. Why does that sound familiar?" Before long he let out an ominous sounding chuckle. When he spoke next, Rosita could picture his charming smile. "I'll take care of this, Scarlett. Don't you worry your pretty little head about it. Why don't you go on home now? You seem a little shaken."

Hearing the two heading her way, Rosita quickly slipped back to her desk.

"I can't go home right now," Scarlett said as she and Braxton walked out. "My car is in the shop. I'll take the six o'clock bus home. I'll get a few things done while I wait."

"No need for that. I'm leaving in a few minutes. Let me make a couple of calls to take care of this situation. When I'm done, I'll drive you home."

Imagining Scarlett ensconced cozily next to Braxton in his sleek silver Jaguar, Rosita felt ill. She rose, being careful to move normally, not letting her distress show. "I can drive her, Mr. Carrington," she said. "I'm finished here, and you have to get home for your anniversary dinner."

There. Mentioning the anniversary would remind Scarlett that Braxton was a married man. Not that the young woman had ever been known for any kind of immorality. Still, it couldn't hurt to remind her.

"No, Ms. DeLuca, I'll do it." Braxton's tone brooked no argument. "Scarlett, go get your things. I'll be ready in about fifteen minutes."

"Well, if you're sure," Scarlett said.

"I never say anything unless I'm sure. Meet me in the lobby."

Rosita, watching Scarlett leave, clenched her fists, digging her nails into her flesh so hard it brought pain almost as severe as that roiling in her heart.

Chapter Eight

In his office Braxton immediately called Viejas Casino and asked for a certain poker dealer named Jim Bowman. Several weeks earlier Braxton and Camilla had joined Victor and Ashley at the casino's restaurant for dinner. Jimbo, in his dealer's apron, visor, red bowtie, and black armband, had stopped by the table. With a knowing look, he'd addressed Victor as "Vicky Boy."

That's the scumbag who's trying to bleed Victor, Braxton thought now as he dialed the casino. *Nothing but a blowhard pretending to be a big man.*

When Braxton had Bowman on the phone, he made short work of tearing the little man apart verbally, ending by threatening to report him to the casino's manager and if necessary to the police.

His last question to Jimbo was, "How much did Victor actually borrow from you?"

"T-twenty thou," Jimbo answered. Braxton could almost hear him shaking in his shiny black shoes.

"And you're trying to get fifty out of him. I'll tell you what, Jimbo, ol' boy. I'll see to it that Victor pays you the twenty thousand, and not a penny more."

Feeling his face harden, Braxton slammed the phone down. Victor was such a stupid weakling. Letting himself be taken in by a punk like Jim Bowman.

And he wonders why I keep him on a tight rein. Well, I won't tell him yet that the problem is under control. He can stew for a few days. Let him wonder if he's going to wind up in a back alley of downtown San Diego with a knife in his back.

That business disposed of, Braxton opened the bottom drawer of his desk and took out a small, exquisitely wrapped package. Inside a diamond and sapphire necklace, his anniversary gift to Camilla, waited to sparkle on her lovely white neck. For a change, he'd picked out a gift himself rather than relegating the job to Rosita.

Braxton knew he was often neglectful of Camilla—even occasionally unfaithful. But he did love his wife in his own way. The sweetness and naiveté she had never lost were as refreshing to him as her stunning beauty. But lately he'd sensed an aura of dissatisfaction.

"Don't worry, Babe," he said, bouncing the small package in his hand and imagining the evening ahead. "I won't disappoint you tonight. I'll give you a romantic evening we'll never forget."

That should fix everything.

Besides, his thoughts continued, *if I want to be Mayor of Coronado—and I do—I can't afford unflattering publicity about my marriage anymore than about my gambling brother.*

For the moment Braxton was being even more discreet than usual in his latest escapade, this one with Erika Weston, wife of cosmetic surgeon Stan Weston. Braxton planned to end the relationship soon after Saturday's party.

Even as he thought of Camilla and Erika Weston, however, he leaned back and for a moment allowed himself to remember how alluring Scarlett had looked in her simple tan suit.

No. Better not go there even in my thoughts—at least not until the mayoral election's in the bag. He slipped the package into his pocket, closed his desk, and locked it. He looked at the wall clock.

Five-fifteen. Plenty of time to drive Scarlett home and still get home for this anniversary celebration Camilla's making such a big deal about.

No need to head for the island immediately anyway. At this hour the traffic on the over two-mile-long curve of the Coronado Bridge would be bumper-to-bumper.

He was about to leave when the window caught his eye. Usually he had a magnificent view of the bay and the bridge, but today the scene was blurred by fog. He could barely make out palm trees bending in the wind. He retrieved an umbrella from a stand and went out to meet Scarlett.

"Good night, Mr. Carrington," Rosita told Braxton as he strode past her desk.

"Good night, Ms. DeLuca." He didn't look around as he spoke.

That's why he didn't see the anguish in Rosita's eyes. He didn't see her rise and enter his office. He didn't see her slip around to the front of his desk and peer underneath to check a tiny tape recorder.

Chapter Nine

After Kate hung up, Cami thought back over her day. In the morning she had spent two hours at her regular salon—hairstyle, manicure, even a pedicure. Next she stopped by Robin's Byrd Cage, her favorite boutique on the island, to pick up the dress ordered especially for tonight. She knew the soft pink silk complimented her pale blond hair and smoky blue eyes, and the softly gathered skirt hung gracefully on her slender figure. Maybe when Braxton saw her in it....

"Everything is perfect," Cami said aloud, trying to infuse a note of confidence into her voice. Instead, rather than enjoying a sense of elation for the coming evening, she felt jittery, as insecure as a teenager getting ready for her first date.

Would Braxton keep his promise? Would he be home in time to celebrate what should be a special day? After his father's death, he had become president of Carrington Investments, so he could pretty much name his own hours. He had promised to be home early tonight—seven o'clock being early for him. He made the same promise last year—and arrived two hours late.

Had he chosen her present himself? Or had he left that to his ever-efficient administrative assistant?

Remembering her conversation with Kate, Cami lifted her head and closed her eyes.

I'm sorry, Lord, for thinking negative thoughts, especially tonight. I've been doing that a lot lately. Please help me be positive about the evening ahead. Help me be witty and charming and all the things Braxton said he admired about me when we first met. Help me—

"Oh, drat!" she said aloud. "I forgot to pick up the Brie."

With only an hour and a half to dash to the delicatessen before Braxton was due home, she rushed to her room. From the bedside table she snatched up a Prada handbag, knocking against the table as she did so. A quick glance in the mirror as she left the room told her she looked quite stylish. Since marrying Braxton and coming under the influence—domination?—of her socialite husband and now-deceased in-laws, she always dressed like a fashion model. Even to run out to the deli.

She pulled the BMW keys out of the purse and hurried outside to the garage behind the house. A strong gust of wind snatched the door from her hand. Dark clouds were gathering overhead. Cami considered running back for her umbrella but decided against it.

***

Upstairs, the telephone receiver dangled lazily off its base.

Chapter Ten

B raxton eased his silver Jag to a smooth stop in front of Scarlett's house. Between the usual rush hour traffic and the beginning of a light rain, the drive had been slow.

"Thank you, Mr. Carrington," Scarlett told Braxton as she reached for the door handle.

"Wait. I'll get that for you," he said, suddenly feeling chivalrous. As he reached for his own door, his cell phone rang. After a quick look at the number, he frowned and shut it off.

"You look serious," said Scarlett. "I'll let myself out so you can take care of your call."

Braxton smiled, warmed by the young woman's sincere thoughtfulness. "They can wait," he said. Moments later, holding an umbrella over her head, he helped Scarlett out of the car and to her front porch.

Back in the car, he pulled out his phone and looked at the number of the most recent call. It brought to mind cool and sultry green eyes, pouty lips, flowing red hair.

He hit the return call button and soon heard the provocatively breathy voice of Erika Weston.

***

Erika Weston, sitting in the furthest, darkest corner of a small backstreet French restaurant, checked her makeup. Perfect. Well, maybe a little more lipstick. She pulled out a tube of Orange Dare and dabbed it on. Hmm. And a touch of mascara. A couple of sweeps of midnight black took care of that. She held her mirror far enough away to see her flowing red hair. The big sunglasses she'd worn to cover her green eyes—despite the cloudy day—now lay on the table. On the back of her chair hung a demure jacket that had covered the low-cut gold lamé blouse she was wearing over snug black pants.

"Mademoiselle," a young server said in a fake French accent, "are you yet ready to order your meal?"

"Not yet. Can't you see I'm waiting for someone?" Erika pointed to the two glasses of wine she'd already ordered for herself and Braxton Carrington.

She tapped her long nails against the table. *Where is he? .... Well, it really hasn't been that long. He'll be here any minute.*

This was far from the first time Erika had rendezvoused with Braxton, and she expected it to be far from the last. But lately—ever since he'd begun to think of running for mayor of Coronado—things had been different, as though he were trying to pull away from her.

That will not happen! I won't let it. She felt her face pulling into a frown and immediately forced it back to a pleasant expression. Braxton hated it when she frowned.

There he is!

Erika's eyes devoured the tall, black-haired, gorgeous man who strode purposefully toward her. He did everything purposefully. That was one of the things she liked about him. As he neared the table, she gave him her sultriest smile and held up her face for a kiss.

"Hello, Erika," Braxton said tersely, taking the seat across from her and ignoring her upturned face.

The sultry smile vanished. Embarrassed and bewildered, Erika lowered her head.

Braxton took a sip of the wine, but it didn't seem to relax him. He pulled out his phone and said, "I need to make a quick call to my wife."

My wife, he had said. Not *Camilla*, but *my wife*, as if to emphasize the point. He had never called *his wife* in Erika's presence before. A pang of panic pricked her chest.

After a few seconds, Braxton said, "The house phone is busy." He pushed another button. Erika could hear Cami's recorded message in the light drawl that still clung to her voice. At the end, Braxton said, "Cami. Where are you? I may be a few minutes late. Don't eat without me."

He laid the phone on the table and made an impatient sound. "Half the time she has her phone turned off." He rose. "Excuse me. I'll be right back."

Erika saw him head for the men's room. She waited till he was out of sight, picked up his phone and held down the "End" button until the screen turned black. With a triumphant smile, she placed the phone back on the table.

As soon as Braxton was back and seated, he asked, "Now, what was so urgent that I needed to come over right away?"

Erika put on a pout. "Not, hello, Erika. You look nice today. I've missed being with you for the past two weeks. Just, 'what was so urgent?'"

Braxton looked her over as if noticing her for the first time. One brow flicked up, and he gave her a slow smile. "You look ravishing. As usual."

There. That was better.

She leaned forward and traced one finger up and down his jacket sleeve. "So, how are the party plans going?"

Braxton's mouth twisted in a sardonic smile. "Let's say that Ashley is going all out to do things the way I want them."

"Doesn't everybody?" Erika asked, continuing to caress his arm and giving him a provocative look.

Braxton pulled back. Hurt and frightened, Erika covered her feelings by picking up her wine-glass and taking a sip.

"Speaking of the party," Braxton said in a matter-of-fact tone, "there's something I planned to discuss with you after Saturday. I might as well go ahead and do it now. But first, what was so urgent?"

Erika had hoped to ease into the subject. "I might ask *you* what was so urgent that you had to call Cami as soon you got here. She's used to you getting home late."

Braxton's face darkened. "If you must know, I'm trying to get home to celebrate our wedding anniversary."

The panic stabbed deeper, leaving Erika unable to comment.

Braxton's expression softened. He took one of her hands between his and massaged it gently. "What's wrong, Erika? Why did you need to see me?"

Placing her other hand over his, she pulled in a deep breath. "I think Stan suspects about us."

At first Braxton didn't reply, but his silence was worse than a violent outburst. At last, he pulled away and spoke evenly. "What makes you think that? We've been extremely careful." He paused. "At least I have."

"Braxton, you know I have, too! But lately Stan has acted kind of funny. He never used to question me when I went out, but now he always wants to know where I've been and who I was with. And the last time you and I were together when he was out of town, he called late at night and didn't get an answer. I had a hard time explaining that one."

"You didn't tell me about that."

"I didn't want to worry you."

"So, what did you tell him?"

"That I had taken a sleeping pill and didn't hear the phone ring. I do take sleeping pills sometimes, so that made sense. But I'm not sure he believed me."

"I see." Braxton leaned back in his chair.

Erika felt as though he were deliberately distancing himself from her, both physically and emotionally. Her insides began to burn.

"Erika." Braxton spoke so abruptly that Erika nearly jumped. "I said I wanted to discuss something with you."

"About the party? Stan and I will be there. I RSVP'd immediately."

"I don't want you to go."

"What?" Erika heard her voice go up several notches. Then thinking quickly, she said, "Don't you see that would make Stan more suspicious than ever?"

"You may be right." Braxton leaned back and studied Erika. She wondered how his face could look both hard and a little tender at the same time. "What I'm trying to say, Erika, is that I think we need to cool it."

"But we have been 'cooling it.' We haven't been together for two weeks. It's been torture for me."

"Well, it's getting too dangerous for us to be together at all. If Stan confirms his suspicions, my bid for mayor is history."

"And your precious *bid* takes precedence over everything else." Erika stuck out her lower lip in a coy pout, hoping a playful attitude would hide her inner turmoil.

Braxton took her hands. He searched her face intently. "Surely," he said softly, "surely you knew this couldn't go on forever."

Erika could hardly believe what she was hearing. "No! No, I didn't." Her voice rose even more sharply. "The only thing that's made being apart lately bearable is knowing that when this mayoral thing is over we can be together permanently."

"Be together permanently?"

She could tell that he was genuinely surprised. How could that be?

"Braxton! That's what you've implied all along—when you're mayor, you'll divorce Cami, and I'll leave Stan, and we can get married."

"I never said any such thing."

"You never actually *said* it, but...." Realization poured over her. "And you never *meant* it, either!"

"Look, this isn't how I planned to end it, but—"

"End it?" Braxton was saying that all along he planned to cut off their relationship one day! The only question being *when*. The panic in Erika became a raging fire as she heard herself stupidly repeating, "*End it?*"

The small bit of tenderness she had seen left Braxton's face. He stood, pulled out his wallet, rifled through the bills, finally shrugged, and drew one out.

"I can't force you to stay away from the party. But I think it would be wise. By the way, I won't be calling you anymore. Please don't call *me*."

He tossed the bill onto the table, picked up his cell phone, and strode away.

Erika sat in stunned silence for several minutes. Her whole being was numb. She could think nothing, feel nothing. Not even panic. Not even pain. Little by little, the numbness wore off and Erika, picturing Braxton's coldness in those last few minutes, thought, *It was just an act, all an act, to get what he wanted. And I was gullible enough to fall for it.*

With that thought, the numbness disappeared and rage set in. It increased when she picked up the bill Braxton had thrown on the table.

A hundred dollars! It felt like some kind of payment, not to the restaurant, but to her.

She sneered and tossed the money back down. Let that little "French" waitress get the biggest tip of her career. Erika rose, not bothering to put on the demure jacket or the scarf or even the dark glasses.

Braxton Carrington would be sorry. Would he *ever* be sorry. Erika's mind was already spinning with plans for revenge—starting with deciding what she would wear to the party at the Hotel Del.

***

As Erika got into her red Corvette, she didn't notice the car parked directly behind her. She didn't see its passenger scribble some notes on a small yellow pad, then lay the pad on his car seat, right next to a camera with a special lens. She didn't notice him pull out only moments after her and follow at a discreet distance.

Chapter Eleven

In her cheerful blue and yellow state-of-the-art kitchen, Cami made one last check of the food for tonight's dinner. She moved to the sunroom and checked the table and the arrangement of mauve freesias. Yes, everything looked perfect. As she had told Kate earlier, as soon as Braxton walked in the door, she could put the chicken in the oven and be ready within half an hour.

Amazingly, her earlier anxiety over the evening ahead had been replaced with a sense of excitement. After running out to the deli for the Brie—and barely missing being caught in the light rain—she had retreated to a small, cozy den in a back corner of the house. There she thought back over her conversation with Kate, whose deep dedication to the Lord almost always caused Cami to examine her own heart.

Odd, she had thought there in the quietness, *I'm the one who took Kate to that meeting where she gave her heart to Jesus. Yet in no time at all she leapt ahead of me spiritually.*

Cami had bowed her head and asked the Lord to quiet her nerves and bless her marriage. As she rose, she experienced a feeling that was almost like peace, something she hadn't known in a long time.

Now she moved the freesias a centimeter, gave a satisfied nod, and headed upstairs to change clothes. She fairly bounced up the steps, feeling a smile tug at her lips at the romantic thoughts tumbling about in her head.

Cami flicked on the light as she entered the large bedroom. Usually the sky was still bright at this hour—about six-thirty—in the summer, but the impending storm had made the atmosphere dark and gray. She took a moment to appreciate the room's mix of heavy, rather masculine furniture set in a stunning and very feminine array of gold and white accessories with accents of black.

A clap of thunder caught her attention. She smiled again, thinking how rare thunder and lightning were in San Diego. Back home in North Carolina, the storm that was brewing would be nothing unusual. Here, the media were full of every detail.

Cami's new dress was spread on a chaise lounge of gold, white, and black floral chintz. As she bent over to stroke the silky pink fabric of the dress, she realized she should have told Braxton to call her before leaving the office. That way she could go ahead and put the chicken in the oven and be ready to eat almost as soon as he arrived. Well, it wasn't too late to call him now. She went to the bedside table. And stopped short.

"Oh, no! The phone's off the hook!" She retrieved the receiver from the floor, pushed the button and got a dial tone. Suddenly another clap of thunder split the air. Cami jumped. The light blinked out. The telephone went dead.

Cami quickly recovered from the slight scare and reached for her purse on the floor. She pulled out her Blackberry. The screen was black.

I can't believe myself, she thought. *I forgot to turn it on. What if someone's been trying to reach me?* It didn't make her feel any better to press the "on" button and see she had forgotten to recharge the battery. The Blackberry was also dead.

***

Meanwhile, Braxton was stuck in traffic on Highway 5 South, still several miles from Coronado. The rain wasn't heavy, but the sky had become unseasonably dark. The combination had caused several traffic snarls, as well as a major accident on the freeway. Braxton had often heard people from other parts of the country say that Southern Californians didn't know how to drive in rain. They must be right.

His conversation with Erika had left him with mixed feelings. He felt relieved to have made a clean break. She could become an albatross around his neck in regard to his political aspirations. Yet, he had enjoyed their secret meetings, and he wasn't one to give up his pleasures easily. He wondered briefly if she would cause trouble.

No, he decided. *Alluring, yes. Bright enough to plan any effective revenge, no. Besides, if I'm no longer available to her, she won't jeopardize her position as wife of one of San Diego's most successful cosmetic surgeons. She'll never risk going back to being poor.*

Braxton dismissed thoughts of Erika. Right now his most urgent concern was getting home for the anniversary dinner Camilla had planned. After spending time with Scarlett and Erika in the past hour, he found himself comparing Camilla to the other two women. She no longer had Scarlett's virginal innocence, but she had kept a sweet naiveté that was a sharp contrast to Erika's bold sensuality. Yet she was poised and confident, as well as savvy in the ways of the island. These, combined with her warmth and delicate beauty, were dynamite qualities for the wife of a political candidate. He needed to make a greater effort to keep her happy.

Rain continued to spatter Braxton's windshield, and traffic had come to a complete standstill.

Better try Camilla again.

He got out his phone and saw it was off.

Erika, he thought immediately. *She turned it off while I was in the men's room. Didn't like my calling Camilla in her presence. Just one more proof that I'm well rid of her.*

He tried calling his home phone. Busy. And he got no answer on Camilla's phone.

***

In the darkened bedroom, Cami felt around in her bedside table for the charger for her Blackberry. She wanted to be prepared when the electricity came back on. Not there. But she did feel a small flashlight, which she used to search the floor. Ah! There it was, wedged between the table and the wall. She picked it up, then sat on the bed holding it and wondering what to do next.

***

Thirty minutes had passed since Braxton left Erika at the restaurant, and he hadn't been able to move ahead more than a few feet. The old cliché "bumper to bumper" was taking on new meaning. Becoming more frustrated by the second, he had tried again and again to call Camilla, with no success.

***

Suddenly the lights blazed on at the Carrington home. Immediately Cami plugged in the Blackberry charger and saw that Braxton had tried to reach her several times.

"Oh, no," she said aloud as she called him back. "Please, Lord, don't let him say he's got a last-minute meeting."

A few seconds later she heard Braxton say, "Finally!"

"I'm sorry," she said. After explaining the telephone problems, she asked, "Are you at the office still?"

"No, I'm stuck in traffic on the freeway. There's been an accident, and I can't get to an exit. I don't know how long it will be."

"The freeway?" Cami asked. She knew Braxton used the freeway for only a short distance before getting onto Coronado Bridge.

"I had to take Scarlett home. Her car wouldn't start."

He had to take Scarlett home? There wasn't anybody else to drive her? No, I mustn't think that way. He must be telling the truth.

"Maybe you can still get home by seven," she said aloud.

"I doubt it. Traffic hasn't moved in the past half hour. But I'll get there as soon as I can."

"Oh, Braxton," was all Cami could think to say. She knew that disappointment was heavy in her voice.

"I'm sorry, Camilla. I really—" His voice began to break up, then faded away. The weather must have caused a bad connection.

Cami sat holding the phone and forcing back tears. She tried to console herself by recalling that Braxton had sounded genuinely sorry and maybe he'd be home soon. But she didn't feel consoled, only more dejected than ever.

Scarlett. Where did Scarlett live? What freeway was Braxton on? Cami opened the bedside table drawer again and pulled out a Carrington Investments employee directory. She opened it and ran her finger down the list of names. Ah, there it was. Scarlett Starling. On Via Santa. Cami had heard that name.

She ran downstairs to the computer in her small office, where she logged onto Mapquest and found Via Santa in San Diego, California. Just as she thought. There was absolutely no need to get on any San Diego freeway to reach that street from Braxton's office. To do so would be ridiculous.

Cami carefully put the map away. She made her way back to the den where she had prayed earlier. The encouragement and elation she'd felt were gone now, replaced by a sick feeling in her stomach.

Braxton had lied.

Chapter Twelve

Kate breathed deeply, drawing in the clean salty air. She lifted her head to the sun, letting her dark hair fall back and not caring if it got tangled by the breeze that Cami had said was cool for August. Reveling in the rhythm of the surf rolling in to shore then being pulled back out to emerald green depths, she swung her Birkenstocks back and forth and scrunched her toes in the damp sand. Cami had already told her that yesterday's "storm" fizzled out after a little rain and a few flashes of lightning. A stronger storm was predicted in a few days.

Kate and Cami were strolling on Coronado Beach across from the large Tudor-style home that had been in Braxton's family for several generations. She would enjoy being here with her dearest friend. For weeks she had looked forward to the long, leisurely chats she and Cami had every time they got together.

And chat they did all the way from the airport—where Cami had made sure to arrive long before the plane's 1:50 p.m. ETA. At least, *Cami* had chatted. She'd been bright and cheerful, talking so much that Kate could hardly get a word in edgewise. Cami had always been loquacious, but not to the point of hardly allowing the other person to speak. It hadn't taken Kate long to see that Cami's cheer rang with a false, brittle note. Not once had she mentioned the anniversary celebration. In addition, the shadows under her eyes were unmistakable.

Kate lowered her head in time to see Cami about to trip over a big clump of thick brown seaweed. She caught Cami's arm and moved her away.

Ugly stuff, she thought.

"Ugly stuff, isn't it?" Cami asked, making a face and not releasing herself from Kate's grip.

"Were you reading my mind? That was my exact thought."

"Really?" Cami laughed, sounding almost like her old self. "Just like the old days at college when—"

"—we were always finishing each other's sentences."

The two friends laughed together, and Kate felt some of the tension she'd sensed in Cami relax.

They were silent again for a while, but now the silence was companionable. In the quiet lull, Kate prayed for wisdom about how to approach the subject she knew was uppermost in both their minds. At last, she felt that the Lord wanted her to simply speak in her usual forthright manner.

She took a deep breath. "So how did it go?"

Kate was glad Cami didn't ask what she was talking about, but sighed deeply and replied, "Disaster-ville."

"What happened?" Kate asked as the two avoided another clump of seaweed.

"Braxton got home nearly two hours late, just like last year. Got stuck in traffic from a big pile-up on the freeway."

"And that was his fault?" Kate asked.

"Yes! Well, no. The accident wasn't his fault, but he should have never been there in the first place."

"I don't understand. I thought you Californians lived on the freeways."

While Kate's heart grew sadder by the second, Cami explained how she figured out that Braxton had lied to her. She ended by saying, "I don't doubt that he drove Scarlett home. But where else did he go? And why didn't he say where he'd been if it was completely innocent?"

"So, did you confront him when he got home?" Kate knew she herself would have lit into Braxton if she were in Cami's shoes.

"No," Cami said, her voice expressionless but eyes hard in a way Kate had never seen them before.

"No?" Kate's voice raised a notch. "Let me get this straight. You had your little celebration as if nothing had happened?"

"Not exactly. I had eaten long before he got home, so I warmed up a plate for him in the microwave."

Chicken Cordon Bleu warmed up! Kate thought.

"Then we exchanged gifts."

"What did he give you?"

"A diamond and sapphire necklace," Cami told her as casually as if she were talking about costume jewelry from Wal-Mart.

"Wow!" was all Kate could think to say.

"I know you're thinking how many women would be over the moon to get a gift like that."

"Exactly."

"And I don't want you to think that I've become so jaded I don't appreciate that fact. The necklace is fabulous. I'll probably wear it to the party Saturday night. It's just that....well, I looked at it and I felt like...like..."

"Like?"

"Like a kept woman. Cheap. Owned by an indulgent master."

"And yet you didn't confront him?" Kate asked in astonishment.

"I know you think I'm a big coward, but I just couldn't. I was too hurt and angry to even think straight. So, while he was taking a shower, I went to bed and pretended to be sound asleep."

"What now?"

Cami shrugged. "I don't know, Kate. I don't know anything—except that I still love him, ridiculous as that may seem."

Kate didn't answer right away. For some reason her thoughts jumped back to the few years she had with Joel. Their time together may have been short, and Joel had been nothing at all like Braxton Carrington, but Kate clearly remembered the intensity of her love for him. How could she judge Cami for feeling the same way about Braxton, even if the man was not worthy of it?

"No, Cami," she said at last. "It doesn't seem ridiculous to me." She paused. "But you can't go on like this. You've got to confront him."

"You're right. I will. After the party. Or rather, after you're gone. I'm not going to spoil our time together by a confrontation with my husband." She took a deep breath. "In fact, let's not spoil another minute together with this. I'm going to trust you to pray for me and not keep on talking about it. Agreed?"

"Agreed," Kate said. But deep down, she knew that was a promise destined to be broken.

Chapter Thirteen

Back from the stroll on the beach, Kate enjoyed a leisurely shower in her elegant guest suite—one of three in the house. This one, on the ocean side of the second floor, featured French doors that opened onto a balcony and gave Kate a panoramic view of the Pacific. She looked forward to being lulled to sleep by the sound of the surf. The light, airy room, done in shades of green and pale yellow, was one that Cami had rescued from its former dark décor. She may seem a bit scatterbrained in some areas, but every detail in the house had been carefully thought out, all without the professional decorator that she could well afford.

After the shower, Kate dressed in navy slacks and a navy and white blouse and made her way down the wide, curving stairs to the family room.

"Aunt Kate!" a lilting feminine voice greeted her. Though Kate was no relation to the Carringtons, Cami's children had always addressed her as "Aunt."

"Debra!" Kate opened her arms wide to Cami's daughter.

After they embraced, Debra's twin brother stepped in.

"Durant!"

"It's great to see you, Aunt Kate." The young man enveloped her in a bear hug.

As Durant released her, Kate stepped back. "Let me look at the two of you."

She studied them for a few moments, struck as ever at how Debra, except for her darker hair, was so much like Cami had been in her college days and how Durant was practically a younger carbon copy of Braxton. Simply looking at them, no one would guess they were twins, nor suspect the deep, almost mystical bond they shared. Debra's casual attitude about spiritual things was one of the few barriers between them.

Kate let out a deep breath of satisfaction. "You're going to have to catch me up on all your doings. Your mom keeps me filled in a little, but—"

"—she's not the world's most faithful correspondent," Cami finished with a smile as she entered the room carrying a tray of lemonade. "Even with email. Come on, you three. Let's get comfortable and have a quick drink before supper."

Kate caught Cami's eye and jokingly groaned at Cami's use of the word *supper* rather than *dinner*. Kate had often teased her about that word and other "Southernisms."

As Cami led them to the cozy, conversation-inspiring sitting area, Kate surveyed her friend, dressed in white pants topped by a navy linen blouse and gold chain belt. She was even more beautiful than she'd been as a young woman, and she had gained a confident but sweet poise that would be any woman's envy. Kate wondered if Cami was wrong to suspect Braxton's whereabouts last night. With such a wife, how could he possibly turn to another woman?

As soon as the four were settled in leather chairs, Debra began to rattle on about summer school at Pepperdine University, the scarcity of cute guys, and the adorable boutique that she *had* to take Kate to. Durant, never as vocal as his sister, was strangely silent, even for him. Kate determined to have a private talk with him as soon as possible.

When Debra finally stopped to take a breath, Kate took advantage of the brief lull. "And you're both getting prepared to head off to the University of Edinburgh in a few weeks," she said. "I can only imagine how excited you are."

Debra and Durant exchanged meaningful looks. Debra cocked her head at Durant, who set his mouth in a straight line.

"Whoops," Kate said. "Did I say something wrong? You are still planning to go, aren't you?"

Again Debra gave Durant that questioning look. "*I* am," she replied.

Looking uncomfortable, Durant said, "Well, I'm not sure."

"What!" Cami leaned forward with eyes open wide. "What do you mean, you're not sure? All the arrangements have been made. I thought you were excited about studying in Scotland for a year."

Durant took a deep breath. "I was. I really was, until—"

"Until what, Durant?" Braxton's demanding voice cut him off.

Kate looked toward Braxton, surprised. She had not heard him come in.

Durant looked so painfully unsure of himself that Kate felt sorry for him.

Looking at her son quizzically, Cami said, "Braxton, could we talk about this later? Maybe after supper? I'm sure Kate is starving."

Braxton seemed to notice Kate for the first time. "Oh, hello, Kate. Camilla's been looking forward to your visit."

Kate noticed that he said "Camilla," not "Camilla and I."

"Good to have you here," Braxton continued. "Nice flight?" He sounded polite but uninterested in Kate's answer.

"Thank you," she told him just as politely. "It's wonderful to be here. And my flight was very nice—meaning uneventful."

"Well, I'm sure you and Camilla have a lot of catching up to do," he said wryly, making Kate wonder if he knew Cami would probably confide in her. "Hi there, Dee Dee," he said to Debra. He bent over to give her an affectionate kiss on the cheek she lifted to him.

"Hi, Daddy."

In the few moments Braxton had been in the room, the affection between father and daughter stood out in stark contrast to the tension between father and son. That was nothing new, but Kate feared that things were coming to an unpleasant head.

Braxton ruffled Debra's golden brown hair before bending over to kiss Cami; but before his lips touched hers, she turned her cheek to him. He paused a second before pecking the cheek. Frowning, he straightened up. "Dinner soon?" he asked Cami.

"Fifteen minutes," she told him.

"Good. I need to go back to the office." He gave his son a hard, cold look. "After Durant and I have a chat."

Cami opened her mouth to speak. Before she could say anything, Braxton strode out of the room, leaving behind the impression that a brief "chat" would take care of any ideas Durant had that were contrary to his own.

He's worried, Kate thought. *He knows that Cami suspects something, and jerk that he may be, he cares enough about her to dread the thought of losing her.* Another thought occurred to Kate. *Then there's the mayoral election coming up. He knows the public doesn't want a candidate with a troubled marriage.* She closed her eyes briefly. *Lord, I don't see how I can be of any help in this situation, and I don't want to add to it. But if there is anything You want me to do, please show me.*

Chapter Fourteen

Durant took a bite of the cook's delicious beef stroganoff, its meat so tender it hardly needed chewing. Unfortunately, the atmosphere in the room was less tender. Though Braxton was cordial, especially to Kate, and the conversation was pleasant, Durant felt a tension thick enough to need a cleaver to slice it.

As soon as the meal ended, Braxton rose and fixed his gaze on Durant. Voice dripping with cold sarcasm, he said. "I'm waiting with bated breath to see what ridiculous reason you have for implying you might not want to go to Edinburgh."

When Durant didn't move away from the table immediately, Braxton said, "Well?"

Durant hated the way his father made him feel like an errant three-year-old. *Lord, help me!*

"Yes, Durant?" Braxton's eyes were as cold as his voice.

Durant lifted his chin, feeling a little confidence from his short prayer. "Is it okay if Debra and Aunt Kate join us?"

"Why in—" Braxton stopped himself and shrugged. "As you like." He headed for the library, clearly expecting everyone to follow on his heels.

Like the obedient puppies we all are, Durant couldn't help thinking.

After everyone else had found seats in the reading corner of the paneled library, Braxton remained standing among the floor-to-ceiling rows of books. He made a point of checking his Rolex.

"Okay," he said to Durant. "Make it quick. No. Wait a minute. What are you doing here in the middle of the week? You and Debra are supposed to be at Pepperdine. Why are you cutting classes? You two don't need to be missing any classes if you want to be ready for the University of Edinburgh."

Durant inwardly flinched at the mention of the Scottish university. But knowing his father was a real stickler for class attendance, he hastened to reassure him. "Neither one of us is skipping class." He stood, hoping that being eye-to-eye with his father would help. "We finished up at noon and drove right down here. We were planning to head back about six in the morning. That'll get us back in plenty of time for our ten o'clock class. We came down so I could have this talk with you."

"You mean you drove down here—and dragged Debra with you with the roads still wet—just to talk with me? Something wrong with your cell phone?"

Durant fought down resentment. His father's main concern had always been and always would be for Debra over him. He hated feeling resentful of the sister that he loved as much as his own soul. Thankfully, he recognized the feeling as being more toward his father than Debra. "I wanted to talk with you in person about this. Something really important has come up."

"It had *better* be important," Braxton spit out.

"Braxton, let him talk," said Cami, surprising Durant by speaking more sharply than usual.

Durant didn't have time to dwell on that. He needed to move on. His father was going to be mad enough when he heard Durant's request. No need to make it worse by making him wait. "I have to get an answer from you before tomorrow. I didn't find out about it until yesterday or I would have talked to you sooner."

"Okay, okay," Braxton said. He gave Durant a long, level look. "If it's about money, you can forget it."

"There is some money involved," Durant said. He had to send up another quick prayer to keep bitterness out of his tone as he went on. "But I've saved up more than enough from my allowance to cover it. It's not *money* I want to talk about."

"Then what is it? Look. I have to get back to the office."

"Tonight, Braxton?" Cami asked.

Durant thought his mother's question had an odd quality to it. His heart sank. This wasn't going well. When he had prayed about the matter, he imagined discussing the situation with his parents for a few minutes before easing up to the heart of the matter. What a dreamer he'd been. He took a deep, steadying breath.

"I want to spend the fall semester in Israel."

There. Now he only needed to wait for Braxton to explode.

He didn't have to wait long.

"You want to do WHAT? Have you forgotten that you're scheduled to head for Edinburgh in a few weeks? You want to waste an opportunity like that for some harebrained idea you heard about yesterday? Why in the world would you want to study over there rather than in Edinburgh?"

"I wouldn't be studying," Durant said quietly.

"What *would* you be doing? Tooling around the country with one of your buddies while your sister goes on with her degree? You're nuts if you think I'm going to allow that."

"I wouldn't be 'tooling around the country.' Not exactly anyway."

"Not exactly?" When Durant didn't answer right away, Braxton spoke again. "Why do I have the feeling I'm not going to like your answer?"

Durant decided he'd better go ahead and get it all out at once. So he talked as fast as he could, trying to allow Braxton no time to interrupt. "I want to go on a mission trip to the Galilee area. It's with the Andrew Club on campus."

"Andrew Club?"

"It's a Christian club. Named for Jesus' disciple Andrew." Durant felt that now was not the time to mention that Andrew was the first person in recorded history to tell another person about Jesus. "We'd be working at a *moshav*. That's a place similar to a *kibbutz*—you know, a communal settlement. Kibbutzes used to always focus on farming, but today they may focus on education or— "

"I know what a kibbutz is, Durant."

"Well, this *moshav* is run by a church rather than the Israelis. It's a few miles from Nazareth. Anyway, the leaders, both here and in Israel, won't accept anyone under twenty-one without their parents' permission. Like I said, I found out about it yesterday, and they have to have an answer by noon tomorrow. I think Mom will say yes if you will." He glanced over at Cami.

Braxton's countenance got darker and darker as Durant spoke. Now his voice became dangerously low. "A mission trip? A *mission* trip? You want to give up a chance to spend a semester in Scotland at one of the world's most prestigious universities for…." His jaw hardened as he continued, "Out of the question! I'm amazed you had the nerve to even approach me. Now, if you'll excuse me." Braxton began to walk away.

"Dad! Wait!" Durant caught his father's arm.

Braxton stopped and, without speaking, glared at his son.

For a moment, Durant considered continuing his plea. Then he noticed that both the maid and cook were pretending to be busy in the next room but were probably hanging onto every word. Feeling utterly defeated, he let go of his father's arm and watched him walk away, shaking his head as if in disbelief. Or was it disgust?

"I'm going upstairs for some papers I have to take to the office," Braxton called back to Cami. "Don't wait up for me."

Berating himself for his string of distinctly ungodly thoughts, Durant rushed out of the library and past the curious servants. He dashed out the back door, slamming it so hard it rattled. A minute later, he had pulled his Beamer out of the garage and was speeding backwards in the lane that ran behind the house. With a roar of the engine and screech of tires, he pulled away.

Chapter Fifteen

Debra Carrington sat cross-legged on her bed. Her lithe young body was tense, not leaning against the pale yellow pillow shams. She stared at the iPhone in her tight fingers, willing it to ring.

When Durant had slammed out of the house, Debra excused herself and went up to her room. There she threw her light summer dress onto the funky lime green love seat and changed into white shorts and a T-shirt emblazoned with a photo of a popular rock band. After pulling up her hair with an elastic band, she called a number on her phone's memory, only to be disappointed by a recorded message.

"Call me back." As she closed the phone, she forced her mind away from the call she awaited.

That was some scene between Durant and Dad, she thought.

Debra adored her arrogant, ruthless, controlling, perfectionist father. As far as she could see, the only people who ever came close to pleasing Braxton were her mother and Rosita DeLuca, who seemingly had made it their life goals to do so. Debra knew she herself came nowhere near Braxton's standards of perfection, yet some tweak in his makeup allowed him to overlook her shortcomings and give her his total affection. Over the nineteen years of her life, she had developed a close bond with him that no one else seemed able to achieve.

Perhaps it was because they were basically alike. Debra saw in herself a drive and ambition that closely matched Braxton's. She also recognized her own tendency toward perfectionism and intolerance, softened somewhat by Cami's tender and fun-loving influence.

One thing—or rather one person—kept Debra from fully luxuriating in her father's love and approval: her twin brother. She loved Durant with a depth that only other twins could comprehend. He was as much a part of her as her arm or leg. She could hardly bear the thought that she would be separated from him if he got his wish to go to Israel. No need to worry about that, though. Their father would never agree to such a plan.

The rejection she saw piled on Durant higher and deeper every year twisted at her heart and at her feelings for her dad. It also made her come as close to praying as anything else in the world. Now, of all things, ever since Durant "turned himself over to Jesus," he had turned into a first-class pray-er. For her. Always wanting her to join him in a dedication to God that struck her as fanatical.

"Lay off me, Durant," she had finally told him. "I'm already a Christian. I was baptized when I was a baby, the same time you were. And Mom took us to church all our lives. She even dragged us to that little Baptist church on Orange Avenue sometimes, in addition to the services at Christ Church." She referred to Christ Episcopal Church, which several generations of Carringtons had attended.

"I keep trying to tell you," Durant had pushed, "being baptized and going to church are important, but they're not what make you a Christian. It's having a personal relationship with Jesus."

"Drop it!" she'd said. "I have no problem at all with you having this *personal relationship*, as you call it. But if it's so *personal*, doesn't that mean I'd have to make that decision on my own—*if* I were so inclined?"

Durant had looked sad but backed off, for the time being at least.

For now, Debra pushed aside her growing irritation at Durant's religiosity. She had a bigger problem on her mind—one that could very well mar the wonderful relationship she had with her father.

***

Debra's phone began to play "Dixie." Her mother always smiled at the tones, and Debra got a quirky pleasure at her friends' expressions when they heard the jaunty tune.

Seeing the name "Frank" on the caller ID, she relaxed and quickly answered. She could hear the spark in her voice as she said, "Hey. Where were you?"

"Just got back from dinner with my parents and another couple and their daughter," the deep voice responded. "You know—I told you about it."

Yes, he had told her about it; but he'd also told her last week that he couldn't go up to Pepperdine to visit her because he had some work to do for his dad. Later Debra learned that "working for his dad" meant lunch at Peohe's, one of Coronado's plushest restaurants, with his father's secretary. Debra knew her to be cute, chic, and witty. The incident planted a seed of uneasiness in Debra's mind.

Pushing aside the thought, she asked, "How was it?"

"Borrrr-ING." The way Frank's voice rumbled on the simple word made Debra's heart skip a beat.

"What's she like?" she asked, determined not to let him know how he affected her.

"Huh? What's who like?"

"The daughter!"

"Oh, yes. The daughter. Well, let me see. She has pale blond hair, down to her waist. Kind of wavy. And she's got huge baby-blue eyes."

"Sounds pretty." Debra hated how catty she sounded.

"Oh yeah. A real babe."

Debra pressed her lips together and didn't say anything.

"Jealous?" Frank asked. Debra could almost see his sensuous lips flick upward in amusement.

"Of course not," she lied. "Should I be?"

"Only if you consider a ten-year-old competition."

"That's *not* funny."

Frank chuckled. "Sorry, Deb. But I'll make it up to you." His tone held promise. "Can you get out tonight? In about an hour, say?"

"Yeah. Durant and I got a call from the school about an hour ago saying classes are canceled for the rest of the week—plumbing problems or something. My mother's friend from Boston is here, so Mom will be occupied talking with her. Soooo, about nine o'clock I'll tell Mom I'm going out for a stroll on the beach—which will be true—and I'll meet you at the usual place."

"What about Simon Legree? Will he be around?"

"I wish you wouldn't call my dad that," Debra said, irritated. "No, he won't be here; he said he was going back to the office. Anyway, he doesn't question me."

"Daddy's little girl, huh?" The tone was teasing and serious at the same time.

"So? What's wrong with that?" Debra felt her temper rising.

"Nothing. Nothing at all. Don't get all worked up. But I'm wondering how the great Braxton Carrington will feel about his little girl—"

"—going out with Francis Paul Giovanni, the son of his number-one opponent in the race for mayor."

***

Kate, who had come upstairs to get some photos of Gunnar to show Cami, was nearly to Debra's room when she heard Debra refer to "my mother's friend from Boston." She had been about to hurry past, but something stopped her. Then she heard Debra say that she was seeing Dominic Giovanni's son.

Kate wished she hadn't heard Debra's words. The possible ramifications of such a relationship were unthinkable. *Ignorance is bliss,* she thought. But she *had* heard. Perhaps the Lord had intended for her to hear. If so, what did He want her to do with the knowledge? Should she face Debra with it?

Definitely, she thought, in her usual decisive way.

Not now, Kate. Not yet, a still, small voice cautioned her. On the way to her own room she sent up a prayer for wisdom about how she'd tell Cami what she'd heard.

Not now, Kate. Not yet.

Then when, Lord? I feel that I need to share this with someone. The unexpected thought of talking to Gunnar about it flitted across her mind.

For now you share it with Me alone.

Her spirit heavy, Kate went into her room and knelt by the bed and rested her head against the coverlet. For several minutes she poured out her heart to the Lord about her concerns, not only for Debra, but for Cami, for Durant, for herself, even for Braxton. Little by little, the heaviness lifted until she was able to end her prayer with heartfelt thanks for being allowed to be on this beautiful island at a time when her dearest friend may need support more than she'd ever needed it before.

She rose and fished the photos of Gunnar out of a suitcase. Holding them close to her chest, she smiled and made her way back downstairs.

Chapter Sixteen

It wasn't hard for Debra to get away from the house. Her father had returned to his office. Her mother, as Debra had foreseen, was spending the evening with Aunt Kate, probably discussing Durant's surprising announcement. She wondered what Cami thought of the idea. She had been thrilled at the prospect of her children studying in Edinburgh—together.

Expecting to see serious expressions on the two friends' faces, Debra was surprised when she poked her head through the doorway. Her mother was staring at a photograph Kate held out for her to see, raising a brow above a twinkling eye and saying, "What a hottie!"

Hottie? Her mother using the word *hottie?* And Aunt Kate was actually blushing! Could she actually have a boyfriend? At her age?

Before Debra could process that thought, Cami looked up and caught sight of her.

Deciding not to go near the subject of the photograph and Aunt Kate's red face, Debra said, "I'm going out for a stroll on the beach, Mom. And I might walk up to Cafe 1134."

"For a vanilla latte," Cami said, smiling. "Where's your jacket? The rain has cleared up, but it's still cool."

"Right here," Debra told her, holding up a dark green hoodie.

"I hear you're in for another big *storm*," Aunt Kate teased, her complexion returning to its normal hue. "I'll never get used to what you San Diegans call bad weather."

"That's what they're predicting," said Cami, pointedly ignoring Kate's gentle jab. To Debra she said, "I hope it doesn't spoil your dad's party."

Debra laughed. "It'd take one of Aunt Kate's New England Nor'easters to keep that crowd away." She blew the two women a kiss and waved goodbye.

"Be careful!" she heard her mother say.

Be careful, Debra thought a few seconds later as she unlatched the wrought-iron gate set into the low brick wall surrounding the property. She crossed the narrow street that separated the house from the beach. Pulling her jacket close around her, she slipped through an opening in the piled-up boulders that edged the sand.

She gazed up at the sky. Washed clean by yesterday's rain, it provided the stars the perfect backdrop to sparkle like a million gems. The moon cast a gleaming swath on the water and lit the tops of the white-caps in the now-gentle surf. Debra loved this island, especially the ocean and all its changing moods. She breathed in the salty air and waited for the feeling of contentment that usually came to her here.

Instead....

Be careful. Her mother's words came back to her again, like a whisper in a ghostly movie. She knew that Cami had meant for her to be careful to stay fairly close to the house and not wander into the lonelier areas of the beach. What would she say if she knew her daughter had come out to meet the son of her own father's major political opponent?

Debra shivered again, this time not from the cold.

She turned abruptly to her left and quickened her pace. At the next opening in the rocks, she left the beach, re-crossed the street and hurried toward The Jackal, a small bar frequented almost exclusively by the under-thirty crowd.

Trying to rationalize her deception to her mother, Debra told herself, *I said I might go to Café 1134, not that I actually would. And when I get to The Jackal, I'll order a coffee. After all, a vanilla latte is just glorified coffee.*

The deception to her father was a little harder to rationalize, but she almost managed it with the thought that most of the crowd at The Jackal had little interest in politics. They'd be unlikely to report to Braxton her presence there with Frank.

Despite her rationalizations, guilt warred with the thrill of the forbidden within her. Thrill gained tactical advantage with every step she took until guilt had retreated from the battlefield by the time she pushed open the door of the bar.

Chapter Seventeen

Frank Giovanni took a few moments to appreciate what he saw in his bedroom mirror. Collar-length black hair swept back from a broad forehead. His olive complexion was the perfect setting for the black hair, thick ebony brows, nearly black eyes, and gleaming white teeth in an expressive mouth. He was no "pretty boy," but his tall, muscular build and rugged looks were perfect for some of the roles he'd portrayed in high school plays and now at Lamb's Players Theater. He ran a comb through his hair, patted one errant strand, and gave a nod of approval to his image, thinking how his looks attracted as many girls as he could handle. He liked that.

Like Frank, Debra Carrington was a lifelong resident of the island, so he had been vaguely aware of the cute young girl and her twin brother most of his life. But it was in March at a Coronado High School basketball game that he really noticed her. Now a student at Pepperdine U, Debra entered the gym minutes after the game began and looked across the crowded bleachers for a seat. Her twin, Durant, had stayed home that night.

Frank took in Debra's red tam atop her golden brown hair and red jacket over jeans and let out a low whistle. Quickly, he shoved the boy next to him over a couple of feet.

Ignoring the boy's complaints, he called out, "Hey, Debra!" and pointed to the newly created spot. For a moment her big blue eyes met his, and it seemed that a laser beam had blazed between them. Neither of them moved, and he sensed that she felt it, too.

"Great!" she finally replied. She joined him, not seeming to mind the tight squeeze.

That had been the beginning of a relationship that was unlike any Frank had ever had. That night he learned that Debra was witty and intelligent and a lively conversationalist. And she was the daughter of the one man on the island his father most despised.

Even before Dominic and Braxton began seriously talking about running for mayor, Frank and Debra knew their fathers would die rather than allow the two of them to go out together. That very fact—along with keeping their relationship from Durant—lent a zing of excitement to his arranging to meet her for their first date—dinner and a movie in Malibu, not far from Pepperdine.

He soon learned that Debra was a "good girl," totally unwilling to engage in sexual activity. At first he credited that to her mother, who had kept her children in church all their lives.

"I believe in God, but I'm not a religious nut like my brother," she told him with a flirty grin. But she turned serious when she said, "I have this romantic and, well, old-fashioned notion of waiting for sex until marriage."

While that frustrated Frank, it added to Debra's appeal. As for the frustration, there were plenty of other not-so-nice girls.

Lately, though, he'd been seeing less and less of the not-so-nice girls. Debra Carrington had gotten to him, and he hardly knew what to make of it. He even wondered if he was actually in love with her. A thrill of excitement ran through his veins as he thought of meeting her at The Jackal in a few minutes. As he ran down the stairs in the ultra-modern Giovanni home, he pulled a warm sweatshirt over his head. At the bottom, there was his mother holding a video store bag.

Oh no. He'd forgotten he'd promised to watch an old movie with her tonight.

"Frank!" she said. "Are you going out?"

"Only for a little while, Mom," he said, kissing the cheek that was almost level with his.

Frank sincerely hated forgetting his promise to her. He knew that despite the busy life she led volunteering at the hospital, keeping up her award-winning garden, and supporting Lamb's Players, she was often lonely. She had plenty of friends but was basically shy and was not close to any of them. As for her husband, Dominic's attitude toward his wife was one of toleration rather than love and companionship. He rarely hid his contempt for his wife's need for medication for her bipolar condition.

"How long will you be gone?" Terese Giovanni asked, her disappointment evident. "This is a long movie, you know."

"About an hour." That was true. Debra couldn't be gone from home longer than that without arousing concern.

"Well, okay," she said, putting on a brave smile.

She always tried hard not to smother him, but he knew how much his company meant to her. And he enjoyed her company. Most of his acquaintances would be astounded at this soft spot in Frank Giovanni's tough persona.

"I promise I'll be back soon. You get the popcorn and sodas ready, okay?"

She brightened. "Will do. By the way, who are you meeting?"

His mother was usually so careful not to pry about his friendships that without thinking Frank said, "Deb—" He gave her another peck and said, "No one you know. Don't forget the popcorn."

***

Terese Giovanni stood at the bottom of the stairs, gazing at the door. What had he been about to say? It sounded like "Deb." Deb who?

Chapter Eighteen

Debra scanned the crowded, smoke-filled room. She didn't see
Frank. She made her way around and between couples gyrating
to a loud hip-hop tune, recognizing a few people, but not finding
Frank.

"Hey, Debra." A boy who had been a couple of years ahead of her
at Coronado High appeared at her side.

"Oh, hi, Keith." Keith was one of those people who was everybody's
friend. "How's things?"

"Pretty good," he answered, then proceeded to update her on his
life since they last met. Eventually, despite Debra's efforts to prevent
it, the conversation turned to her father's possible mayoral candidacy.
That, in turn, led to mention of one of Braxton's opponents, Dominic
Giovanni.

"Speaking of Dom," said Keith, "look what just drifted in." He
nodded toward the door. As Debra had done earlier, Frank was scan-
ning the room. Soon their eyes met. Debra's heart quickened.

"Oh ho," said Keith. "So that's how it is."

"That's how it is." Debra waved at Frank and started to move away.

Keith became serious. "Be careful, Debra. Don't play with fire."

Debra stopped. *Be careful,* he had said. *Be careful.* She wiggled her
head, trying to shake the words out of her brain. Deciding to turn the
warning into a joke, she jabbed Keith in the chest with one finger and
said playfully, "Maybe it's Frank who should be careful."

Unhurriedly, his eyes never leaving hers, Frank wove his way
through the crowd. His slow, languid pace shouted out his total confi-

dence of her reception of him. That arrogant assurance both irked and excited Debra. As Frank drew near, she made a silent vow to keep a better rein on his growing hold on her.

With that in mind, when he stopped, took her face in both hands, and bent his head for a kiss, she twisted slightly to one side, causing the kiss to land at the corner of her mouth.

He chuckled, as if he read her mind. Then he turned her head back toward him and planted a kiss directly on her lips. Automatically she responded.

"That's better," he said, his dark eyes caressing her face.

Mmmm. It sure was.

He lowered his hands and took hold of her elbow. "Come on. I've snagged a table for us over in the corner."

Seeing all the other tables occupied and dozens of people standing at the bar or around the floor, Debra asked, "How'd you manage that?"

"Oh, I have my methods," Frank said, grinning.

His "method" became obvious when a petite but shapely blue-haired waitress in skin-tight jeans approached the table immediately. "How's this?" she asked Frank, openly flirting as she gestured toward the small table.

"Perfect," he told her. "I owe you one."

"You don't owe me anything," she said, patting a back pocket of her jeans. "What can I get for you two?" For the first time, she looked at Debra. Recognition and astonishment flickered in her eyes.

"Aren't you...."

Panicked, Debra couldn't answer.

"You got it right," Frank told her. "Now, how about a beer?" He quirked one eyebrow. "And a Diet Coke for the lady."

"Make that a coffee," said Debra, remembering her earlier rationalization. "It's cold tonight," she added lamely.

"Got it," the waitress said. "Be right back." Then, before turning to go, she leaned over and whispered loudly, "You two sure like to live dangerously." She straightened up. "Your secret's safe with me. And the rest of this crowd could care less." She sauntered off toward the bar.

"Any trouble getting away?" Frank asked.

"None at all, but I hate lying to my mom."

He leaned so close to her that she felt he'd speared her with the fervor in his dark, dark eyes. Trying to maintain her emotional equilibrium, she touched the mole near his mouth and joked, "I know girls who would kill for a natural mole like that. It's totally wasted on a guy."

"I'm thinking about something else that's totally wasted." He came still closer. "Wanna know what?"

Debra's heart nearly stopped. She had no doubt what he referred to. She felt giddy with excitement—and fright.

"Time to come up for air, you two." Debra wanted to hug the waitress for rescuing her. Instead, she said a shaky "Thanks."

"You're welcome. Enjoy yourselves." The waitress touched Debra's arm lightly and looked directly at Frank. "Better be careful with this one, honey."

Be careful. Her mother's words came back to Debra like a jolt of electricity.

"What's wrong?" Frank asked her.

Annoyed with herself, she shrugged. "Oh, nothing."

But she felt shaken and irrationally angry at Cami for intruding on her adventure.

"I don't believe you," Frank said.

"Huh?"

"I don't believe that it's nothing." He covered her fingers with one large hand. "I think you're worried about your dad finding out about us."

"Let's not forget about *your* dad. He wouldn't be anymore pleased about his son dating Braxton Carrington's daughter than my dad would be about me seeing Dominic Giovanni's son."

"You might be surprised," Frank said. "Dad might find a way to turn the situation to his advantage. You know—the liberal-minded, tolerant father and all that. He might even like the idea."

"Well, my dad wouldn't. I can guarantee you that."

Frank chuckled.

"What's so funny?"

"I'm imagining ol' Braxton's face if he walked in right now and saw us together."

Debra drew in her breath sharply. "That's not a pretty picture."

Frank sobered. "No, it isn't. Let's not talk about the old men anymore. Let's get out of here."

Debra rose. "That's the best idea you've had all night."

Outside the bar, Frank leaned against the wall, crushed her to him, and began to kiss her. At first Debra responded, but as his kisses became more and more urgent, she became frightened by the feelings stirring in her. With a major force of will, she finally forced herself to remember her earlier resolve. Breathing heavily, she placed both hands on his chest and pulled away. So far, she had resisted giving in to his urgent demands—sorely tempted though she was. Instinctively, she felt she needed to—*be careful.*

Chapter Nineteen

"Get your hands off her!" A profane name followed the command.

Frank stumbled, as much from the force of the words as from the hand yanking the neck of his sweatshirt. The next thing he knew he was reeling from the impact of a fist slamming into his face.

"Dad!" Frank heard Debra shriek.

Frank lunged at Braxton Carrington with all his weight. The older man, nimbler on his feet than Frank would have imagined, easily stepped to one side. Frank flew forward, his head crashing into a light post. Ignoring the searing pain and Debra's cry to stop, he swung around and lunged toward Braxton again. Again, Braxton stepped nimbly to one side. Frank fell against the stucco wall of The Jackal. The rough surface cut into his right cheek, dampening his face with blood.

"Frank! Dad! Stop!" Debra demanded, her voice desperate but not loud, as though not to attract attention. Fortunately, the cool weather was keeping the thin-blooded San Diegans inside tonight. Few were on the streets, none near The Jackal at the moment. She stepped between Frank and her father and stood straight and stiff, her very body language daring either of them to make another move toward the other.

Not that Braxton seemed inclined to make another move. Only his eyes bespoke his anger. That and his steely tone when he told Frank, "If I ever see you near my daughter again, your life won't be worth the price of the college diploma your father *bought* you."

Frank froze. How did Braxton know about that? He tried to think quickly of a way to divert Debra's attention from the subject. It wasn't necessary.

"Dad! What are you talking about? Don't speak to him that way. Anyway, what are you doing here?" As she spoke, Debra stepped to Frank's side. She pulled a tissue from her pocket and began to dab at the blood on his cheek.

"Let's say that I got a very interesting phone call a few minutes ago," Braxton replied. "And I'll speak to that jerk however I please." Then, flicking his eyes briefly toward Debra, he said, "And *you* will stay away from him."

Debra bristled. "Dad! You can't—"

"Look here, Carrington," said Frank. He roughly slung one arm around Debra and pulled her close. "Debra's an adult. She can see anybody she wants to."

Debra, rather than lean into him, stiffened. He tightened his hold and glared defiantly at Braxton, expecting him to shove his daughter aside and strike out again. He hoped that would happen. He would love an excuse to pound Braxton Carrington into the ground. And he could do it. He tightened his fists in preparation.

But Braxton, though his eyes blazed like bullets, only sneered in Frank's direction. "That's right," he said coolly. "She can. But I think she has the right to an informed decision."

"What are you talking about, Dad? That's the second time you've—"

"Why don't you ask *him* what I'm talking about?" Braxton's gaze pinioned Frank. "Ask *him* about the huge donation his father made to that college in Washington. Ask *him* why his dad had to *buy* his son's Business Administration degree."

Debra looked at Frank, her brows drawn together in puzzlement. "Frank?"

Frank felt cornered. "So what?" he answered, trying to make light of his answer. "So my dad put out a few bucks for his son's sake. What's the big deal?"

"The local high school girl who wound up with mass infections from an abortion after her relationship with you thought it was a big deal," said Braxton. "The only reason the family didn't turn Frank in for statutory rape was to protect the girl's reputation. Afterwards, with only a few weeks left before graduation, the school politely—or maybe not so politely—asked Frank to withdraw. That's when Daddy Giovanni stepped in and made a donation that assured his son of a diploma. The school was hurting for money, so they agreed to the diploma request, but they still insisted that Frank vacate the premises."

"Frank?" Debra repeated, eyes pleading and voice sounding as though she were saying, "Please tell me that isn't true."

Braxton answered before Frank could speak. "It's true, Debra. And there's a lot more—things so sordid that I don't want to speak of them."

"Frank?" Debra pled once again.

Frank tried to bluff it out. Half expecting her father to attack him again, he took Debra's face in his hands and caressed one of her cheeks with his thumb. "Do you really believe that, Deb? You know I'd never do anything like that. He's mad because you're going out with Dominic Giovanni's son."

He tried to ignore the sure knowledge that Braxton could easily get proof of his allegations.

Braxton remained eerily still. And Debra hesitated. Not a good sign. Frank watched in disbelief as she moved his hands from her face and stepped away. Anguish twisted her face, and tears pooled in her eyes.

"My father has never lied to me," she said, the tears spilling over onto her cheeks. She tilted her delicate chin upward in that patrician gesture that had so often both repelled and intrigued him. It was as if she were on a pedestal looking down on him, though he was several inches taller. Her voice only slightly unsteady, she added, "And you have."

"Ready to go home, Dee Dee?" Braxton asked quietly, not moving toward her.

"Yes, Daddy." She gave Frank one last sorrowful look. "I'm ready."

Too stunned to speak, Frank watched Braxton lead his daughter to the silver Jaguar parked at the curb. He opened the door for Debra, who looked like a princess getting into a silver carriage. Seconds later, they drove off at a sedate speed.

In those few seconds, Frank's rage built to a near bursting point. He had never in his hate-filled life loathed anyone as much as he did Braxton Carrington.

***

Not until she was sure they were out of Frank's sight did Debra break down. All the tension of the evening—from lying to her mother, to Braxton's dramatic appearance, to learning about Frank's escapades—it all coalesced and burst forth. Without warning, she found herself sobbing.

Braxton patted her knee but didn't speak.

Her words broken and barely coherent, she told him, "I'm—so—sorry, Dad. I didn't realize...." She couldn't go on.

"I won't say it's all right, Dee Dee." His tight voice above her sobs confirmed his words. "But if it taught you a lesson, the experience served a purpose."

Since the drive from The Jackal to her house was short, Debra knew she needed to get herself under control. Gradually, she forced her sobs down to a hiccupping sniffle.

"What about Mom?" she asked at last. Though Debra considered her Mom terribly old-fashioned, she loved her and valued her opinion. It was her *Be careful* that had hounded Debra all evening.

"I don't see that your mom's knowing about this would be of benefit to anyone involved." Braxton pulled the car into the driveway behind the house and activated the garage door opener. Inside the four-car structure, he turned off the motor and reached into his back pocket. "Here," he said, handing Debra a handkerchief. "Wipe your face."

Still sniffling, she obeyed. A thought occurred to her as she handed it back. "Dad, who called you tonight?"

"I don't have any idea. They didn't give me a name."

"Was it a woman?" Debra thought of the waitress at The Jackal.

"Hard to tell. The voice was muffled, like a cloth was over the mouthpiece. I don't really care who it was. I'm glad they called."

"Me, too," Debra whispered. Her head bent, she went on, "Thank you, Dad. I love you."

"I love you, too, my little Dee Dee," he told her softly.

Debra had a sudden desire for her brother to experience the love she felt emanating from their father. But now was not the time to express that thought. Instead, she planted a kiss on Braxton's cheek, got out of the car, and ran into the house.

Inside she called out "I'm home, Mom!" and slipped up the back stairs to her room.

***

As Debra got out of Braxton's car, her phone fell onto the seat. Braxton picked it up and started to call her back to retrieve it.

No. Wait. He searched the contact list and found Frank's number.

Seconds later, he heard, "Frank. Leave a message."

Good. This was better than getting into a conversation with that lowlife.

"Stay away from my daughter," Braxton said into the phone, "if you don't want your little escapades splashed over the front page of the *Coronado Eagle.*"

He erased the record of his call then got out his own phone and called Dominic Giovanni's office. As expected at this hour, he again got a recorded message, but he knew his cryptic words would be heard the next morning.

"Giovanni. Braxton Carrington here. Be at my office at 8:30 this morning."

Braxton knew that Giovanni was in town and that he always went to his office by 7:00 a.m. and would hear the message in plenty of time.

He had no doubt that Giovanni would be there.

Chapter Twenty

At the desk in her office, housed in a delightfully restored 1920s craftsman-style cottage, Ashley Carrington reviewed the neat stack of plans for Braxton's political "coming out" party. Her company, SeaView Ventures, was putting on the event for little more than the cost of basic expenditures. Her three employees assumed Ashley was settling for such minimal profit as a favor to her brother-in-law, though they must have wondered why one of the wealthiest men in California would need to economize.

Little did they know the perverse enjoyment Braxton Carrington derived from lording it over people, from having them at his mercy.

Ashley pushed aside an artist's rendering of an ice sculpture shaped like the crown that was the motif of the Hotel del Coronado. Propping her elbows on the desk, she pressed her fingers to her forehead. She didn't even try to stop memories of the shock, the anger, the fear that had been uppermost in her thoughts for the past several weeks. In her mind, she could hear her intercom buzzer announcing the first inter-ruption that June afternoon.

She had punched the button and said, "Who is it, Mindy? I thought I told you to hold all calls. You know I'm buried in the initial planning for Mr. Carrington's party."

Ashley knew that her no-nonsense speech coupled with her brisk English accent terrified her young receptionist.

"That's why I put the call through, Ms. Carrington," Mindy said.

"What's why?" Ashley snapped.

"I-it's Mrs. Carrington calling. The other Mrs. Carrington, that is."

"Cami?"

"Yes. I think she wants to ask you a question about the party."

"Put her on hold, Mindy. Tell her I'll be with her in a minute."

"But, Ms. Carrington...."

"Do as I said, Mindy. Put her on hold." Ashley cut off the intercom connection.

Ashley Carrington hated her sister-in-law Cami. And she did little to hide the fact. She ran her fingers through her very short black hair and stared at her short, neat, square-cut fingernails and thought about all the ways she hated Cami. She held up one thumb and began to tick them off on her fingertips.

One. She hated Cami's blond beauty. Ashley pulled a small mirror out of a desk drawer and stared into it. Although at forty-seven she was five years older than Cami (and four years older than her own husband, Victor), her face was even more youthful looking than Cami's: baby-bottom smooth and lineless thanks to various cosmetic "procedures" by Coronado's own Dr. Stanley Westcott.

Two. She hated Cami's innate sense of style, a style that, despite her middle-class upbringing, was both classic and up-to-the minute. Somehow, no matter how long and hard Ashley worked or how much money she spent on her wardrobe, her own efforts always seemed cheap and tawdry in Cami's presence.

Three. She hated the faint Southern drawl that clung to Cami's accent even after twenty-plus years in California. Ashley delighted in mockingly referring to Cami as a "Southern Belle."

Four. She hated Cami for her popularity despite her refusal to drink alcoholic beverages or light up a cigarette or use even the mildest swear words—facts Ashley attributed to Cami's church-going.

Five. Most of all Ashley hated Cami for being married to Braxton Carrington, President and CEO of Carrington Investments, while she, Ashley, was stuck with Braxton's weakling of a younger brother, Victor.

Five years ago, Ashley met Victor at Chicago's famed Top o' the Mart restaurant where the events planning outfit she worked for at the time was hosting a cocktail party. Ashley, like every other woman in the room, was attracted by Victor's tall, dark good looks and boyish charm—and by the fact that he was vice president of one of the most successful investment companies in the country. Newly divorced, he was "fair game." Not that a little thing like a wedding ring had ever deterred Ashley in the past, but Victor's being single simplified matters.

Having grown up in a rowdy neighborhood in London, Ashley was nothing if not street smart. Victor, with all his poise, charm, and "old money" breeding, seemed surprisingly naïve in comparison. Not once did he suspect a secret that Ashley knew would cause him to reject her as a possible future wife.

That night at the Chicago cocktail party, Ashley set her sights on Victor and his money and position. Within a month she married him and acquired all three. Not till she got to Coronado did she realize that Victor's title as vice president of the company was almost meaningless. The real prize, she soon saw, would have been Victor's brother Braxton—who was already married to Cami Carrington with her sugary "Southern charm."

Enough of that. She touched the intercom button and told Mindy to put Cami through. Without apologizing for keeping her waiting, Ashley said, "Hello, Cami."

"Hi, Ashley, how are you today?"

For heaven's sake, couldn't the woman get to the point? Did she always have to make polite conversation first?

"I'm quite well, Cami." She deliberately allowed her irritation to come through. "What can I do for you?"

"I'm looking for Braxton. An important package came for him, and there's no answer at the office or his cell phone. I thought maybe he dropped by your office to discuss the party."

"You mean his oh-so-efficient secretary, what's her name? Conchita? Lolita? .... What's that? .... Oh yes, Rosita ... you mean she's fallen down on the job? Will wonders never cease?"

"Rosita's probably on a break," said Cami evenly.

Of course, Cami would stand up for Rosita, or almost anybody else for that matter, Ashley thought, freshly irritated. She wondered if Cami was the only person in the firm who didn't know Rosita was in love with Braxton.

She felt like putting on an exaggerated Southern accent and saying, "Sorry I couldn't he'p y'all, honey." She knew that last bit would tick Cami off. It would also earn her a lecture about how most Southerners never use "y'all" when referring to only one person. Besides, she didn't need to antagonize Cami before she was paid for Braxton's party.

So, instead, she simply allowed a little irony in her voice as she said, "Yes. I'm quite sure Rosita is on a break."

In her maddeningly polite manner, Cami said thank you and hung up.

Ashley had barely put down the phone when Mindy buzzed her again.

"Mindy! Must you keep interrupting me?"

"I'm sorry, Ms. Carrington, but this time it's Mr. Carrington."

"Victor?" Ashley asked. Her husband did have a habit of calling at inconvenient moments, but Mindy was usually able to put him off if Ashley was busy.

"No. It's Mr. Braxton Carrington."

"All right," Ashley said, wondering why Braxton was calling. He was known for making an assignment and then expecting it to be carried out to perfection or else. He rarely checked up. She hit the intercom button.

"Hello, Braxton," she said. Unable to totally avoid a derogatory tone, she told him, "Cami called looking for you. Something about a package arriving at the house."

"Probably her anniversary present," he said. "They were supposed to deliver it to the office. They'll hear from me about that."

"I was working on your party when she called. I think you're going to be really pleased."

"This is not about the party," Braxton said. "I'm sure it's fully under control in your capable hands." Ashley didn't like the smug, almost gleeful sound of his voice. He continued with, "I called to discuss a certain person who…." he paused, "…*rang me up* this morning." He paused again, clearly waiting for a response.

Ashley nearly choked at his use of the British term *rang me up* for *telephoned*.

"It was morning *here*," Braxton continued smoothly. "That would make it early evening in London. Maybe you'd better drive over to my office and discuss the, uh, matter in private."

Ashley knew she had to gain control. She couldn't let Braxton sense the extent of her fear. So she cleared her throat and was amazed at her own normal sounding voice when she said she'd come right over.

She hung up and, momentarily paralyzed, looked out her window at the overcast skies that were typical of June. "June gloom" the locals called it, the follow-up to "May gray." It amused Ashley how quick they were to declare that the rest of the year was near perfect.

Before leaving to meet Braxton, Ashley opened a desk drawer and took out the small mirror again. She held it up and shuddered. Her hazel eyes were dull, her fair complexion ashen. The gloomy skies were bright compared to her face.

***

Now, six weeks after that conversation, Ashley raised her head from her hands and tried to think what she could do to prevent certain disaster and the loss of everything she had worked so hard to gain.

Chapter Twenty-One

"You're not going to like these, Dr. Weston."
Stan Weston watched Lucas Richards' dark, slender hands toss a thick manila envelope onto the table in the dimly lit restaurant. Knowing what it must contain, Stan looked away from the envelope as Richards took a seat. He studied the man before him. Richards' appearance was perfect for his job as a private investigator. An African-American, he was medium height, medium weight, plain featured. His thick black hair was cut short, but not too short, and he wore thin-rimmed glasses. In his charcoal slacks and conservative gray print shirt, open at the neck, he blended into the darkness of the restaurant as if he were part of it.

Nondescript. That was the word that came to Stan's mind the other two times he and the private detective had met. Yet, Stan knew that Lucas Richards was anything but nondescript when it came to his job. He knew he had hired one of the best in the field.

Richards sat silently, giving no indication that he was aware of Stan's scrutiny and making no attempt to urge Stan to open the envelope. At last, with a sense of certainty and dread, Stan pulled it toward him. He fingered the clasp but didn't open it.

"How many photos?"

"I printed a dozen. I have others, but they're—"

"More of the same?"

Richards nodded.

Stan waited a few more seconds, then opened the envelope and pulled out the eight-by-ten photographs. Even in the dim light, Erika's bright red hair and sultry face were unmistakable. As were the features of the man with her.

Erika and Braxton Carrington, faces close together, their fingers entwined, at a restaurant that looked Italian.

Erika and Braxton embracing beside a pool at a motel, a huge Las Vegas casino marquee in the background.

Erika and Braxton entering the door of a tiny inn.

Stan felt as if he'd been stabbed in the stomach with one of his own scalpels. He couldn't look at anymore photos of his wife with another man right now. He stuffed them back in the envelope and looked at Richards.

"You'll forgive me if I don't say thanks."

"Hardly anyone does."

Stan pulled a folded-over check from his shirt pocket and handed it to Richards. The detective opened it, looked at it briefly, and slipped it into his own pocket. With that, he rose, shook hands with Stan, and left.

For a long time, Stan sat motionless, unable to command his legs to stand. Nor could he command his mind not to wander back to the day he had met Erika Morgan. Stan had been mesmerized by her and within a year had freed himself of his obese wife and married Erika. He was not stupid. He knew that his attraction could not lie in his balding head, ordinary face, and short, slightly dumpy stature. Nor could it lie in his somewhat taciturn personality. No, it lay in his money. Period.

Yet, he had been pathetically willing to take a chance with her. And he had not been sorry, the only thing marring his pleasure being the constant gnawing dread that a younger, more charismatic man would steal her from him. Not only had he enjoyed Erika's physical attractions, but he knew she had made a real effort to be a good wife to him. She had made him happy.

Until several months after they moved to Coronado. And met Cami Carrington and her multi-millionaire husband, Braxton.

Now Stan held in his hands photographs that confirmed suspicions he'd entertained for at least three months. Like a martyr deliberately flogging himself with a whip, he tore open the envelope and pulled out the photographs again. He forced himself to look at them one by one, turning each one over to read Richards' notes: locations, dates, hours.

His emotions whirled as he stared at the photos again and again. Humiliation battled heartbreak, and disgust fought against wounded pride. But little by little, rage took root and grew and grew until it overcame every other emotion.

Braxton Carrington would pay for spoiling the most beautiful thing that had ever happened to Stan.

Chapter Twenty-Two

Kate and Cami strolled down Orange Avenue, Coronado's major thoroughfare. Pleasure shone on their faces as they bit into three-scoop ice cream cones.

"This island is such a mix of charming retro and contemporary," Kate said. She pointed to the street. "Look at that. Four lanes. I remember how that surprised me the first time I saw it. I'd expected nothing but narrow lanes, some not even paved."

"I felt the same way the first time Braxton brought me here," said Cami, licking some cherry nut ice cream from around the edge of the cone.

"You got some on your nose." Kate swiped the tip of Cami's nose with a napkin. "And yet," she went on, still thinking about the idiosyncrasies of the island, "the palms and other trees and flowers do give it a quaint, cozy feel. So many exotic flowers everywhere you look. And I love the architectural mix—Spanish, Victorian, craftsman cottages from the twenties, and buildings that obviously come from the forties and fifties."

"You should apply for a job at the Coronado Chamber of Commerce."

Kate grinned sheepishly. "Sorry. I have a tendency to get carried away."

"I do, too, sometimes. I love this island. I decided long ago that if I'm not going to live in the South, San Diego is the next best place—and specifically Coronado. " She stopped in front of an upscale boutique, where a clerk was arranging a colorful display of summer dresses and beachwear.

Kate stuffed the last of her ice cream cone into her mouth and wiped her lips. "Thanks for taking me to the RV sales lot this morning."

"You're more than welcome. That was fun. I always thought I'd like to make a motorhome trip—as long as somebody else did all the driving and hooking up and—"

"—and everything!" Kate laughed and added fondly, "Some things never change, Cami."

"I hope the RV shopping didn't tire you out, being only your second day here. We must have looked inside twenty of them."

"That wasn't tiring. It was fun. Especially since I found the one I want."

"On your first day of looking. Amazing."

"Nineteen feet long. Long enough to have a fairly roomy sleeping area, a small kitchen—with microwave and fridge, built-in TV—yet a length I can handle on the road."

"My favorite part is that pull-out bathroom and shower," said Cami. "You'd never even know it was there, it's so well hidden."

"I like that, too, but it *is* tiny. Showering may prove to be a challenge. I might wish I were an acrobat."

Cami laughed. "You're the only person I know—with the possible exception of Braxton—who could make such an important decision in such a short time."

Kate was not especially pleased at being compared to Braxton, even in a favorable way, but she ignored that. "I pretty much knew what I wanted. I spent hours online researching. I knew I wanted one big enough to have a few amenities, but small enough to maneuver easily. The road test cinched it for me."

"Too bad they'd sold the only one like it on the lot."

"Actually, I don't mind that it's going to take several weeks for another one to come in. That way, it should be here about the time I return from teaching that seminar in Portland."

"Well, better you than me. I can't begin to imagine traveling around the country for months in a motorhome. Especially alone. Tell me again why you're doing this?"

"You sound like Gunnar."

"Sensible guy. By the way, I noticed there's plenty of sleeping space for *two*." Cami cast Kate a sly look. "You know…as in honeymooners?"

Kate blushed and ignored Cami's none-too-subtle comments. "As for my reasons for doing this, for one thing, I've never taken a sabbatical. For another, I've been in several foreign countries, both in Europe and Asia, and even Australia. But I haven't seen that much of my own country."

"I'm surprised. You travel around giving seminars and lectures at universities and colleges all across the U.S."

"But it's always in and out. I rarely have time to stay around and explore. Most of the time, I see little more than the route to and from the airport."

"Well, I don't have to ask why you've chosen traveling in a motorhome rather than a car."

"Which is?"

"You like the idea of being free to travel at your own leisure. Not being at the mercy of motels or restaurants. You'll have your own bed and your own food and cooking facilities."

"Got me figured out, haven't you?"

"Sure. Even in college you never liked the restraints of rules and regulations—unless you made them."

"Is that your nice, polite Southern way of saying I'm a control freak?"

"Possibly. I mean, you always did like having things in order—your own order, that is." Cami put one finger to her forehead and pretended to consider the matter deeply. "Mmm. I think I'd describe you as a *free-spirited* control freak."

The two friends laughed. It felt almost like the old days back at Compton College.

Chapter Twenty-Three

"Match point!" Cami shouted across the net from Kate and Durant at the Coronado Tennis Center that overlooked waving palm fronds, moored pleasure boats, and the glistening water of Glorietta Bay.

While Debra, her doubles partner, bent forward clutching her racket, Cami let fly a perfect serve to Durant. With a sure backhand slice, he returned the ball far past Debra to the backcourt. Cami sprinted and caught it just in time to send it back toward Kate. Puffing, Kate hit it straight to Debra, who snagged it before it bounced, then slammed it down close to the net on Durant's side. Durant lunged. And missed.

"Good game!" Kate said. Tucking the racket under one arm and breathing hard, she leaned over to rest both hands on her knees. The sun that earlier had hidden behind a cloud was now, about ten-thirty, out in full force. Kate could feel perspiration rolling down her face, arms, and every inch of her body.

"Okay, Aunt Kate?" Durant asked as he strode to her side.

"Fine," Kate said. She let out a whoosh of air, then stood up and brushed her forearm across her brow. "Just fine." She shook her head ruefully. "I used to be able to beat your mother once in a while. If you hadn't been playing with me, I'd have lost every game."

"Don't forget—Mom plays twice a week. And Debra was fierce today."

"What's that about Debra?" Durant's twin asked, following Cami around the net.

Kate heard a tightness in Debra's voice that had not been there yesterday. She sounded … angry? Hurt? Both? Kate wondered if it had anything to do with the young girl's outing last night.

"Just saying you were really *on* today," Durant said.

"You really were!" Cami agreed.

Debra smiled and said thanks, but her eyes looked bleak.

"Hey!" Kate said, trying to lighten the mood. "I think I recall the Del's Boardwalk Café serving killer smoothies. And it's only a couple of blocks from here. How about I treat us?"

Cami shook her head. "I need to get back to the house and check on a couple of details for the party, though Ashley probably has it all under control. But you and the kids go on."

"Not me," said Debra. "I, uh, have some homework to do. But thanks, Aunt Kate."

"Of course," Kate told her.

"But you said you got a call that all classes are canceled for the rest of the week. Plumbing problem or something," said Cami.

"They are. But this…this paper I'm working on is giving me some trouble."

"Looks like it's you and me, Durant," said Kate. "You game for a smoothie?"

"Only if you twist my arm." Durant grinned.

"Consider it twisted." Kate turned to Cami and Debra. "See you two back at the house."

Chapter Twenty-Four

Sitting on a bench between the Hotel Del and the beach, Kate slurped up the last of her strawberry banana smoothie. She licked her lips and tapped her empty cup.

"It's everything I remembered. I'll give it to you Californians. You know how to make smoothies."

Durant patted his stomach. "No lie. Thanks."

"Now this is what people envision when they think of Southern California," said Kate, gazing out at the dark blue, white-tipped waves beneath a sky dotted with wispy clouds. To the north, the Point Loma Peninsula, with its two lighthouses, jutted its slender finger into the water. Closer in, after a day of rain and another of cool weather, today's balmy warmth had brought out hordes of sunbathers, swimmers, and surfers.

Durant nodded. "I can't imagine living anywhere else." Suddenly, he leaned forward. "Look, Aunt Kate!" He pointed to a surfer who'd caught a curling wave. "I think he's gonna ride it all the way in."

Kate smiled inwardly, thinking that Durant would probably rather be surfing than having a smoothie with an "aunt" whom he likely thought of as middle-aged. She had to admit to herself that she remembered being nineteen and thinking of forty-two as quite old.

"He made it!" Durant pumped one fist in the air. "What a ride!"

"Just missed destroying that little girl's sandcastle. She doesn't look too happy. And look at her dad."

Durant took in the beet-red back of the man lying face down on a beach towel next to the little girl. "Ouch. I wouldn't want to be him tonight."

Kate shifted her chair and turned her gaze back to the sprawling Victorian hotel with its gleaming white walls and bright red roof. She knew the islanders felt affectionate pride for their historic landmark.

The Hotel del Coronado opened in 1888 and, because of having its own generator, had electricity before the city of San Diego did. Over the decades, its world-famous visitors had included such diverse characters as Babe Ruth, Charles Lindbergh, Thomas Edison, several presidents, and innumerable Hollywood personalities, including the ill-fated Marilyn Monroe. In 1920, England's Prince of Wales—then in line to become King Edward VIII—attended a party at the Hotel Del. According to island lore, that night the prince met Wallis Spencer Simpson, a Coronado divorcée he later gave up his throne to marry.

Kate looked forward to again strolling through the Hall of History with all its wonderful photos and other memorabilia. But now, more current matters came to mind.

"Where is your dad's party being held?" she asked Durant.

"Right over there." Durant pointed upward to a bank of floor-to-ceiling windows in a large, gazebo-like protrusion.

"The Oceanfront Ballroom," said Kate.

"When everyone first arrives, it'll still be light—if the storm holds off—so they'll be able to enjoy the ocean view."

"Wonderful."

After a few moments of companionable silence, Durant said, "Sorry you had to witness that little episode between Dad and me last night."

Kate merely gave him a sympathetic look and nodded.

"I really lost it, didn't I?"

"Actually, I thought you handled it well at first."

"Too bad I ended up stomping out."

"You didn't exactly keep your cool, but I certainly understand your reaction."

"Not too great a testimony to my sister, huh?"

"Uh-uh."

"Thanks for praying for me." At Kate's questioning look, he grinned and went on, "I knew you would."

"You're right, I did. And I still am." She gave him a look of sympathy. "I guess you'll have to give up your trip to Israel."

"Maybe not. They might give me a little more time to get Dad's permission." Durant looked hopeful for a moment, then his face darkened. "Fat chance."

"Durant," Kate said, "have you really prayed about this trip to Israel?"

Durant looked surprised at the question. "I guess so. A little at least. It seemed so right that I guess I didn't think I needed to pray about it that much."

She patted his hand and, hoping not to sound too preachy, said lightly, "Well, be sure you do."

"Will do." His tone matched hers for lightness, yet held a serious undercurrent. "Now let's talk about something else." He sat back and gave Kate a long, appraising look.

"What?" asked Kate.

"I've been wondering something. But you might think I'm prying."

"Go ahead. Pry. If I don't want to answer you, I won't. Agreed?"

Durant gave her arm a playful jab. "That's what I like about you, Aunt Kate. You're completely straightforward. Agreed."

"So, which one of my deep, dark secrets are you curious about?"

"Your love life."

A vision of Gunnar immediately popped into Kate's head. "Talk about *my* being straightforward. Are you serious?"

"Completely."

"I'll answer the question, Durant. But why do you want to know?"

"Maybe it's just that your leading me to the Lord makes me have a special concern for you. Mom says there's a man in your life. Do I need to fly to Boston and knock his lights out?"

Kate laughed till a young couple at a nearby table began to dart questioning looks at her. She forced her laugh down to a chuckle and said, "I can assure you that Gunnar Volstad is a fine Christian man with the most honorable of intentions. I'd appreciate it if you'd just leave his lights on."

"Tell me about him."

"He's from Minnesota. He's a widower with two grown sons. He works with Hub Digital Corporation."

"'The Hub' being a nickname for Boston."

"Right. Gunnar is a gas turbine software developer there. He's very involved in the church we both attend—and he teaches an adult Bible study. As for looks, he's, um, what your mother called a, um, a hottie."

"Mom said that?"

"She did."

Durant shook his head in disbelief. Then he grinned. "I'm sure he wants to marry you."

Touched by Durant's assumption, Kate gave him a grateful smile and said, "Yes. At least he *did*. We had an argument the night before I left."

"About Joel?"

Kate nodded.

"How long were you married to Joel?"

"Only five years." An incredible sadness came over Kate. "But they were the five most wonderful years of my life. When he died, only my faith in Christ kept me going." She took a deep breath. "Joel was a war correspondent with the *Boston Globe*, you know."

"And he was killed on assignment in…Peru? Ecuador?"

"Colombia—during a minor skirmish between the government and some terrorist-type insurgents. It wasn't even a major conflict. A bullet caught him just as he snapped a government soldier being shot. The picture was published in the *Globe*."

"He was a converted Jew, right?"

Kate smiled. "He liked to call himself a 'completed Jew.' Meaning that he had come to realize that Jesus fulfilled—completed—the prophecies and requirements for the Messiah the Jews have looked for for centuries. And he felt that Jesus completed *him* by saving him." Sweet nostalgia tugged at Kate. "He was more on fire for the Lord than anyone I've ever known." For a moment Joel's thin, intense face with its sharp features, olive complexion, and piercing dark eyes seemed to float before her so clearly that she wanted to reach out and touch his tight black curls.

"More than Gunnar?" Durant asked.

The question stopped Kate. In an instant the picture of Joel dissolved and again she saw Gunnar's big smiling face. She saw his twinkling blue eyes, his slightly crooked smile, his straight, pale blond hair. Memories of his strong but gentle testimony—so different from

Joel's intensity—invaded her heart. She shook her head and tried to get back the picture of Joel.

But she could only see Gunnar. As though she'd been slammed by a twenty-foot wave, she felt the...the *wrongness* of clinging to a memory and rejecting a very real, flesh-and-blood, wonderful man who sought her love.

"Aunt Kate? Is something wrong?"

With Durant's words the vision of Gunnar dissolved.

"Uh, no. No. I'm fine. Just fine." But she wasn't fine. She was shaken to the core. Abruptly, she stood up. "Durant, do you mind if I run along now?"

"Well, no. Sure. If that's what you want. Did I say something wrong?"

Kate planted a kiss on the top of Durant's head.

"No. You said something exactly right."

Chapter Twenty-Five

"Sure you don't mind walking to Stan's office?" Cami asked Kate as they strolled down one of the charming side streets of Coronado.

Kate took in the lush semitropical greenery dotting the landscaping of the houses on the street and deeply inhaled the scent of jasmine on a picket fence.

"And miss seeing all this up close? You miss so many details when you're driving. Like the bird of paradise tucked behind that trellis." Kate tilted her head toward the Victorian style home they were passing. "Or the bougainvillea spilling over the top of that doorway." She waved her arm at a tall Spanish-style house across the narrow street.

After a few minutes of strolling in silent companionship, Kate spoke up. "Cami, I need to tell you something."

"Sounds serious."

"It is. I'll get right to the point. I'm thinking of backing out of the motorhome deal."

"What!"

Kate told Cami about her discussion with Durant at the Hotel Del. At the end, she said, "So, you see, I think I want to go back home and seriously consider marrying Gunnar."

Cami gave Kate a hug. "Now that's what I've been waiting to hear all along."

"I knew you'd be pleased."

"I am, but more importantly, I see that you're happy."

A few minutes later, Cami stepped onto the walkway of a low, discreet stucco building with a red-tiled roof and an arched entrance. "Here's Stan Weston's office," she said, "He's expecting us in a few minutes,"

"Tell me again why we're here," Kate said, looking doubtfully at the small brass plaque affixed to the door. The top line read, "Weston Clinic." Below, in much smaller letters were the words, "Cosmetic Surgery."

"Well," said Cami sheepishly, "I ran into Stan and his wife at a dinner party a few months ago. They've only been in Coronado a couple of years—came here from your neck of the woods. He's done amazingly well, but he's still trying to build up his business."

"By practicing on you?" Kate stared at her friend's smooth complexion and slender face. "What could you possibly want done?"

"Oh, I don't know." Cami's reply was evasive.

"Cami! You're not thinking of *enhancement,* are you?"

Cami giggled. "Me? The original pain baby? Don't you remember how you had to hold my hand that time I came down with bronchitis and had to get an antibiotic shot?"

"Then what? Botox?"

"No way. That requires shots."

"So, no Botox. Then what?"

"I've heard of a painless laser procedure that zaps lines around the eyes."

Kate squinted and gazed at Cami. "What lines?"

"Just kidding. Stan invited me to come by and see his office. And I'll admit I'm curious."

Kate had to admit she was curious, too.

"Maybe his wife, Erika, will be there," Cami went on. "And you can judge his work."

"He operates on his own wife?"

"Probably not himself. Probably lets one of the other two doctors do it. Or maybe she's naturally beautiful."

Kate, shaking her head, followed Cami into the clinic.

Chapter Twenty-Six

Stanley Weston stared moodily at the certificate on the wall opposite his desk. It named a school in Boston and proclaimed that Stanley Richard Weston had completed the requirements to perform cosmetic surgery.

Stan's office décor was like everything else about this building—discreet. He was well aware that the women, and even a few men, who availed themselves of Weston Clinic's services were in no hurry to advertise the source of their improved looks. So he deliberately chose a building on a little-traveled side street. It had once been a private residence and, like most of the homes on the island, the garage and parking area were in an alley running behind it. Tall bougainvillea bushes hid most of the area from view, and his clients could enter the back door virtually unobserved.

Very few came in the front as Cami Carrington and her visitor Kate Elfmon just did. When Stan's receptionist announced their presence, he instructed her to tell them he would be with them in five minutes. Actually, there was no practical reason to make them wait; his last client for the day had left half an hour ago.

When Stan invited Cami Carrington to visit his office all those months ago, he hadn't yet begun to suspect that his wife was involved with Cami's husband, Braxton.

He recalled talking with Cami at a home cocktail party. The guests were all Coronado residents who opposed many of the plans that mayor hopeful Dominic Giovanni espoused for the island. It soon became obvious that the main purpose of the "party" was to introduce Braxton

125

Carrington as a possible alternate candidate. Dan Clark, the third hopeful, also opposed the controversial changes; but many thought he didn't have the charisma to beat Giovanni.

Stan wasn't particularly taken with Carrington as a person. To him, the man seemed several shades too self-assured, to the point of arrogance. But Stan fully agreed with Braxton's determination to find ways to boost the city's economy without destroying its unique island flavor. He put forth some excellent proposals that night, and Stan had to admit that Braxton, with his good looks, assurance, and longtime family connections, would make an excellent candidate.

Another major asset for Carrington was his lovely wife, Cami, who exuded openness and friendliness. Even now, he recalled their conversation at the party that night with a kind of melancholy pleasure.

"Hi, Stan," Cami had said warmly. "So good to see you and Erika here." She inclined her head toward Erika several feet away.

Stan, seeing his wife's bright head nodding and full lips smiling at something Braxton was saying, felt a moment of pride in her.

"I hear your business is going very well," Cami said, "even though you've only been here a couple of years."

With a strictly professional eye, Stan took in Cami's flawless features and complexion.

"If all the women in San Diego looked like you, I'd be out of business." He clinked his wine goblet to her glass of sparkling cider. "To natural beauty," he said. "May it never catch on."

Cami laughed. "Why, thank you, Stan." He noticed that she made no self-deprecating remarks as so many of his clients did when given a compliment. "Now I'd like to hear all about your clinic."

Something about Cami had broken through Stan's usual reserve, and he went into much more detail about his work than he usually did. Cami displayed such genuine interest that when he finally apologized for talking so much, he invited her to stop by for a personal tour.

"One of my oldest friends is flying out to visit in a few weeks," Cami said. "That would be a fun thing to do with her. Something different from a trip to the zoo or a day in Tijuana."

"Call my office and set it up with my receptionist," Stan told her. "I'll tell her you'll be calling."

Later, when he began to have suspicions about Braxton and Erika, he realized that Erika had hovered near Carrington all that evening. Stan became so obsessed with learning the truth that his casual invitation to Cami completely slipped his mind.

Then a few minutes ago, his receptionist buzzed him and told him that Cami and her friend were in the waiting room. Cami had called while he was out and asked if the two of them could come over this afternoon and take him up on his offer of a tour of his facilities. Stan's first reaction was horror. At that very moment, he was staring at one of the incriminating photos of Erika and Carrington that Lucas Richards had given him yesterday. How could he be genial and friendly, or even be in the same room with Braxton Carrington's wife?

The same perversity that made him repeatedly review the soul-sickening photographs took over. He buzzed his receptionist and told her to admit his visitors.

Chapter Twenty-Seven

In the Weston Clinic reception room, Kate and Cami relaxed in soft armchairs covered in floral print tapestry of delicate burgundy, soft gold, and sage green. The walls echoed the gold in the tapestry, while the carpet picked up the green. Floral prints on the walls and several potted plants, including two small trees, completed the garden atmosphere. The only hint that this was a cosmetic surgery clinic was the literature neatly spread on the coffee table.

Kate's eyes swept the room. "Nice," she said softly to Cami. For some reason, the room seemed to call for quiet conversation.

"Mmm," Cami replied. "Classy, but subtle."

Kate was silent for a few moments—and wondered why she felt uncomfortable. Though she herself had no desire for any kind of cosmetic surgery, she wasn't opposed to it. She picked up several leaflets and scanned them. One described rhinoplasty and pictured a woman who certainly looked better after having her large nose turned into a perky small one. Another touted a "tummy tuck" achieved through liposuction. Yet another proclaimed the convenience of permanent makeup: eyeliner, lip color, eyebrow enhancement, even cheek color.

Glancing at the pretty auburn-haired receptionist behind a delicate cherrywood desk, Kate wondered if the young woman had achieved her perfect makeup in her employer's clinic.

Cami looked up from a pamphlet and said, "They do a little of everything, don't they?"

The receptionist spoke up pleasantly. "Dr. Weston will see you now."

As the two friends entered Stan Weston's private office, Kate found herself hoping that the receptionist didn't think *she* was considering some kind of cosmetic procedure.

"Ladies!" Stan Weston said from his desk. He held both arms out from his short, plump body and said heartily, "Welcome to my humble headquarters."

Welcome to my parlor, said the spider to the fly, Kate thought, surprised at the thought. Somehow, Weston's effusive greeting seemed insincere. *I must be wrong. After all, he did invite Cami here.*

After Weston acknowledged Cami's introduction of Kate, he said, "I really want to show you around, Cami. We have three state-of-the-art procedure rooms where we use the latest technology and newest, most effective anesthetics. But something has come up unexpectedly, so I'll have to give you a brief overview of what we do."

"Oh, no, Stan," Cami told him. "You don't need to take the time for that. We saw your fliers in the reception room. They give a pretty good idea of the scope of your work."

"Well, if you're sure."

He doesn't want us here, Kate thought. *That doesn't make sense.*

Cami, in her gracious way, said, "We'll be on our way, Stan. Thanks for seeing us when you're so busy. Will we see you and Erika at Braxton's party on Saturday night?"

A steely look crossed Weston's eyes. "Wouldn't miss it for the world." Then his expression turned jolly again as he apologized profusely for not being able to give them more of his time, all the while ushering them out of the room.

Seconds later, outside the building, Cami frowned. "We got kicked out, Kate!"

"Uh-huh," said Kate, looking back at the clinic.

"Let's get away from here. This place gives me the creeps."

"You felt it, too?"

"I don't know what I felt. Maybe it's all that emphasis on physical beauty." She paused. "You know what I mean."

Cami smiled at her friend, and Kate thought, *Now there's true beauty, outside and in.*

***

In his office, Stan stood for a full minute clenching the knob. He'd been ruder to Cami and her friend than he'd intended. He had meant to show them around the clinic, but the very sight of Cami conjured up images of her husband and his wife together.

He released the knob and, trembling a little, walked to his desk. He sat down, took a deep breath and let it out slowly to steady himself. Cami Carrington was a nice lady, but he couldn't allow her to stand in the way of seeking his revenge.

Chapter Twenty-Eight

Erika Weston sat at her dressing table brushing her luxurious red hair. The mirror reflected the pale Danish-style furnishings set amidst a sleek black and aqua décor. When house-hunting in Coronado, Erika had steered Stan away from the older, historical homes that dominated the island. She fell in love with Coronado Cays, on the San Diego Bay side of the Silver Strand causeway that connected the "island" to the city of Imperial Beach. She adored the Venice-like inlets and peninsulas and the huge Tuscan and Caribbean-style homes that filled up most of their tiny but lushly landscaped lots. She talked Stan into a peach-colored stucco with a red-tiled roof and its own boat slip.

Erika immediately proceeded to fill the house with ultra-chic furniture and splashy modern art and accessories. Nothing old for her. She'd had enough of that when she was growing up in a rundown neighborhood on the south side of Boston where the predominant furniture style was best described as early Salvation Army.

She'd also had enough of the religion that was stuffed down her throat during those years. Constantly rebuked and severely disciplined for her sins—ranging from such "crimes" as leaving her bed unmade to sassing her father—Erika eventually became immune to the punishment. By the time her father caught his seventeen-year-old daughter in an extremely compromising situation in the back seat of her boyfriend's car and kicked her out of the house, Erika felt freed rather than punished.

Various friends took the young but rebellious girl in for a while, but each time they asked her to leave because of her negative influence on the family. Meanwhile, she finished high school, got a low-paying secretarial job, and found a cheap room in a boarding-house.

Then she began haunting the doors of the modeling agencies in Boston. Despite her exotic appearance, the modeling jobs never amounted to much. The best one was at an exclusive restaurant in the Beacon Hill area of the city. There Erika slinked her way about the room in outrageously expensive clothing that she drooled over but couldn't begin to afford.

And there, when she was twenty-one, she caught sight of Stan Weston.

Another model, a tall, sloe-eyed African-American named Tasha, pointed Stan out to Erika right before they were to begin modeling.

"Look at his wife," Tasha said. "Would you believe she's married to a plastic surgeon? You'd think she'd at least let him do a nose job on her, if not a full-body liposuction."

Erika studied the plain, uneven features, including the overlarge nose, of the extremely fat woman Tasha pointed out. Then her eyes shifted to the surgeon. Though round-faced and slightly chubby, he still looked to be half the weight of his wife. A fringe of light brown hair encircled his bald pate. Behind his thick glasses, Erika detected a look of discontent.

"And look at her clothes," Tasha continued. "Did you ever see anything so dumpy? If you don't count the rocks on every finger. With her money…." Tasha rolled her eyes.

"Really wealthy, huh?" Erika said.

"Filthy rich is the word, honey. Word is, she practically paid Stan Weston to marry her."

A cue from the *maitre d'* ended the conversation, and both women made their way onto the floor.

Filthy rich, Erika thought as she posed and turned and answered questions about the slinky orange lounging pajamas she was modeling.

Filthy rich, she thought while accepting the oohs and aahs and comments about how surprisingly attractive the orange looked with her red hair.

Filthy rich, she repeated to herself, her eyes constantly wandering toward the Westons. Little by little, a plan began to form in her mind.

At last she reached her destination and slowed to a stop at the cosmetic surgeon's table.

"This one is part of Luis Bandini's latest collection," she said to Stan's wife.

The wife looked up briefly, then went back to her two desserts, first forking in a huge bite of chocolate cake with one ring-laden hand, then cutting into her cherry cheesecake. Erika was not insulted; her germ of a plan was only furthered by Mrs. Weston's indifference to the world of fashion.

Erika gave her full attention to Dr. Stanley Weston, making sure he got a view of her outfit—and more importantly, of *her*—from every angle. The models had strict instructions not to engage in chit-chat with the diners, but she had learned long ago how to speak volumes with her emerald green eyes and body language.

So she was not surprised to get a phone call from Dr. Weston that very evening, especially not since she'd easily sweet-talked the Westons' male server into supplying her phone number if the good doctor asked for it.

***

Less than a year later, by then free of his obese wife, forty-eight-year-old Dr. Stanley Weston married twenty-two-year-old Erika Morgan and moved her to Coronado, California.

Now another year had passed and Erika sat at her dressing table, brushing her luxurious hair and trembling with anger at Braxton Carrington and with fear of being found out by her doting husband.

Over the past two days she had called Braxton's cell phone repeatedly, each time hearing his deep, recorded "Leave a message." Erika knew he was deliberately not answering the phone when he recognized her number on his caller ID. She even called the office twice. Both times that uppity Mexican secretary gave her a terse "Mr. Carrington is busy. I'll tell him you called." Erika doubted that.

Worst of all, though, was this morning. She went to the drugstore and bought a cheap pay-as-you-go cell phone; Braxton wouldn't recognize that number. Sure enough, he answered. But no sooner had she said his name than she heard a click, then a deadly silence. He had hung up on her!

She called back. This time he spoke to her.

"Why are you calling me during office hours?" He was abrupt, cold. "I thought we agreed you'd never do that."

"I wouldn't if you'd answer your phone." A clear note of pleading filled her words.

"I'd think you'd get some kind of hint from that fact."

The conversation ended in less than three minutes. When it was over, a hopeless reality swept over Erika. Her emotions became a reeling jumble. Devastation. Anger. Revenge. All tumbled around in her head and chest. Then a new thought hit her.

Stan. What if Stan found out?

As long as she had thought Braxton wanted to marry her, Erika wasn't overly worried about her adoring husband. Yes, he'd be hurt, and yes, his money would no longer be available to her. Well, he'd get over the hurt. As for the money, Braxton was incredibly wealthy. What would she need with anyone else's money? But now....

Chapter Twenty-Nine

Remembering the humiliating phone call to Braxton, Erika slammed down her hairbrush, imagining the dressing table to be Braxton Carrington's head.

"Careful. You'll break something."

Stan! He was home. Erika was glad her head was down so he couldn't see the fear in her eyes. Taking a deep breath, she willed away the trembling inside.

"You're home early," she said in the sultriest tone she could conjure up. She raised her head and in the mirror saw him standing in the bedroom doorway, a ray of sunlight from the window touching a spot on his bald head, another bouncing off his thick glasses.

He stood there and stared at her for a few moments, as he often did before approaching her. Over and over he had told her that he took great pleasure in drinking in her beauty. So now she gave him a slow smile in the mirror, one calculated to entice and invite him. Slowly, he moved toward her, his eyes locked with hers.

Good. As usual, she had him in the palm of her hand. She relaxed and slowly pulled up her hair, baring her neck and deliberately letting some tendrils fall provocatively across her face. As she expected, he bent over and kissed the little indentation at her nape.

"You'll be the most stunning woman in the room at Braxton Carrington's party Saturday night," he said as he kissed her neck a second time. "Every man there will envy me." He paused. "Even Braxton."

Erika could feel the blood drain from her face.

Stan kissed her neck a third time. "Thought I didn't know, didn't you?" His words were soft, like silk.

Behind the silk, Erika heard iron and steel. It took every ounce of her willpower to relax and ask innocently, "Didn't know what?"

Stan's right hand flew out and struck her square on one cheek. Stunned as much as hurt, Erika swung away from him, rubbing her cheek. She felt like screeching at him, but she had to keep up her charade of innocence.

It wasn't hard to force tears to her eyes and let her voice tremble. "What have I done? Tell me what I've done, Stan! You've never hit me before. Tell me what I've done!"

Stan stepped toward her, his hand upraised again. He stopped and pressed his arms tightly to his sides, as if trying to keep from hitting her again. His mouth curled. "Don't try to play innocent with me, Erika. Do you think I don't know what's going on?"

Thinking quickly, Erika opened her eyes as wide as possible. "What are you talking about, Stan, sweetie?" She forced out a pitiful sob. "I don't know what you're talking about."

"What I'm *talking* about," Stan said between clenched teeth, "is your little romance with Braxton Carrington. No, don't deny it," he said when she opened her mouth to do that very thing. "I've known it for a long time, even before I found that matchbook from the inn at Cardiff by the Sea."

"But, Stan, I explained that to you. Remember? I got it when I had lunch up there with Cheryl Larkins. I told you about her. We became friends when they moved to the Cays a few weeks ago."

"Some friend you are. You didn't even know that Cheryl Larkins has been in San Francisco for the past month, caring for her mother, who had a heart attack."

Erika felt trapped, but she was an expert at thinking quickly. "Oh yes, I forgot. It wasn't Cheryl Larkins I had lunch with up there, it was Cheryl *Lawson*. Their names are so similar I get them mixed up."

"Good try, Erika." Stan let out a mirthless laugh. "There was a time when I would have believed you. That time is past—especially now that I have these."

For the first time, Erika noticed the manila envelope Stan held. Dread enshrouded her like a fog rolling in from the ocean.

"W-what's that?"

Turning to the bed, Stan undid the envelope and pulled out a stack of papers. Erika moved closer to see them better. They weren't mere papers; they were photographs! The top one was of her and Braxton entering the inn at Cardiff by the Sea.

In horrified fascination, Erika watched as Stan laid the photos out on their bed in four neat rows of three each. Though none of them was graphic, several showed her and Braxton embracing or kissing. She was caught. There was no use denying anything now. She had only one chance to redeem the situation.

She sank to the dressing table stool, buried her face in her hands, and began to cry softly. "Oh Stan! I'm sorry," she said brokenly. "So sorry! I never meant for it to happen. But, but Braxton kept on after me until I gave in." Wailing, she continued, "When I told him I would never love anyone but you, he threatened to tell you."

"Shut up, Erika. You're only making it worse."

Erika uncovered her tearful eyes. "But it's true! Finally, two days ago, I told him I wouldn't see him anymore, no matter what."

Stan seemed to be wavering. "And what did he say to that?"

Erika sniffed. "At first he was mean. Said he'd tell you about us. I reminded him that a scandal would hurt his political ambitions. Finally, he agreed to stop trying to see me."

"Is that the truth, Erika? Is that really the truth?"

He looked so pathetic that Erika felt sorry for him. Taking a chance, she reached up and pulled him down until he knelt at her side and buried his head in her lap. "It really is the truth, Darling."

His voice began to shake with sobs. "I can't lose you, Erika. I'd die if I did!"

She kissed his shiny head and made cooing, soothing, repentant noises for a long time. Meanwhile, her mind was racing. After several minutes, when Stan had calmed down, she said hesitatingly, "Something's occurred to me, Darling."

Stan lifted his head. "What is it?"

"Well, no, you won't like it. Never mind."

"Tell me."

"No, I can't. I was silly to even think of such a thing."

"Tell me," he repeated. "I insist. And I promise I won't be angry."

"Well, it's just that.... Stan, we can't let Braxton Carrington win."

"What do you mean? Are you talking about the election?"

"No. I'm talking about us. We can't let him win over us. We have to go to his party."

Stan jumped to his feet. "Are you crazy? How can you even suggest such a thing?"

"You said you wouldn't get mad."

Stan stared at Erika in disbelief for a few seconds. He slowly moved his head from side to side and said, "You're right. I did. Go ahead, finish what you were saying."

Erika let some of the anger she felt toward Braxton show through. "If we don't show up, he'll think he has some hold over me. On the other hand, if he sees us there together, he'll know for sure that I'm finished with him."

Stan stared at Erika without speaking for a few seconds. He seemed to be thinking hard about her suggestion. She held her breath. At last, his mouth twisted in a sly grin. "You know," he said slowly. "You might be right. Let's do it." He pulled her up from her vanity bench and gave her a long kiss.

Whew! Erika thought even as she returned Stan's kiss. *That was easier than I would have thought.*

***

After ending the kiss, Stan continued to hold Erika, hoping she didn't recognize the loathing for Braxton Carrington that grew with every thump of his heart. His straying wife didn't know that she had played right into his hands with her suggestion to attend the party. She wasn't the only one who could put on an act.

Chapter Thirty

Rosita DeLuca let herself into the two-bedroom condo she'd bought ten years ago. It was in a then-new development in Chula Vista, a suburb bordering San Diego on the south. It was only a ten-minute drive from the border town of San Ysidro, where Rosita was born and grew up, but it might as well have been a continent away. When she went to work at Carrington Investments, she was living with her prostitute mother on the upper floor of a dingy two-story apartment building whose walls hadn't seen paint in years.

As for her father... Rosita's mouth turned down in a sneer. *Mamá couldn't even tell me who he is.*

Occasionally as she was growing up, she'd longed for a father to love her and lend stability to her life. Her grandfather had done his best to fill that role, but he died when Rosita was a young teen. Even while he was alive, she had gotten so used to fending for herself—and fending off the attention of her mother's boyfriends—that eventually her longing for a father disappeared into a determination to be completely independent and never allow a man to rule her life or her emotions.

Then she had literally bumped into Braxton Carrington the very day she went to his company to apply for a job. From that moment on, the second part of her determination was as if it had never been.

Yes, she became Braxton's personal assistant in record time.

Yes, she eventually saved enough money to buy this near-luxury condo.

Yes, she was financially independent and free of all ties to her old life.

But, Rosita often admitted to herself, *emotionally I'm so dependent on that man that to lose the opportunity to be near him would bankrupt my soul.*

She set the chain on her door and dropped a handful of mail on the sofa.

Just advertisements and bills. No need to look through them now. I'll pay the bills by the end of next week.

Rosita had an obsession about paying her bills on time. No matter how much money she made, memories of her growing-up years never erased the recollection of her mother's calls from bill collectors and of angry landlords threatening eviction.

Tonight, however, Rosita didn't want to think of bills. Tonight she felt a sense of excitement.

Friday! she thought. *Friday! Tonight I will listen to the tapes recorded this week.*

Usually the tapes were full of dull conversations between Braxton and a client, but now and then Rosita got a reward for her patience: bits of information with which she could ruin certain people if she so chose. She had no desire to do so, yet she fed on the sense of power she felt from her knowledge. That no one suspected her knowledge only added to that sense of power.

Six weeks ago Rosita heard a bit of information that was a jewel in the crown. First there was a telephone conversation between Braxton and a man in London. A couple of hours later, she heard Braxton telephone Ashley and hint at the content of the London call. Within minutes, Ashley Carrington breezed past Rosita's desk and into Braxton's office. Rosita, pretty much inured to shock by now, was stunned when she heard that conversation. She made sure not to erase it from the tape, and she gleefully tucked its contents into the computer of her brain.

Now for the ritual that drew out the waiting time and added to the pleasure. First Rosita took off her ultra-conservative gray suit and hung it carefully in the closet. Next she removed a bright red and yellow blouse, trim black pants, and shiny gold-colored sandals. After slipping on the colorful outfit, she loosened her thick dark hair from its constricting bun and shook it loose so that it fell several inches down her back. A few touches of makeup enhanced her nearly black, slightly almond-shaped eyes and brightened her full lips. The final touch was a pair of large, gold hoop earrings. Looking into her dresser mirror, she tossed back her hair and imagined the reaction of everyone at Carrington Investments if they saw her like this.

"Olé!" Rosita told her mirror, snapping her fingers in Spanish dancer style.

She left to join a friend for dinner and a movie.

Chapter Thirty-One

"Kate?"

Kate could tell that Gunnar was incredulous to receive a call from her.

"It is I," she said jokingly.

"I—Is—." Gunnar cleared his throat and began again. "Is anything wrong?"

"Does something have to be wrong for me to call you?"

"Considering our last meeting, yes."

Kate felt a pang of guilt at the pain she heard in his terse reply. "Well, nothing is wrong—not with me anyway. Braxton's party is tomorrow night, and the tension around here is thicker than Boston fog."

Gunnar cut her off. "I see."

"No. No, that's not the reason I called." The resounding silence from Gunnar's end suddenly made Kate feel insecure. "It's that…well…."

His tone a little softer, Gunnar asked, "Why did you call, Kate?"

Kate hesitated.

"You can't bring yourself to say it, even after going to the trouble of calling me, can you?"

"Can't say what?"

"That you miss this big, loud Norwegian. That you wish you'd never left him languishing in Boston."

Kate giggled like a teenager. "Languishing? You? I can't picture that. Oh, Gunnar, it's so good to hear your voice."

"And yours." He paused. "You still can't say it, can you?"

Kate took a deep breath. "Yes, I can say it. I miss you, Gunnar."

"Ahhh. That's more like it."

"Gunnar?"

"Yes?"

"I've been thinking about this RV trip. Cami and I found the perfect motorhome a couple of days ago. The only model I liked had been sold, but they're ordering me another one that should be here by the time I get back from Portland."

"I see."

"No, you don't. You don't see that I'm having second thoughts. I'm thinking of backing out of the deal."

"Why?"

"You … you can guess why."

"I don't want to guess. I've spent the past several months guessing and hoping. I want to hear you say why."

Kate saw that Gunnar wasn't going to make this easy for her. She took another deep breath and let the words rush out. "Because I don't want to travel around the country all by myself. I don't want to be away from that big, loud Norwegian."

"Why not? Tell me why not. Say it, Kate. Say it."

"Okay! I'll say it. I love you, Gunnar. I love you, I love you, I love you!"

Gunnar's voice turned husky. "Now, that's what I've been wanting to hear. You already know how much I love you. So. When are you coming back to Boston so I can tell you—and show you—in person?"

"Cami's expecting me to stay here for another week. And despite the tension—I'll explain all that when I see you—I'm having a great time with her. Then I'll be in Oregon for a month. After that, I'll let you know when I've arranged a flight home."

"Home. That sounds good. The first thing we'll do when you get back is talk about what *home* means to you and me."

"The very first thing?" Kate asked playfully.

"Okay. The second thing."

The laughter they shared made Kate feel so at one with him that she wondered how she ever could have imagined anything else.

Gunnar turned serious. "One more thing."

"About Joel?"

"About Joel."

"We'll talk about that, but for now, let's say I thank the Lord for the years I had with Joel. He will always be a wonderful memory in my heart."

"And?"

"And I'm tired of living on memories."

Chapter Thirty-Two

Rosita returned from dinner and a movie with her friend. The friend's company had been dull, and the movie duller. She was eager to listen to this week's tapes. In one corner of her bedroom, she opened a mahogany file cabinet, took out a plastic shoebox, and removed several tapes from the front. She took them to the living room and set them on the coffee table in front of the couch, next to a small tape recorder. She settled herself comfortably on the couch and inserted the first tape.

The first one was duller than usual. She was glad she could look forward to the one that recorded Thursday's conversations first with Victor, then with Scarlett Starling. Right now, she listened as Floyd Owen, whom Braxton had chosen as his political advisor, droned on about plans for the mayoral election.

Then they began to talk about the three candidates' wives. The incumbent's wife, they concluded, was a pleasant enough woman but had several health problems that prevented her being a real presence in the campaign.

"In her unobtrusive way, Terese Giovanni will make up for that," said Floyd, "what with her volunteer work at Coronado Hospital and her association with Lamb's Theater. And she's president of the Garden Club. People like that kind of community involvement."

"Then there's that son of theirs," said Braxton.

"Frank. Only child. Much adored by Mama and Papa Giovanni. Arrogant, spoiled trouble maker."

"Right," Braxton replied tersely.

149

"Well, maybe we can make sure he's their loose cannon," said Floyd.

The men went on to several other dull subjects. At last, Rosita heard the sound of both men getting out of their chairs as Floyd prepared to leave.

"You've come up with some great strategies," she heard Braxton say. "I'll study your suggestions and give them to Rosita so she can note the changes we discussed." Braxton paused. "Speaking of Rosita...."

Rosita started at the change in her employer's tone.

"What about her?" asked Floyd.

"I'm getting a little weary of her. As soon as this election is over, win or lose, I'm replacing her."

Rosita grabbed the tape recorder and stared at it wildly.

"Got a replacement in mind?" Floyd asked.

"He doesn't know it yet, but I'm planning to steal my brother's secretary from him. I'm going to let Rosita go and hire Scarlett Starling."

Floyd let out a wolf whistle. "Well, you're wise to wait till after the election!"

Horror rolled over Rosita. She jabbed the stop button. For the next several minutes she was too stunned to think or feel.

Little by little, the numbness began to wear off. As it did, she experienced the deepest hurt she'd ever felt. Even worse than when her grandfather died. This too was a kind of death. The death of the life she'd built for herself, the death of a dream. She'd been smart enough to realize she'd never be Braxton Carrington's wife, so her dreams had rarely gone in that direction. But for years she'd been even closer to him than a wife in many ways. And she'd envisioned becoming ever more indispensable to him, until the thought of not having her around would be unthinkable to him.

And now this. And for Scarlett Starling! Beautiful, yes. Intelligent, yes. But practically a baby, not only in age, but in the ways of the business world. How could he? How *could* he?

The more she agonized, the deeper the hurt cut into her. Then another emotion trickled in and strangely cleared her thinking. Anger. Some of it was directed toward Scarlett, but mostly it centered on Braxton. The trickling stream bubbled up and began to steam and boil, like a witch's cauldron. As it did, Rosita sprang into action. She flung the tape recorder against a wall, then stomped over to it, took out the offending tape and hurled it onto the couch.

"Eso diablo!" she shouted. That devil!

She spun around and through the bedroom door caught sight of the framed photograph of Braxton she kept on her bedside table. Her face contorting and her body trembling, she charged into the room and shook her fist at the photo. *"Vas a pesar esto!"* Then, as if translating her words to the photo would make Braxton himself understand, she shouted, "You're going to regret this, Braxton Carrington!"

Chapter Thirty-Three

After talking with Kate for half an hour, Gunnar hung up the phone. He felt a silly grin spread across his face. He pulled in a deep breath, relishing the very oxygen he breathed.

It seemed he had waited a lifetime to hear Kate say she was putting memories of Joel in the past. He understood her reluctance to a point. After all, he'd felt disloyal to Brita the first time he was attracted to another woman. Three years later, he struggled with guilt again when he was first drawn to Kate. He had discussed it with his two sons. Both twenty-five-year-old Hans and twenty-three-year-old Peder had assured him they only wanted to see their father happy and they were sure their mother would have felt the same way. He still wrestled with guilt over his budding feelings for Kate for several weeks. But little by little he realized his sons were right: Brita would want him to go on with his life.

Now it seemed that Kate—after four years of clinging to a memory—had come to that same conclusion for herself. He felt that silly grin spreading ever wider. He even did a clumsy two-step across the small den where he'd taken Kate's call, laughing at himself all the way.

He raised his large arms toward the ceiling and cried out, "Thank You, Lord!"

Then a sudden awful thought slammed into him. He dropped his arms.

What if Kate changed her mind? What if she'd only been caught up in the tension of the Carrington household and clutched at him as a kind of lifeline?

No. Too uncharacteristic. Kate's too sensible for that. That thought eased his concern for only a couple of seconds before another one occurred. *So? Sometimes people act out of character.* What if she called him tomorrow? He could almost hear her saying, "I'm so sorry for acting impulsively. I hope you'll forgive me."

"No!" he said. "I won't let that happen."

But what if the Lord didn't want him and Kate together? What if he had misread all the signs he thought he'd seen leading to the two of them as a couple?

Again he turned his eyes toward the ceiling. "Lord, am I being dumb? Or is there something I should do?"

Silence. Both outwardly and in his heart.

"*Nothing?* I should do *nothing*, Lord?"

Gunnar dropped into a brown leather chair chosen especially for his large frame. He closed his eyes and tried to push down the impatient, almost urgent, desire to make a move to assure that Kate would not back out on him. Several minutes later, with much effort, he said, "Okay, Lord, I give up. If You want me to trust You to work in Kate's heart, that's what I'll do. And if You don't want us together, I'll try to accept that."

Despite his promise to the Lord, Gunnar began to relive the conversation with Kate. To distract himself, he reached for today's mail on the table beside his chair. He rifled through the small stack: a dental appointment reminder, a couple of bills, a business letter, several advertisement fliers. He separated the fliers from the other mail and took them to the wastebasket near his desk. As he dropped them in, one fluttered to the floor. He stooped, picked it up and started to add it to the others.

Then his eye caught sight of the picture of a large red, white, and blue airplane with a stylized blue eagle between huge red and blue A's on the tail. American Airlines. It was the carrier Kate had taken to San Diego. In the advertisement a slogan stood out beneath the plane: "Something special in the air." A flutter of excitement touched him.

"Something special in the air," he read aloud.

Was this a sign from God? Did He want Gunnar to fly to San Diego?

I sure hope so, he thought with a rush of adrenaline. *Because I'm going with it.* He moved toward the telephone on his desk.

He stopped.

Impossible. Too much going on at work to up and fly across the country. **What about Johnson?**

The thought seemed to pop out of nowhere. Keith Johnson was a young ambitious assistant who had been with the company for only a year.

You've been wanting to pass on more responsibility to him. *Perfect!*

Although Gunnar had a lot of work, Johnson could handle part of it, and Gunnar could catch up on the rest fairly quickly when he got back.

He raised his eyes to the ceiling once again, this time an eager question in them. With a small feeling of confirmation, he picked up the phone directory and quickly found the number for American Airlines. If he couldn't get a flight out to San Diego tomorrow, he would take that as a definite answer. But if he could....

With trembling fingers he punched in the number.

Thirty minutes later he was packing his bags, relishing the surprise he'd see on Kate's face when she saw him.

Saturday, August 16

Chapter Thirty-Four

Cami's hands clenched the wrought-iron railing of the balcony outside the sitting room of the master suite. Beyond her, past the street, past the pile of huge rocks, past the stretch of sand, steel-gray waves rose and fell, then spread across the shore. Though the sun would not set for another two hours, only a faint glow penetrated a black cloud that hid it from the world it was supposed to warm.

A chilly swish of wind blew the cold diamonds of Cami's dangling earrings against her cheeks. She shivered and wished she'd chosen a warmer dress for Braxton's party. She remembered choosing it. The silky steel-blue fabric shot with silver, the long straight skirt that flared at the hem, the form-fitting top with rhinestone spaghetti straps, the diamond and sapphire anniversary necklace—they all seemed perfect at the time. Elegant but understated, Cami's trademark style. Now it just felt cold.

Like me, she thought, wishing she could get back the sense of optimism she'd felt last night. She and Kate had sat up late talking, and Kate had encouraged her to hold onto her faith and seek the Lord's direction. Kate had also encouraged her to fight for her marriage with all that was in her.

"Sometime soon, after this party is behind you, face Braxton with your suspicions, Cami," she'd said. "Much as you hate confrontation, you've got to do this. Your marriage and—I believe—even your relationship with the Lord depend on it."

"But how, Kate? How can I find the strength to face him?"

Kate's eyes had twinkled. "Well, you could Philippians 4:13 it."

Cami smiled at her friend. "You're right—I can do all things through Christ, who gives me strength."

That was last night. Now, staring into the gloomy sky, she felt no strength, only emptiness.

Another swish of wind, this one colder, sent another shiver through her. Time to go in. As she stepped into the frame of the French doors leading into the suite, Braxton turned toward her.

He stopped in the middle of adjusting the bowtie of his tuxedo. His intense blue eyes widened in appreciation.

"Stunning!" he said, his eyes sweeping from the top of her pale blond hair pulled back into a classic chignon to the tip of her silver sandals and back up again. "Stunning," he repeated. "Come here." He held out a hand to her.

Slowly, her chin up and her heart heavy, she went to him, but when he pulled her to his chest, she stiffened.

He held her away from him. What she saw in his eyes startled her. Surprise? Confusion? Had the coolness she'd shown him for the past few days made him lose a little of his confidence of her?

When Braxton brought his lips down to hers, she turned her head.

"What's wrong?" The question was demanding, not solicitous. Braxton was used to getting his own way, even with Cami.

Especially with me. Sudden visions of the many, many times she'd gone along with Braxton in nearly every area of their lives, whether she felt like it or not, tumbled about in her brain. She was tempted to go ahead and pour out all the hurt and anger and confusion she felt. She opened her mouth to do so. No. She couldn't do it now and put a pall on the party. She'd wait—but not till after the election, as she'd told Kate she planned to. She now realized she couldn't hold it in that long—but at least till after Kate was gone.

"It's that Elfmon woman, isn't it?" Braxton asked.

Cami looked at him in surprise. How did he know she was thinking of Kate?

"Her name is Kate," she said stiffly. "I wish you wouldn't speak of her in that sneer. Anyway, what do you mean?"

"Every time you spend a little time with her, you turn into a different person. You think differently about me. Even turning away from me just now."

"That's ridiculous. I didn't want to get lipstick on you."

"It's more than that. Every time *Kate* shows up, you start getting religious and pious. I can see it now. You'll start going to church every time the doors open."

"Braxton!"

"The same thing happened to Durant when he visited Kate in Boston. All he can talk about is how 'accepting Christ' changed his life. Now he's wanting to throw away a chance to attend Edinburgh University," Braxton said, his voice dripping with scorn, "and go on a *mission* trip to Israel."

Feeling her eyes go as cold as the air on the balcony, Cami said, "I'm not sure how the conversation came around to this, but I think it's something we need to discuss later." She lifted her chin and turned away. Picking up the silver chiffon stole that lay across a chair, she said, "Time to go."

"Right," she heard him say in a tight voice as she left the room.

Chapter Thirty-Five

"Carrington's the only one who can beat out Giovanni and his crowd," Cami heard one tall, bearded guest say as he tugged at the lapels of his tuxedo.

Nearby, a plump woman clad in black velvet slapped one multi-ringed hand to her heart. "I hate to imagine what that man would do to our island."

As the two moved away, Cami surveyed the Oceanfront Ballroom of the Hotel Del with an appreciative eye. Shortly Braxton would announce his intention to run for mayor of Coronado, and the two hundred elegant guests milling about seemed eager to witness his official venture into politics.

Even after twenty-two years of living a life of luxury, Cami had rarely seen so many diamonds, rubies, and emeralds; so many dazzling dresses; so many perfectly coifed heads and expertly made-up faces.

This is what they mean when they refer to the beautiful people, she thought.

Just then Robin Byrd, owner of Robin's Byrd Cage, Cami's favorite island boutique, came up. Robin liked to wear the red color that reflected her name and that of her shop. Tonight her off-the-shoulder dress was trimmed with red and black feathers and sparkled with red sequins.

"This is amazing!" Robin said, lifting her hands and turning her head from side to side. "Ashley's work, of course."

Cami flashed Robin a smile. "She really outdid herself, didn't she?"

"I like how she knows where to decorate and where not to." Robin looked toward the huge plate-glass windows overlooking the ocean. "Those certainly didn't need any adornment, but I love what she did with the tables. Using not just one but three gold-plated bowls with floating water lilies. And the crown-shaped brooches and tie tacks were a great idea, too." She kissed her fingertips in appreciation.

"Yes, they do carry out the crown motif of the hotel. I'm so glad you like them."

"I should." Robin placed one hand beside her mouth and whispered, "She ordered them from me."

Both women laughed, and Robin headed for the appetizer table with its silver platters of fresh fruits, raw vegetables, and oysters on the half shell flown in from Cape Cod. Amidst all this sat a huge, crown-shaped ice sculpture surrounded by tropical flowers typical of the island.

A dozen waiters and waitresses circulated with trays of drinks sparkling with lighted ice cubes. A dozen more stood ready to serve a five-course gourmet meal. Two bartenders manned the fully stocked bar, which included sodas and sparkling cider for the teetotalers like Cami and Kate.

Cami caught sight of her husband. He turned, gave her a sardonic smile, lifted his champagne glass to her, and turned away. Hurt, Cami felt torn between sharing his moments of glory and resenting them. Still, she knew Braxton had an excellent chance at the bid for mayor—despite the many people who had reason to resent him. She hoped none of them would cause a problem tonight.

Suddenly a streak of lightning flashed through the already brilliantly lit ballroom. Lights flickered. A crash of thunder shook the tall windows and bounced off the walls.

Cami shivered.

***

Kate had never seen Cami look lovelier. With her pale blond hair, porcelain complexion, and smoky blue eyes, Cami had always been beautiful. Tonight she was breathtaking. Apparently the photographer from the local newspaper thought so too. He must have snapped at least a dozen pictures of her.

Yet behind her friend's apparent high spirits, Kate recognized the bleakness in her eyes.

***

Rosita knew people thought of her as a colorless if formidable fixture in Braxton's office. She also knew how uninteresting she looked in her simple black dress and dark hair in the usual plain bun; so she was surprised when the newspaper photographer snapped a picture of her.

Frowning at the young man, she moved toward Braxton and his "admirers." Once she would have relished the thought that she alone knew which ones were true fans and which ones despised her boss. She would have fed on the little "secrets" she'd learned through the tapes she listened to every Friday night.

That was before she heard the tape that involved herself and turned every hope and dream of the past twenty-four years into a pile of ashes. For a moment she relived that moment in her apartment when horror had poured over her like hot oil and transformed her love for Braxton into paralyzing hatred.

Hatred that demanded action.

***

Dr. Stan Weston's eyes followed his fiery-haired wife as she swayed across the crowded ballroom in slinky bronze colored pants almost indecently snug. When Erika reached the group near Braxton Carrington, she latched onto his arm and gave him a provocative smile.

What was she doing? *This* was how she let Braxton know she was no longer interested in him? Ha.

Stan saw Braxton give Erika a cool, dismissive expression and loosen himself from her grip. At that moment, Stan hated Braxton almost as much for snubbing Erika as for luring her away from him.

***

Trembling, Erika moved away from the group. Braxton had all but pushed her away! He'd been colder than the nearby crown-shaped ice sculpture. Burning with humiliation, she fought back bitter tears that threatened to spoil her makeup. She felt a fresh stab of pain remembering their last time together at the small French restaurant where he ended their relationship as casually as he would have ended a business meeting.

Minute-by-minute since then, her hurt and anger had coalesced into one thought: revenge. Nobody brushed off Erika Weston and got away with it.

***

"This is one of Seaview Venture's best efforts, Ashley," Robin Byrd said, patting Ashley's hand.

Ashley forced out a thank you as Robin, whose red and black feathers fluttered in the breeze she created, hurried on. However, Ashley's insides twisted with fear and anger, rather than pride and satisfaction, as she studied Braxton across the room. With his commanding height and athletic build, combined with jet-black hair, piercing blue eyes, and strong but patrician features, he was considered a "man's man" as well as every woman's dream.

And then there was Victor, who looked so much like his older brother, but somehow missed.

Like a smudged copy of the real thing.

Ashley was unable to quash that thought despite the loathing she felt for Braxton tonight. Because of the call she received from him a few weeks ago, she was losing money on this event that should have raked in a huge profit from one of the wealthiest men she knew. But worse, much worse, was the fear that accompanied every moment of her existence, waking or sleeping.

Her mouth twitching in an ugly smile, Ashley swirled the amber liquid in her glass, making the lighted ice cubes clink against the side. Braxton Carrington may feel an almost god-like invulnerability, but he was wrong. Soon he'd know how wrong.

***

Victor stepped near his wife. "What's the matter? Sorry you went to all this work for your brother-in-law instead of your adoring husband?"

"Shut up, Victor. Haven't you caused me enough grief getting yourself in debt to that creep at Viejas?"

"Shhh!" Victor looked quickly around. "You want to announce it to the world?"

"No," Ashley hissed. "What I want to do is kill both of you."

"Both of us?"

For a moment Ashley looked startled. The look disappeared, and she shrugged. "Sorry. I'm really tired."

Not for a second did Victor believe her.

He stared at Braxton and his entourage, imagining the reactions if people knew how the *great man* forced his younger brother into subjection. Made him account for every cent. Made him crawl for help—then refused him.

His mouth curled downward. "Things are about to change around here," he told Ashley. "You'll see."

As he walked away, he paid little attention to the photographer eagerly snapping him and Ashley.

***

Durant fastened his eyes on his father and frowned. He had rarely felt such inner turmoil. Longing for his father's love and approval one second, hating him the next. He couldn't understand how his own deep love for God could dwell in his heart right next to an anger that threatened to destroy him.

A light kiss on the cheek from Debra interrupted his thoughts.

"Hey," she said. "You okay?"

"Not really."

"You're upset because he refused your request about Israel. Right?"

Without looking away from Braxton, Durant gave a casual shrug, but his words held a bitter bite. "Nothing new there." Abruptly he faced Debra and spoke in a harsh whisper so as not to attract attention. "He's said no to nearly everything I've requested since I was three! Why should anything suddenly be different?"

"Whoa! Calm down. This is the first time I've seen you this angry in more than a year—since Aunt Kate talked you into that *religious experience.*" Debra's voice softened. "Sorry. That was kinda lame. I thought you were a pretty good person already. But now aren't you supposed to start loving everybody?"

Again, Durant looked long and hard at his father. His mouth tightened. When he spoke, it was as if he were talking to himself rather than to his sister.

"I don't know how many more rejections I can take!" He stomped off.

***

As Debra watched her brother stride away, she knew she couldn't hide her own inner turmoil from him much longer. It was amazing that she'd managed to keep her relationship with Frank a secret for so many months. She hated deceiving Durant. Soon—maybe tomorrow, with this party behind them—she'd tell him everything, from that first night she met Frank at a basketball game to the recent fight between him and their father.

Their father. How she loved him, despite all his flaws. Now he was surrounded by a group that—in addition to a couple of waiters, the photographer, the television cameraman, and several sumptuously-dressed guests—included Victor and Ashley, the Westons, Rosita, and Victor's secretary, Scarlett Starling. Feeling oddly protective, Debra moved nearer.

Chapter Thirty-Six

"And now, I think—"

A clap of thunder interrupted Victor Carrington's words. Many of the two hundred guests in the Oceanfront Ballroom of the Hotel del Coronado started at the sound. A murmur of concern came from others who cast worried glances at the sky outside. A few nervously fingered diamond necklaces or tugged at gold cufflinks. Yet all seemed eager for what they knew they were about to hear.

The thunder died down, and Victor continued, "—my brother has a few words for you." He made a sweeping gesture toward the dark-haired, aristocratically handsome man to his right.

Braxton Carrington stood leisurely to warm applause. Dignified, smiling, nodding left and right, he accepted the acclamation as his due.

"Thank you. Thank you all for coming tonight." His rich baritone voice filled the room as he spread his arms and took a slow, deliberate look around. "What better place for this event? What better place than the *Hotel of the Crowned* to announce my intention to press for the honor of mayor of Coronado, the world's greatest little island, the very crown of America's Finest City? My own great-great-grandfather, William Carrington, attended the Del's grand opening in 1888. And I'm proud to say that Carringtons have been active in island civic activities ever since."

Braxton paused, letting the words sink in, subtly reminding his guests that Dominic Giovanni, his major opponent in the mayoral race, was only a second-generation Coronadan.

A ripple of good-natured laughter filled the room, and Braxton thought of how this gala had been a huge success so far. All the right people were here: most of the local elite, several San Diego and State of California officials, and a number of officers from North Island Naval Air Station, all carefully chosen. Even those who didn't particularly care for him agreed that Braxton was the man for the job. Admittedly, a few had good reason to dislike him, but he had them under control.

The laughter died down, and he continued, "Now. Let's get down to the nitty-gritty. Let's talk about where I, as your future mayor, plan to take the island of Coronado."

At that moment, a streak of lightning lit up the moonless sky beyond the huge windows facing the water.

Braxton chuckled. "The weatherman was right for a change. Looks like that storm they've been predicting has hit us."

Smiling at his beautiful wife Cami, seated next to him, he reached for his flute of pink champagne, gave it a little swirl, and took a sip.

Suddenly pain slammed his chest. His glass clattered to the table as both hands clutched the tuxedo fabric over his heart.

"Cami!" he cried out.

The pain sharpened—like someone had stabbed him. He felt himself losing control.

"Cami!" This time the word came out in a coarse whisper.

He groped toward a white-faced Cami, who had half risen from her chair.

"Ca...."

He collapsed.

Amidst gasps from the guests, a crash of thunder shook the room, and the lights went out.

Chapter Thirty-Seven

It was close to midnight when Gunnar slowed his rental car to a stop and put it in neutral in front of the Carrington house. Even in the dark downpour, it looked more like a mansion than a family home. Yet the wooden beams of the Tudor-style architecture, along with tall, diamond-paned windows, lent a softening touch. Because of a long layover in Denver, made even longer by a delayed flight, he was so late getting to San Diego that he'd had to forfeit his hotel reservation near the airport. He planned to check out the location of the Carrington home, then look for a room on the island. Though Kate was an early riser, she would need extra sleep after a late-night party, so he would force himself to wait till mid-morning to call her.

He had expected to find the house dark, but lights—made wavy by the rain—shone through the downstairs windows. Also, several cars lined both sides of the street, and Gunnar could see people moving around inside.

Braxton's party must've been pretty successful for them to be celebrating this late.

His first thought was to dash to the house and find Kate. No. He shouldn't crash their party. It would be awkward for everyone. Besides, he wanted a private reunion with Kate. He shifted into drive and started to pull away.

At that moment, he saw a familiar figure move close to a window. Even through the wavy lights, the profile and the dark bob that was Kate's signature hairstyle were unmistakable. She stretched her arms out as though to receive someone into them. Then another woman, blond and taller than Kate, moved into her arms and dropped her head onto Kate's shoulder.

Something was terribly wrong in that house, Gunnar realized with mounting unease.

Go to her, Gunnar.

Kate needs me?

Go. Now.

Unable to ignore such a definite impression, Gunnar jammed the car into drive and drove a little way down the street, thanking God for the parking space he found right away. Seconds later, he stood at the elegant double entrance with the stained-glass panels on either side and a fan-shaped window above. He jabbed the bell with his large thumb.

A few seconds later a middle-aged woman in a light-blue uniform appeared. She coolly appraised him, clearly concluding that he was a stranger. "This is not a good time to be calling," she said in a stiff, formal voice. "The family—"

"Who is it, Edie?" a trembling feminine voice called out.

"Gunnar!" Kate rushed into view, surprise and joy in her eyes.

Gunnar dropped all restraint and shoved past Edie to envelope Kate in his arms.

"Gunnar! What are you doing here?" She pulled back a little to look into his face. "Never mind. Never mind. What's important is that you're here, when I need you most."

High-spirited, independent Kate Kelly Elfmon—who rarely admitted to needing anyone but God—needed *him*! Needed Gunnar Volstad! The knowledge was almost too much for him. He pulled her close again, and for a full minute ignored the people milling about the room and simply reveled in Kate's nearness and the force of her embrace.

At last he released her and looked down into her eyes. Those eyes. Those amazing brown eyes looking back at him with such love. He wanted to gaze into them forever. Nice thought, but not very practical. He forced himself to look around the room.

For the first time, he took in the quiet voices, the somber faces. He turned back to Kate. "What's going on here?"

Kate shook her head. "It's Braxton."

"Braxton?"

Nodding, she lifted her hands in a gesture of disbelief. "Braxton is dead."

"Braxton? Dead?" Gunnar could hardly believe what he was hearing.

"It looks like he had a heart attack. It happened at the party."

Clinging to his arm, Kate led Gunnar across a high-ceilinged, marble-tiled foyer. "He just collapsed," she said. "He was still breathing, barely. He died in the emergency room."

Gunnar and Kate entered the large formal parlor in solemn silence. In the room, Kate stopped. Her back to them, a slender blond in a long, silver-blue dress rested one hand on the carved back of a chair and seemed to be staring into space.

"Cami?" Kate said softly, touching her friend's arm.

The woman turned. There, before the background of gracefully carved furniture and soft lighting, stood one of the most beautiful and saddest looking creatures Gunnar had ever seen.

Chapter Thirty-Eight

"How dare they come here?"

Gunnar, standing by the cavernous marble-mantled fireplace, looked toward the voice. He saw that it belonged to Debra Carrington, whom Kate had pointed out as one of the twins. Her forlorn, tear-streaked face turned upward to the pale one of her brother. She inclined her head toward the couple talking with their mother. Gunnar looked in that direction.

Unlike the partygoers still in formal clothing, these visitors were dressed casually. Only their manner was formal. The stocky, medium height man with thinning black hair wore chinos and a navy blue polo shirt. He shook hands with Cami and said a few words. The tall, slim, dark-haired woman standing stiffly beside him wore black pants, a pin-tucked white blouse, and a lightweight black cardigan.

Durant's eyes flicked to the couple. "The Giovannis!" he said. Then he shrugged. "I guess they have as much right as anyone else to be here. Just because Dominic is—was—Dad's main opponent doesn't mean—"

"Well, I don't want them here! I never want to look at another Giovanni as long as I live!" Debra twisted away from Durant and headed toward the offending visitors.

Durant seized her arm. "Stop. Don't make a scene. I don't like them being here either. But you didn't seem to mind Dan Clark stopping by earlier, and he's the other opponent. What's up?"

"I'll tell you what's up. Frank's what's up."

"Frank? The Giovannis' son?" Durant looked puzzled.

"Yes, Frank. Their darling son. He—" Debra stopped, her face turning more forlorn than before. She began to cry. Durant put one arm around her waist and led her away.

As they left the room, Gunnar saw Kate watching them. He caught her eye and questioned her with his own. Briefly she nodded to the twins and put her hands together in a quick prayer-like gesture. He nodded back and sent up a silent prayer.

Upon meeting Cami, Gunnar had offered what felt like extremely inadequate condolences. Now he stood beside the fireplace and sipped a cup of coffee. He usually stayed away from caffeine late at night, but his tired body reminded him that it was three hours later in Boston, and he needed the kick to stay alert. He felt like an observer from a foreign planet, taking in vignettes of extraterrestrials.

He had already met Pastor Oates of the Baptist church Cami sometimes attended and learned that the minister of the Episcopal church where she and Braxton were members was out of town. The Baptist pastor's presence seemed to be a comfort to Cami. After explaining the church situation to Gunnar, Kate filled him in on the others present. He tried to remember who everyone was.

Victor and his wife Ashley stood in a corner of the room. Their facial expressions and tense body language suggested an argument.

Victor's pretty secretary, Scarlett Starling, unobtrusively gathered up empty glasses and cups and handed them to the maid.

Braxton's administrative assistant, Rosita, had made a surprisingly brief stony-faced appearance before rushing out.

The Giovannis moved away from Cami and stood near Gunnar. Though they kept their voices low, by moving two steps closer he could hear what they said.

"There I was, Terese, about three minutes past eleven, flipping on the news and seeing my own face on the screen and hearing that my major opponent is dead," Gunnar heard Dominic Giovanni tell his wife. "Then Carrington appeared on the screen." He shook his head. "I can hardly believe it."

"Me either. Poor Cami. And those twins! What will this do to them?"

"Durant won't be too torn up—he and Braxton were always at odds."

"But I've heard that Debra adored him," Terese said. "Anyway, it really is hard to believe. I was appalled when I heard the news on the radio driving back from the hospital."

"Well, now that I've put in my appearance," said Dominic, "I'm going to say a word to Victor and go on home. Coming?"

Terese gave Dominic a reproachful look. "I'll be along in a few minutes."

As the Giovannis went separate ways, Gunnar looked back at Cami. Looking almost ethereal, she listened to—without seeming to hear—a stunning young redhead in tight bronze-colored pants, accompanied by a short, balding man.

His curiosity piqued, Gunnar moved closer. At the same time, Kate did likewise and stood next to him.

"We're sorry if we're intruding," the man was saying. "I wanted to wait till tomorrow or the next day to come by, but Erika—"

"I insisted we come over right now," the red-haired woman said in a low, husky voice. "Stan and I thought so highly of Braxton that we wanted to offer our condolences right away."

Gunnar thought he'd never heard anything so insincere sounding.

"Besides," she went on, "Stan being a doctor...."

"Erika, I'm a cosmetic surgeon, not a family doctor," the man snapped. Then he spoke gently to Cami. "But if there's anything at all I can do, I'd be happy to. Like—well, I keep sedatives in my car."

Cami, who looked as though she could use a sedative, simply gave the doctor a weak smile of appreciation. "Thank you so much, Stan, but no."

Kate stepped close to Cami and said, "You may not need a sedative, but you do need some rest. Why don't you let me help you get into bed?"

Cami's eyes widened in horror. "No, no, I couldn't. Not—not there."

The master bedroom, Gunnar surmised.

"I know," said Kate. "I don't blame you. You could sleep in one of the guest bedrooms for a few nights."

"Kate?" Cami's voice and eyes were pleading. "Will you...."

"Yes, you can sleep on the other bed in my room tonight. I won't leave you alone for a minute."

Pastor Oates came up at that moment. "That's a good idea, Cami. But, before you go up, would you like me to pray with you?"

"Yes. I'd like that. Let's go in the den." Cami turned to Kate. "You'll come, too, won't you? And the twins." She looked around and frowned. "Where are the twins?"

"They left the room together a few minutes ago," said Gunnar.

The doctor cleared his throat. "Erika and I will be on our way now. Please call if we can help."

"Yes, please *do*." His wife slung back her fiery mane and led her husband away.

"I'll be going, too," Gunnar said, though he wondered where.

"Where are you staying, Gunnar?" Cami asked.

"At a local hotel, I guess."

"You don't have a reservation?"

"Not anymore, but I'm sure I can find something."

"Not on the island," Cami said. "This is the height of the tourist season. Besides, there aren't that many choices." She touched Gunnar's arm. "We have plenty of space here. I'll tell Edie to get a room ready for you."

Scarlett came up at that moment and said, "I'll tell her for you, Mrs. Carrington."

"Thank you, Scarlett. I'd really appreciate that."

"You don't need to do that, Cami," Gunnar protested. "I'm sure I can find a place on the mainland."

"No. I want you here. Please don't argue." She straightened herself and lifted her delicate chin in a determined way that surprised Gunnar a little. This was not the frivolous, weak-willed woman he'd imagined Cami to be. He was touched at her consideration for him when she herself was so grief-stricken.

"Thank you," he said simply.

Chapter Thirty-Nine

Debra, her long yellow silk skirt dragging in the water and one hand holding her spike-heeled, backless sandals, was drenched and shivering with cold.

A few minutes ago, when she told Durant all about her relationship with Frank Giovanni, he wasn't shocked.

His lips had tightened and his eyes glittered. "I knew something was going on with you. What'd you see in that loser anyway?"

Debra thought for a few seconds before answering sheepishly, "Probably the forbidden fruit"—she made quotation marks in the air—"more than anything else. And well, he is kind of good-looking."

Durant gave her a doubtful look. "You should have confided in your brother sooner. I'd have warned you off him." He paused. "The only thing that surprises me is Dad decking Frank. That's not his usual style." Durant touched Debra's cheek and added, "But then he would never stand for anybody messing with his little girl."

His sweet tone was so opposite of the one Frank had used when he'd called her "Daddy's little girl" that she broke down sobbing again.

After Durant's totally unsuccessful attempts to comfort her—at least he'd not tried to tell her that her father's death was "God's will" as she'd feared he would—Debra left him and threw her hoodie over the thin, sleeveless gown she'd worn to the party. She slipped out of the house and ran across the street toward the beach. The rain had slackened only a little and she was thoroughly soaked by the time she reached the sand.

Now a flash of lightning briefly lit up the sky above the dark, roaring waves. The ensuing crash of thunder stabbed at her heart, reminding her of the similar crash that had immediately preceded her father's collapse. She wondered how she was going to get through this. It seemed impossible.

For the first time she envied Durant his convictions. Yes, he was clearly devastated and feeling guilty because of the arguments he'd so recently had with Braxton. Yet, beneath it, Debra sensed a calmness and strength that she wished she could latch onto. His faith seemed as sure as the tide that was now moving in. Maybe he had something there.

She stiffened. Someone had come up behind her. She hadn't heard anything; the noise of the pounding surf covered most other sounds. But she knew someone was there. Not knowing why, she felt an immediate sense of danger. Steeling herself, she twirled around in time to see a hand raised above her head. The hand held a rock!

The rock smashed against her forehead.

She crumpled to the ground. Before deep blackness overtook her, she was vaguely aware of footsteps running lightly away—and of the tide moving ever closer.

She lay still.

Chapter Forty

Debra's attacker looked back while dashing down the beach. *What luck! Never thought I'd get two of them tonight. One more to go.*

Chapter Forty-One

"Lay off me, will you?" Victor Carrington said to Ashley. "My brother's only been dead a few hours, and already you're nagging me about *taking my rightful place* in the company."

"Oh, don't give me that sneer," Ashley hissed. "And keep your voice down." Her eyes scanned the people in the room, repeatedly returning to her sister-in-law. She edged closer to him. "It may be a good idea to play the grieving brother to this crowd, but don't put on your act with me."

"It may surprise you, dear wife," Victor hissed back, "but I do feel grieved. Braxton and I rarely saw eye-to-eye, but he *was* my brother." Victor stopped, biting his lower lip.

"Right-o," she said, her British accent strong. "That would surprise me all right. Seriously, try to tell me it hasn't crossed your mind that you're slated to step in as president of the company."

"And you? You aren't already picturing yourself as the president's wife?"

"Touché. And why not, may I ask? You can bet I wouldn't be a helpless, pretty figurehead either." Again Ashley stared at Cami.

"You really hate her, don't you? You're so jealous it oozes from your pores."

Ashley's eyes sparked as she opened her mouth to reply.

Victor looked toward Cami, poised and serene even in her grief, and back at Ashley. "And it's easy to see why." He abruptly turned his back and walked away.

Chapter Forty-Two

Rosita kept to the speed limit as she drove across the soaring Coronado Bridge to mainland San Diego. She had turned her windshield wipers to the fastest level, and each rapid swish seemed to beat in time with her heart. Everything in her cried out to press the gas pedal to the floor, but she didn't want to get pulled over.

Going to the Carrington home and expressing condolences to Braxton's family was the hardest thing she had ever done. Accepting Cami's expression of concern for her had been the most difficult part of all.

"I know this is as hard on you as anybody," Cami had said. "No man ever had a more faithful—and helpful—administrative assistant."

For a brief second Rosita had nearly folded, had nearly let herself give in to Cami's thoughtfulness. Then the past twenty-four years streaked through her mind like the streak of lightning in the stormy sky. Faithful? Yes, she'd been faithful, more faithful and helpful than anyone realized. And what had she got for it? An employer who was ready to dump her for a younger, prettier assistant.

Anger and bitterness boiled up in her again—against dead Braxton Carrington, against everyone connected with him.

Throwing caution to the wind, Rosita pressed her foot hard on the pedal. Like a mad woman she took the remaining dangerous curve of the bridge high above the churning waters of the bay. She had to get away.

Chapter Forty-Three

Weariness seeped through every inch of Cami's body. Weariness so deep it nearly matched her grief and confusion. Sleep. That's what she needed. Kate had said so. Pastor Oates had said so. Even Gunnar had said so after joining them for prayer in the den. The prayers—to which she listened silently, but didn't join audibly—had been some comfort, but at the back of her mind she'd kept wishing her children were at her side. She'd had only a few moments with them since… She couldn't bear to put the thought into words.

At the same time, Cami couldn't shut out the vision of Braxton splayed across the table, pink champagne spreading across the snowy white cloth. She had bent over him immediately. Someone cried out, "I'll call 9-1-1!" Victor yelled for a doctor.

The rush to the emergency room, pacing the floor in the waiting area with Victor and Ashley, Scarlett, Rosita, and of course the twins and Kate: it was all a blur. But the ER doctor's words—"I'm sorry, Mrs. Carrington. We did all we could, but it was too late"—were etched into Cami's brain.

Everyone had accompanied Cami and the twins back to the house. Now only Kate and Gunnar remained with them. Final funeral arrangements would have to wait until after the required autopsy. Then Braxton's body would be taken to the funeral parlor.

His body—alone, covered in a shroud in a cold, impersonal room in a mortuary—waiting to be reduced to ashes in a crematorium, as Braxton had arranged long ago. Cami shuddered and slammed that thought shut.

The children. No matter how weary she was, she had to see Debra and Durant before she went to bed. Scarlett and Edie had prepared a guest room for Gunnar, and Kate was in the den saying good night to him.

What a nice man, Cami thought. *And it's so obvious that he loves her deeply. And she loves him.* Even in the midst of her sorrow, Cami was able to think how perfect Kate and Gunnar were for each other and to pray, *Please, Lord, give Kate the happiness she deserves.*

The children. Cami's jumbled thoughts swung back to them again. With a surprising burst of energy, she climbed the curving staircase to their rooms. She tapped on Debra's door first.

"Debra," she called out softly. When she got no answer, she quietly turned the knob and stepped inside.

From the light in the hall, she could see the room was empty and the bed unruffled. Debra must be with her brother. Cami had seen them clinging to each other. She knew, though she felt she'd never fully understand, that the bond between them as twins was inexplicably powerful. They were probably able to comfort each other more than anyone else could, even their mother. Cami turned down the hall to Durant's room.

"Come in, Mom," Durant told her, pushing himself up from a beanbag chair emblazoned with a San Diego Chargers emblem.

Cami saw that he had flung his evening clothes on the bed and was wearing long pajama bottoms and a T-shirt. His eyes were rimmed with red, and his dark hair was awry, as though he'd pushed his hands through it over and over. He looked so much like a young Braxton Carrington that Cami thought her heart would stop. He pulled her to him and held her silently for a full minute.

"The Lord will help us get through this, Mom," he said at last.

"I know He will," Cami whispered. "I know He will." She stepped back and looked around the room. "Where's Debra?" she asked, her heart quickening for some reason.

"Debra? I guess she's in her room."

"No, she isn't."

"You sure?"

"Of course. I looked a couple of minutes ago. She's not there, and her bed hasn't been touched."

"She's probably downstairs."

"She's not downstairs," Cami snapped. "I was just down there, making sure the lights were off. I sent Edie to bed some time ago."

Durant frowned. "Well, she's got to be somewhere in the house. Come on. I'll help you find her."

When a quick search of the house showed Debra wasn't there, Durant called her phone, only to get her voice message.

"I don't like this, Durant."

"Me either."

"What's going on?" asked Kate, coming out of the den with Gunnar.

"Debra's not in the house," Durant told Gunnar. "Mom and I looked everywhere. And she's not answering her phone."

Gunnar spoke up. "How long ago did you see her? Did you ask the maid if she'd seen her?"

"We were together about an hour ago," Durant answered. "I didn't talk with Edie yet, but I did look in the garage, and her car is still there."

"Then we'd better search the grounds," Gunnar said.

"You think she would have gone outside in this weather?" Cami asked.

"We have to at least look, Cami," said Kate. "And if she's not near the house, you can call a couple of her friends. Maybe she went to see one of them."

"No way," said Durant.

"I know that seems unlikely under the circumstances," Kate told the distraught young man, "but maybe she felt she had to talk with one of her girlfriends."

"Let's quit wasting time," Durant commanded. "Everybody get a raincoat, and let's start looking." He dashed to a nearby closet. Before he ran out, he turned to Cami. "Mom, you stay here."

No! Cami thought. She opened her mouth to protest, but Kate stopped her.

"He's right, Cami. Someone needs to be here in case Debra calls or shows up."

Cami wanted to protest again, but she saw the wisdom of staying at the house. Instead, she went to her favorite chair in the den, where she sent up a volley of prayers for her daughter—and for herself.

I don't think I can take it, Lord, if You let Debra be taken from me, too.

Chapter Forty-Four

Debra tried to rise out of the fog that enveloped her brain. Couldn't do it. Head hurt too much. Such pain. Such horrible pain.

And wetness. Cold, cold wetness. Rain from above and shallow water in the sand beneath.

Water beneath her? Sand? Why? Why was she lying in wet sand?

She felt icy water touch her toes.

Why?

Ocean water. Tide coming in.

Have to move. Have to get away from the water.

She tried to push back the pain in her head and will herself to move. Finally she managed to raise up on her elbows, but couldn't get to her knees. She dragged herself forward a little. Then a little more. Inch by excruciating inch she crept forward.

"Help!" she cried out, but her voice was barely a croak that could never be heard above the pounding surf. Still, she tried again. "Help! Help me. Somebody help me."

She inched forward again. "Help me, Lord! Oh God! Please help me."

She collapsed. Cold, wet sand met her face. The water slapped against her feet again. A few minutes later it reached her knees. As it touched her waist, she blacked out.

Chapter Forty-Five

Durant and Gunnar rushed out of the house first. Kate dashed upstairs for tennis shoes and sweats—"I can move faster that way," she said—and joined the search in record time. Though the Carrington acre of property was bigger than most home sites on the small island, even in the rain it didn't take long for the three of them to search it thoroughly. They looked among the palms and pepper trees, inside the gazebo, and under the cabana that covered the outdoor kitchen. Debra was not there.

Chapter Forty-Six

The long yellow silky skirt of Debra's party dress floated atop the water as a wave subsided and flowed back into the sea. The next wave, bigger than the one before, rushed in immediately and reached her shoulders. Only her face remained uncovered by water.

Chapter Forty-Seven

A sense of urgency so strong that it felt like a physical blow hit Durant. He sent up a desperate plea. *Help me, Lord!*

Almost as soon as the words formed in his thoughts, he knew where to look. He berated himself for not thinking of it sooner. Debra loved to retreat to the ocean when she was upset! He ran to the front gate. In his haste, he fumbled with the latch.

Chapter Forty-Eight

Another wave rushed over Debra's body, this one reaching her chin.

Chapter Forty-Nine

The gate latch gave. Durant shoved it open. He ran with all his might across the street and through the opening in the large rocks. When his feet touched the sandy beach, he ran several feet to the right.

Nothing.

He retraced his steps. Debra's favorite spot was right in front of the house. No need to search far in either direction. He ran a little past his starting point.

Nothing.

He stopped and looked around, hardly aware of the water dripping from the hood of his raincoat and flowing into his flip-flops. The moon that usually made a path of light across the sea was hidden behind storm clouds. He walked forward. Another wave flowed over his feet.

Nothing. He couldn't see anything unusual. Heart sinking and tears joining the rain on his face, he headed back to the house. They would have to call out a search team for Debra.

Chapter Fifty

A wave ebbed away from Debra's chin, and another swept in and covered her face. Her long skirt swirled about her.

Chapter Fifty-One

A flash of lightning brightened the sky. For a moment, Durant could see the area around him better. To his left something was floating in the water.

A piece of seaweed? No.

A scarf? No.

Debra's skirt!

Heart pounding, Durant ran toward her shouting, "Debra! Debra!"

A wave retreated to the sea, and he saw her still, pale face. He bent over and scooped his sister out of the water.

Chapter Fifty-Two

How much more can she take, Lord? Kate's heart wrenched help-lessly at the sight of Cami's drooping slender shoulders.

Cami stood by Debra's bed in Sharp Coronado Hospital and stroked her hand. She had refused to leave her daughter's side for more than a couple of minutes since Durant, wet hair plastered against his head, rushed into the house. In his arms his sister lay limp and drenched. Blood dripped from her forehead onto Durant's raincoat.

"She's alive!" he shouted. "I'm gonna take her to the hospital. I can drive there quicker than waiting for 9-1-1. Somebody get my car keys. They're on my desk."

"Mine are right here," Cami said, retrieving her small evening purse from a nearby table.

"Good. Let's go."

Durant and an ashen-faced Cami, still in the dress she'd worn to Braxton's party hours earlier, rushed through the house to the garage.

"I'll phone the hospital and tell them you're on the way," Kate called out after them.

They had arrived at the emergency room about midnight. Now the mid-morning sun shone brightly through the hospital window. The storm had dissipated so thoroughly that it may as well have never occurred.

Please pull Debra through, Lord, Kate prayed. *And please give Cami Your strength.*

Before she and Gunnar drove to the hospital, Kate quickly found a deep blue summer jogging suit for Cami in her cavernous closet. Now Gunnar, along with Victor and Ashley, were in the waiting area.

Pastor Oates had rushed over as soon as he heard the news and stayed with the family until he had to leave to preach at his church. He said his congregation would pray for Debra to recover and for Cami and Durant to feel God's comfort and strength. Kate knew what that meant: the people in the church would spread the word, not only to others on the island, but to friends and acquaintances all over the country—even around the world.

Someone had called Reverend Fitzgerald, the family minister, vacationing in Hawaii. He sent his sincere sympathies and prayers and said he would cut his vacation short and be home in time to perform Braxton's funeral service.

Cami agreed to change into the comfortable clothes Kate brought but refused any kind of sedative. "I want to be fully aware when Debra comes to," she insisted.

Cami was frighteningly calm, Kate thought. Only the grief etched in her face and that melancholy droop gave her away.

"God is going to bring her through this," Cami said suddenly and definitely. "He didn't help Durant rescue her only to let her die. She's suffering from hypothermia and will probably wake up with a raging headache, but she's going to be all right."

"Sure she is," Durant spoke up from a chair in the corner of the room. For most of the past hour, he had sat there, elbows on his knees, head in his palms, lips moving silently. His dark hair was askew and his young face drawn. His voice broke a little as he said, "But it was close. So close, Mom. Her face was *in* the water."

Cami let go of Debra's hand and went to Durant's side. She leaned over and put her face next to his. "You saved her life, Honey. The doctor said you apparently got to her right after the water covered her face, so she ingested very little." Her face took on a puzzled look. "I guess she stumbled over her own feet and fell on that rock. Or maybe she fell over another rock." She shook her head and went back to Debra's bedside.

Kate stood abruptly. "I think I'll go get a soda. Durant, you want to come with me?"

"Sure. You want one, Mom?"

"No. Wait, yes. Bring me a Diet Coke."

"Will you be all right for a few minutes, Cami?" Kate asked.

"I'll be fine. Go ahead."

Outside the room, Durant asked, "What's going on, Aunt Kate?"

"Debra didn't stumble and hit that rock," she told him.

"Sure she did," said Durant, puzzled. "How else would she have fallen?" Then his eyes widened.

"She was hit with that rock. She didn't fall on it."

"Why do you say that?" Durant demanded.

"Think about it. Where is her wound?"

"About here," Durant said, touching his head right above the center of his forehead.

"Exactly. Don't you see how hard it would be to fall and hit your head right there? You'd have to practically bend over and do it on purpose."

"But it could happen," Durant insisted. "If she stumbled over another rock hard enough, that could cause her to fly upwards and land that way." He paused. "But wait. There weren't any other rocks near her."

"Are you positive? You must have just grabbed her up and run."

"It took me a couple of seconds to get a good hold on her. In that time, the water receded, and I could see. There were no other rocks."

He stared at Kate.

Chapter Fifty-Three

A groan sounded from Debra's bed.

"Debra!" Cami slammed down the soda Durant had brought her. "Can you hear me, Honey?" She furiously rubbed Debra's arm up and down. "It's me. Mom."

"I'm here, too," Durant said, leaning over the other side of the bed.

Debra groaned again. "My head. My head." She tried to raise her arm but was stopped by the IV. Her long dark lashes fluttered open. "Mom," she muttered. "Durant."

"I'm here," the two said in unison.

Debra's next words sent a chill down Cami's spine and caused Kate and Durant to stiffen.

"Dad. Where's Dad?" Fright and confusion filled her eyes as they darted from Cami to Durant and back again. "I want Daddy!"

Her lashes fluttered closed again.

Chapter Fifty-Four

"I'm going home," Ashley told Victor. The two stood outside Debra's room. "The doctor says it will be several hours before she wakes up again, and we've been here all night. I'm exhausted." She looked at the leather-banded watch that complimented the brown and blue pants outfit she'd put on when Kate called to tell them about Debra's accident. She and Victor had barely settled into their separate bedrooms when Victor got the call.

Victor studied his wife's face. "You do look tired. Tired and worried."

"Of course I'm worried—about Debra."

Victor, whose face had settled into lines of fatigue over the past few hours, said, "What's with this sudden burst of compassion?"

Ashley started to give him an angry retort, then thought better of it. Victor seemed to be taking Braxton's death much harder than she would have expected. She looped one arm into Victor's and looked up at him. "I'm not a monster, Victor. I may not care much for the precious Carrington twins, but I don't wish them harm."

Looking doubtful, Victor hesitated but then said, "Sorry."

"It's all right. Come on, let's go home."

Victor grunted agreement. "I told Cami I'd take care of Braxton's funeral arrangements. There's not a lot to do; he had everything set up already, down to the last detail, including the urn for his ashes."

"That's not surprising." Ashley couldn't keep a touch of asperity from her voice. "Braxton liked to have everything under control. Including the people in his life."

Oh, no! I shouldn't have said that. I've got to be more careful.

211

"You're right. He did like to keep me under his thumb."

Ashley could barely hide her relief. *He thought I was referring to him, not myself.*

"Unfortunately," Victor went on, "we have to wait for an autopsy."

"An autopsy? Why? The doctor said Braxton apparently had a heart attack."

"It's a requirement when someone dies suddenly away from a hospital or a medical specialist. Especially a man as well known as Braxton. A formality, that's all."

"I should hope so."

"Why do you say that?"

"No reason." Ashley shrugged nonchalantly. *That could mean an investigation!* She forced that thought away.

"I'll go ahead and make a couple of calls," said Victor.

"Remember," Ashley told him as they walked away, "whatever happens with Debra, her father can never control us again."

Victor stopped. "Us? Why do you say us? It's me Braxton kept on a puppet string. He never did anything to you."

Ashley mentally kicked herself for her second slip in the past couple of minutes. She gave Victor what she hoped was an innocent-looking expression. "Anything that hurts you ultimately hurts me, Victor."

Victor gave her a long, appraising look.

Ashley felt anything but assured.

Chapter Fifty-Five

"Cami, you've got to go home and get some rest."

Cami turned to Kate and saw eyes filled with concern. *Thank You, Lord, that she's here.*

"The doctor said Debra would sleep for several hours," Kate continued, "and she's out of danger."

"I can't leave. She may wake up while I'm gone and need me."

"I'll be here with her, Mom," said Durant. "I took a long nap yesterday afternoon before the party, so I'm okay for now. Anyway, when she does wake up, she'll need you to be alert."

The events of the past hours were catching up with Cami. She could hardly think, could hardly process all that had happened. Surely it wasn't possible her husband died and her daughter nearly drowned—in the same night!

The doctor was certain Debra was not seriously injured. Cami couldn't begin to express her relief about that. But now she must face the fact of Braxton's death. For all the distress he caused her over the years, there had been good times, and she had loved him deeply. How was she going to go on? Did she have the faith she needed? Would she be able to stand tall and strong, or would she fold like the weak kitten most people assumed she was?

Oh, God! Please hold me up. Please give me Your strength. I don't have any of my own.

"Cami? Are you all right?"

Kate's words brought Cami back to the moment. She searched Kate's face and was again grateful for the love and support she saw there. She shook her head slowly.

"No. I'm not all right. I feel like I may never be all right again. I— No. I can't leave. I won't be able to rest till Debra wakes up." She expressed a thought she'd tried to push aside. "She'll be asking for her father again. I don't know how I'm going to tell her." Cami faltered and looked at her son, her daughter's twin.

"Mom," Durant said softly, "the Lord will show you what to say, and I'll be here with you."

This is backwards. I'm the mother. I'm the one who should be offering spiritual comfort to my son.

Gunnar spoke up from the far side of the room. "I spoke to a nurse a few minutes ago. They're bringing you a recliner that folds down almost flat."

Cami's heart filled with appreciation for Gunnar's thoughtfulness. How had Kate held herself back from him for so long?

"Oh, Gunnar, thank you so much. But *you* should go on to the house and get some sleep. With the time difference between here and Boston, you've been up even longer than we have."

Kate reached up and stroked Gunnar's two-day-old stubble. "Yes, you should do that," she told him softly.

Cami watched as Gunnar looked deeply into Kate's eyes. In a near whisper, he asked, "What about you?"

"I'll be okay, but I can't leave yet," she said, caressing his cheek. Then she cleared her throat and became her usual practical self. "Maybe you can take Cami's things back to the house."

"Sure." Gunnar gave Kate a crooked grin.

Cami picked up the hospital bag containing the gown she had worn to the party. A bit of the silky silvery-blue fabric peeked from the top of the bag. The sight brought on a fresh onslaught of grief. Cami felt her face contort as tears sprang to her eyes. As she wiped them away and handed the bag of clothing to Gunnar, a tap sounded at the door.

"I'll get it," said Kate.

A few seconds later, Cami heard a strong male voice say, "I'm Detective Carlos Lopez from the Coronado Police Department." Cami turned to see a muscular, pleasant-looking man in a Coronado PD uniform. "I need to talk with Mrs. Carrington."

Gunnar scrutinized his identification badge, comparing the man's Latin face, rimless glasses, and dark hair slightly tinged with gray with the photo on the badge. He nodded in satisfaction.

Struggling to find her voice, Cami invited Detective Lopez in.

"I know this is a difficult time for you, Mrs. Carrington," the detective began.

A difficult time? A difficult time? What an understatement.

Cami refrained from expressing the thought. "Yes, Detective, it is a rather difficult time."

Lopez seemed to be waiting for her to go on. When she didn't, he cleared his throat.

"I'm afraid I have some news that will be distressing."

"What do you mean?" Cami wondered how much more distressed she could possibly be.

Complete silence reigned in the room as all awaited the detective's reply. Lopez cleared his throat a second time. "Well, you see, Mrs. Carrington, we have reason to believe your husband didn't die of natural causes."

No! That meant— Cami felt weak. Unable to speak, she waited for the detective to put her dreaded thought into words.

"We believe Mr. Carrington was murdered."

It was too much. Cami felt her consciousness fading. She heard Durant cry out, "No!" Then she slid into Detective Lopez's arms.

Chapter Fifty-Six

"Someone call a nurse!" Kate commanded as Detective Lopez helped the drooping Cami into a chair.

"No. No, Kate." Cami's voice came out in a raspy whisper. "I'll be okay."

Kate turned to the policeman. "Couldn't this have waited, Detective? Don't you think Mrs. Carrington and her son have gone through enough?"

Lopez spoke kindly but decisively. "I'm sorry. But the timing is very important. We have to speak with everybody involved as soon as possible."

Durant strode to Lopez's side. "My father died of a heart attack."

"We don't think so."

"What do you mean?" Cami rubbed her forehead and sat up straighter.

"We believe your husband was poisoned, Mrs. Carrington."

Shock-waves shot around the room. Cami let out a heartrending sob. Kate reached out a protective hand. Durant rushed to his mother's side.

It was Gunnar who addressed the issue. "What makes you think that?"

"The coloration around his mouth indicated possible poisoning. It was probably in the champagne."

Kate felt Cami stiffen herself into composure. Then she stood. Her face was chalk white, but her words were steady.

"If what you've said is true, we've got to find who did it, Detective Lopez. Tell us what you want us to do."

"First everyone will need to be questioned."

"Everyone?" Kate asked. "A couple of hundred people attended Braxton's party."

"We can cross off most of the names," Lopez told her, "but that'll still leave a lot of questioning. And, as I said before, timing is crucial. It's too bad, I know, but we have to begin with family."

"Why?" Durant spat out.

"Those closest to the victim are always the first suspects," Kate said.

"Suspects!" Durant's voice sharpened.

"At this point, everybody and nobody is a suspect," said Lopez. "Right now, we're trying to find out a few facts."

Durant exchanged a look with Kate. "There's something else, Detective," he said.

"Something else?" asked Cami. "What do you both know that I don't?"

Still Durant and Kate hesitated. She faced her son. "Durant! I insist you tell me."

Durant's face was so miserable looking that Kate answered for him. "We think Debra's accident was—"

"Debra didn't have an accident, Mom," Durant said. "Somebody attacked her." Over Cami's protesting cry, he spoke to Lopez. "I'm sorry I overreacted before. My mother and I will answer any questions you have. The sooner the better."

"Wait!" Cami took hold of Durant's arm. "What do you *mean*, Debra was attacked?"

Looking more miserable than ever, Durant said, "A little while ago Aunt Kate told me that she didn't think it could have been an accident."

"And you didn't tell *me*?" Cami asked.

"Sorry, Mom. I'm really sorry."

"We didn't want to worry you more than you already were," Kate told Cami.

Cami pressed both hands to her temples and closed her fingers around the hair there, further mussing the perfect coiffure she'd worn for Braxton's party.

Lopez spoke up. "We'd already started thinking it was suspicious that Mr. Carrington's daughter had a life-threatening accident the very night he was killed."

Killed. The word hung ominously in the air.

Apparently recognizing the effect it had produced, Lopez cleared his throat and hurried on, speaking to Kate. "What made you think she was attacked?"

"Look. I'll show you." Kate led Lopez to Debra's bedside. Though a white gauze bandage was wrapped around her pale forehead, she was able to point out the location of the wound and explain her theory that it couldn't have gotten there accidentally.

Nodding in agreement, Lopez took a notepad from his shirt pocket and jotted a few notes. Then he turned to the group in the room. "I'm sorry, but I need to go ahead and ask you all—including Miss Carrington when she wakes up—a few questions."

Chapter Fifty-Seven

Detective Lopez's questions didn't take long. Yes, Cami and Durant had been at Braxton's party. Yes, Cami had sat at his right side at the head banquet table. Durant, then Debra, were next to her. Victor had sat to Braxton's left, with Ashley beside him. However, they had not been the only ones with easy access to Braxton's glass.

"Now," Lopez said to Kate. "Let's talk about Debra. You're really observant. Not everybody would notice that it would've been hard to get a wound in that spot on her head accidentally."

Kate nodded, looking glad the detective saw her point.

"But I get the idea there's more," Lopez went on.

Kate gave Durant a questioning look.

"Durant," Cami said sharply, "if you know something, you've got to tell the detective!"

"We don't know anything for sure," he said.

"But you have suspicions," Lopez prompted. "Do you know anyone who would have a reason to want to hurt Debra?"

Durant pressed his lips together and looked at his mother, his eyes full of concern.

"Whatever it is, I can take it," she said. "Tell him."

"Well," Durant said, still hesitating, "there's Frank."

"Frank?" asked Cami. "You mean Frank Giovanni?"

"Yes, Frank Giovanni, Mom," Durant told his mother miserably. "Debra had been seeing him."

Over his mother's astonishment, Durant told her about Debra's infatuation with Frank and Braxton's violent confrontation with him.

As Durant spoke, Lopez's pen flew across the page of his notebook. At the end, he addressed Cami and Durant. "Can you think of anyone who may have wanted to end Mr. Carrington's life?"

Cami lifted her chin and looked directly at Lopez. "A lot of people had reason to dislike—even hate—my husband. He could be very charming, but he was also ambitious, sometimes to the point of ruthlessness. But the people who disliked him most were not invited to a party designed to promote a possible political career."

Lopez considered her words silently for a few seconds. He nodded, but his expression was guarded. A couple of minutes later he left, telling Cami to let him know when Debra awoke.

Chapter Fifty-Eight

For the moment, with Gunnar back at the house, Aunt Kate gone to buy sandwiches at the hospital cafeteria, and his mother finally sleeping on the recliner, Durant was alone with his thoughts. His father was dead. It seemed impossible that this man who had dominated nearly every situation and person in his life was gone forever. Durant was torn between genuine grief and a guilty hope he could live his own life now, especially since Victor would be in charge of Carrington Investments for several more years. It didn't ease Durant's feeling of guilt to remember the battle over the trip to Israel and the way he had stormed out of the house and never resolved that difference.

His head aching from his jumbled thoughts and emotions, along with a lack of sleep, Durant rose from his chair on one side of Debra's bed and walked to a window. Hands in his back pockets, he stared at a colorful bed of mixed flowers several floors below. He was having trouble praying. Not for Debra; that was easy. He had been pouring out his heart to the Lord for her recovery ever since he'd scooped her from the hungry mouth of an oncoming wave. And not for his mother. That, too, was easy, if a bit complicated. No, it was himself he had difficulty praying for. Pleas for forgiveness over some of his recent attitudes and feelings fought with a need for God's guidance.

In the recliner behind him, Cami began to stir. After a few seconds, she spoke groggily. "I can't believe I actually slept." She looked to Debra's bed. "She hasn't woken up yet?"

"Don't you think I'd tell you if she did, Mom?" Durant snapped, immediately regretting his sharp tone.

Instead of rebuking him, Cami asked softly, "What's wrong?" When he didn't answer, she said, "It's more than grief for your father and worry over Debra, isn't it?"

Durant pivoted, pleading with his eyes for her help. She held out her arms. In two long steps, he was across the room. Kneeling at her side, he buried his head in her lap, much the same way he had as a five-year-old smarting from his father's criticism.

Now as then, she whispered, "There, there, my precious boy."

Feeling her tears drip onto the hair she stroked, he lifted his head and poured out his heart to his mother.

At the end, she said, "I'm afraid I can't give you any advice. My own emotions are too mixed up right now. But you know what Aunt Kate would tell us, don't you?" A tender smile touched her eyes if not her lips.

"Sure. She'd tell us that sometimes God hears most clearly when we're the most confused."

"Right," Cami agreed. "And she'd say He already knows everything that's on our hearts—including every doubt and every smidgeon of anger."

"And since He already knows, we may as well talk with Him about it," said Durant.

"Why don't we do that right now?" Cami took his hands and bowed her head.

Chapter Fifty-Nine

"I'm sorry, Detective Lopez. I don't remember a thing beyond getting my hoodie and running out to the beach." Debra shook her head, wincing at the pain, both physical and emotional.

When she had awakened last night, her first thought had been the memory of her father's death, accompanied by overwhelming anguish. Then she realized she was in a hospital, and her mother explained that she'd been in a light coma for most of the past twenty hours. She had looked at the wall clock. Eight o'clock in the evening. She couldn't fathom that she'd lost all those hours.

Almost immediately, Durant had told her why she was there. Now that she was awake, he'd said, they needed to contact Detective Lopez at the Coronado Police Department. Durant called Lopez, but the detective was interviewing Victor and Ashley at the time. He said he'd come by in the morning about nine o'clock.

Now Debra felt her mother's and Aunt Kate's eyes intently on her. She wished Durant were here. He had spent the night by her bedside, then finally was persuaded to go home after two days without sleep.

Still trying to fit everything together in her mind, Debra scanned the faces in the room. "Are you sure I was attacked? I didn't fall?"

The detective answered her. "Ninety-nine percent sure." Lopez's no-nonsense, don't-try-to-get-away-with-anything gaze speared her. "You positive you're not protecting someone?"

Her reply came immediately. "You mean Frank Giovanni?"

Lopez seemed surprised at the quick, direct response. "Well?"

"Look, I admit I had a crush on him—well, maybe more than a crush. But after the things my dad told me and the way Frank talked to Dad, I never want to see him again. The last thing I'd do is try to protect him."

"What kind of things, Debra?"

Debra winced again. "Huh?" She was having trouble concentrating.

"What kind of things did your father tell you about Frank Giovanni?"

Debra squeezed her eyes shut. Her head felt like her brain was swelling out of it. She couldn't believe she could experience this much pain.

"Debra?"

She opened her eyes slowly and said truthfully, "I can't remember. I know they were—they were things that made me never want to have anything to do with him again." She lay back on her pillow, suddenly exhausted.

"Detective, isn't that enough for now?" asked Cami. "We promise to let you know the minute she remembers something specific."

Lopez stared long at Debra. She was glad she wasn't trying to hide anything from him. She really wanted to be helpful. At last he seemed satisfied that she was being completely truthful. He turned to respond to Cami's words.

"Be sure you do. You have my cell phone number; that's the best way to reach me." He looked back at Debra. "And don't wait for something specific to come to you. Even the vaguest memory could mean more than you think."

At that moment and for the briefest second, Debra saw a flash of something shiny in her mind. She sat up with a start.

"What is it?" asked Cami. "Are you remembering something?"

Lopez bent toward her, his stance tense and alert. Durant and Kate stepped closer to the bed.

Debra shuddered, then gave Lopez a look of apology. "No. Not really. Only a shiny flash. Nothing more. I'm sorry." She *was* sorry. And for some reason, frightened.

Surprising her, Lopez patted her hand. "That probably means you'll be getting more and more flashes of memory. I've seen this kind of thing before. Do your best not to force it. And before you know it, the whole thing will come back to you."

Debra wondered if she wanted it to.

***

Lopez gave Debra Carrington another pat on the hand. He didn't see the person who had been listening outside the room duck into an alcove as he was leaving.

Chapter Sixty

Cami straightened Debra's hospital bedsheet and brushed aside a thick lock of hair that had fallen over the bandaged forehead and across the closed eyes. For a moment, she studied the long, dark lashes that lay against Debra's pale face.

How precious she is to me, Lord. Thank You for sparing her life.

Speaking to the others in the room—Durant, Victor, Ashley, Kate, and Gunnar—she let out a hopeful sigh. "She slept well last night. The doctor says she's going to be okay."

"Yes, she is," said Victor, patting Cami's hand.

"Thank God," Durant whispered.

Ashley let out an impatient sigh.

Cami steeled herself for her sister-in-law's sarcastic comment about the prayers for Debra being answered. Instead, Ashley averted her face, but not before Cami caught a quick glimpse of what could be nothing but fear.

She and Kate exchanged questioning looks. Gunnar tilted his head as though he, too, had caught Ashley's expression of fear.

Victor, seeming not to notice, said, "Has anybody seen the estimable Ms. DeLuca?"

"No. She hasn't been seen since the night of the party. "

"A little strange, don't you think," said Ashley. "I mean Rosita, excuse me, *Ms. DeLuca,* the oh-so-faithful administrative assistant."

"That's enough, Ashley." Victor's tone matched the warning in his eyes.

Ashley shrugged and closed her lips tightly.

A light knock was followed by a woman's Spanish-accented voice. "Mrs. Carrington?"

"Rosita! Come in," said Cami, wondering how much Rosita had heard. She stopped, speechless.

Nobody spoke for a moment, all taking in Rosita's appearance. She was dressed in black, as expected. But instead of the usual conservative business suit with a mid-calf skirt, she wore a smart-looking pants outfit—with a *red* shell beneath the close-cut, collarless jacket. A wide gold necklace shone at her neck, and from her ears hung gold hoop earrings edged in tiny rubies and diamonds. Splashes of color played against her lips and cheeks, and mascara enhanced her large brown eyes.

Most surprising of all, Rosita's thick black hair had been released from its tight bun and flowed back from her face and down her back.

She's beautiful! I never noticed before. "We were—" Cami said again.

"We were wondering when we would see you, Rosie," said Victor, an appreciative gleam in his eyes.

Lifting her chin, Rosita shot Victor a look of disdain. "Well, I'm here now, Mr. Carrington." Clearly dismissing Victor, she spoke to Cami. "I'm sorry I did not come sooner, Mrs. Carrington."

Cami moved quickly to Rosita and took both her hands. "Please don't apologize, Rosita. I understand. I really do."

"Thank you." Rosita pulled her hands away. "How is Debra?"

"She's in pain, but she's going to be fine," said Cami. She looked down at her now-empty hands, hoping to hide the brief resentment she felt at Rosita's implied rejection of her empathetic words.

"I cannot imagine how difficult this is for you," said Rosita.

"I won't pretend it isn't, Rosita. It's horrible." *And it's horrible for you,* she thought, her resentment fading at the bleakness in Rosita's eyes. Cami had long known that Rosita was deeply in love with Braxton, but the fact had never threatened her. Braxton, despite his wandering eye, had been too smart to become embroiled in an office romance.

"How much longer will Debra be hospitalized?"

"We thought she would go home today, but the doctor wants to keep her one more night."

Rosita took in the slim, still figure in the bed. "Has she got back her memory about the attack?"

"How did you know about that?" Victor asked sharply.

"Oh. On my way in, I overheard a nurse's aide talking about it."

"Why don't we hang out a sign?" asked Ashley. She extended her arms, pretending to hold a large banner. "I can see it now: *Local debutant loses memory.*"

"It's okay, Ashley," said Cami. "This is the kind of thing that *is* going to become known."

Victor spoke up. "Cami, I need to go to the mortuary. The minister will be in from Hawaii tomorrow to perform the memorial service, but we'll have to wait for autopsy results before we can make final arrangements for the cremation."

"Oh!" Rosita clapped her hand to her mouth. Quickly recovering, she spoke to Cami. "Is there anything I can do, Mrs. Carrington?"

"I can't think of anything right now, Rosita."

"I can," said Victor. "I need to get some papers from Braxton's office. As you know, we're closed for a couple of days, only keeping a skeleton staff. Scarlet isn't there. Cami asked her to design the program for the service, and she's doing that from home." He glanced at Cami. "I haven't had a chance to go by there yet. And I'm going to be busy this afternoon. Maybe you can get them for me, Rosita."

"Me?"

"Is that a problem?" Victor asked

"Oh, no. I haven't been there either since Mr. Carrington—died." She seemed to force out the last word. "But I will go this afternoon and get the papers and drop them by your house."

"No need for that, Rosita," said Cami. "Debra is out of the woods now, so I won't mind leaving the hospital for a short while. I'll meet you at Braxton's office and bring the papers back for Victor."

"Oh, no," Rosita protested.

"Mom. No," Durant agreed.

Cami ignored her son and continued speaking to Rosita. "I'd offer to save you a trip to the office, but I'm afraid I wouldn't know where to look for the papers Victor wants."

"Mom, you can't go there."

"I need to, Durant," Cami said simply.

"Then I'm going with you."

"I don't think you're ready for that." His silence confirmed her observation. "Besides, one of us should stay with Debra."

Kate stepped forward. "Gunnar and I will go with her, Durant."

Gunnar nodded his assent.

"Well, okay," said Durant. "But I don't like it."

"I'll be fine," said Cami. "Like I said, this is something I need to do. You stay here and get some rest in the recliner while Debra is asleep." Giving her attention to Rosita, she spoke briskly. "When should I meet you?"

Rosita hesitated. She looked at her watch. "It is eleven-thirty. I must run an errand. I will meet you at Br— Mr. Carrington's office at one." She spun around and left.

Chapter Sixty-One

Debra awoke but didn't open her eyes. Maybe if she kept them shut, she'd escape the onslaught of memories of the past several hours. The throbbing in her head wound was excruciating, but she knew it would heal in a few days. Emotionally, however, she felt as if she'd been slammed by a tsunami and would never heal.

Could it be that less than twenty-four hours ago, she'd stood at her father's side at the Hotel Del and felt his strong arm pull her to his side? Remembering the twinkle in his startling blue eyes as he looked down at her brought on a fresh wave of pain. The thought of never again seeing that twinkle was unthinkable, too much to bear. Against her will, her eyes flew open.

Only Durant was in the room, and he was asleep in the recliner. Wondering only vaguely where her mother was, Debra gazed at her twin.

Even asleep, he looks like Dad. The thought brought a new wrench to her heart.

One thing was different, though. Durant looked peaceful. Braxton's face had taken on many aspects in life—anger, playfulness, disdain, even love—but never peace, even when Debra had seen him sleeping. She found herself wishing he had experienced the inner serenity his son knew. Oh sure, Durant had his moments of frustration and anger. Look how he'd stomped out of the house the other night. But eventually the calm expression always returned to his countenance. She had no doubt why.

Again, her heart wrenched, this time at the knowledge that her father would now never experience what Durant had.

But you can, Debra.

The thought startled her. Frightened her. Where had it come from? From God? No. Why would He speak to her when she'd derided her brother so many times for his faith?

But you can, Debra. There it was again. She pulled in her breath sharply.

"Debra!" She saw that Durant was suddenly fully awake. "What's wrong?" He was immediately standing by her bed.

Debra looked him full in the face. That concerned, somewhat frightened, but...peaceful...face. Suddenly she wanted that for herself.

Chapter Sixty-Two

At one-fifteen Gunnar stood with Cami and Kate at the entrance to Braxton's office suite. He saw Cami reach for Kate's hand as the three entered the subtly elegant reception area.

Looking toward Rosita's desk and its empty chair, Gunnar said, "I thought Rosita was supposed to be here."

"She must be in Braxton's office," Cami said. "I'll look."

She touched the knob. Immediately, she pulled back, as though it were red hot.

"I can't do it," she said, the relief she'd shown from Debra's improved condition now missing. "I'm scared."

"You can do it, Cami," said Kate. "The Lord will give you the strength you need. Gunnar and I are here, too."

Cami searched Kate's face as though trying to draw courage from it. Gunnar had rarely seen such suffering as he now saw on Cami's countenance. After a moment she set her mouth in a firm line and twisted the knob.

The room was dark.

"That's odd," said Cami, switching on the overhead light.

With the flooding of light, the mood of the room changed. It seemed to Gunnar that though he had never met Braxton Carrington, he knew something of the dead man's energy and power and ambition because it lived on in this room.

Cami frowned. "Rosita said she'd be here and have the papers ready for me."

"Maybe she stepped out," Kate suggested.

"No. Rosita is the most precise person I've ever known. If she said she'd be here at a certain time, she'd never just step out."

"At times like this, people don't always hold true to form," said Gunnar. "Maybe even Rosita."

Gunnar knew that all three of them were thinking of the transformation in Rosita's appearance when she visited the hospital. At the same time, there was the stone-like, seemingly emotionless face she had presented since the night of Braxton's death.

Almost like she expected it. The thought surprised Gunnar.

"Anyway, I guess she's not here," said Cami. "I think Braxton keeps—kept—personal papers in that file cabinet over there." Pulling out the list Victor had given her, she walked to an oak file cabinet in the corner of the room. After extracting several items, she said, "One's missing."

"Which one?" Kate asked.

Cami looked at the list again. "The will." In the silence that followed her words, she looked as though she were about to crack.

"Maybe it got moved to another folder or to his desk," said Kate.

"No," said Cami. "Rosita would never do that."

"Let's look around," said Gunnar. "You check the file drawer again and I'll look in Braxton's desk."

"I'll take the file cabinet near Rosita's desk," said Kate.

Several minutes later, Cami said, "It's not here."

"Maybe it's at home," Gunnar suggested.

"I don't think so. His lawyer would have a copy, and there would be some kind of record on the computer. I'd be able to find that. But where is the actual hard copy?" She frowned. "I guess I'll have to call Rosita."

Gunnar, standing behind Braxton's desk, could tell that Cami dialed Rosita's number with reluctance. Kate, standing beside him, reached out and squeezed his fingers. Touched, he returned the gesture and moved nearer. As he did so, he brushed against a round brass paperweight and knocked it to the floor, where it rolled far under the desk. Gunnar, feeling slightly ridiculous because of his bulk, got on his hands and knees and eased himself under the kneehole. He grabbed the paperweight and began to move back. As he raised his head, something jabbed his scalp.

"Ouch!" he said, touching his head.

"What is it?" Kate asked.

"I don't know." Gunnar, still on his knees, felt under the bottom of the desk. "Something's attached here." He bent over and peered. He saw a small metal case with an opening on one end. He reached into the opening and removed the object inside.

Kate dropped to her knees beside him. They stared at what he held.

"A mini tape recorder!" said Kate.

"Rosita's not answering," said Cami. "Hey. Where are you two?"

She leaned over the desk and began to laugh hysterically.

Stunned, Gunnar looked first at Cami, then Kate, whose face registered shock. This was the first time either of them had heard Cami laugh since Braxton's death. Unfortunately, it was not a laugh of enjoyment and relief, but more of despair. Kate jumped to her feet.

"What is it?"

"You two! You look so funny down there on the floor! Especially Gunnar. You look like a great big teddy bear." She laughed again—and again and again.

Gunnar sprang up and joined Kate at Cami's side.

"Cami. Stop," Kate commanded. "Stop it. We've found something you need to see."

Still laughing, Cami asked, "What? What could you possibly have that I want to see? All I want to see is my husband!" As suddenly as the laughter began, it stopped and turned into sobbing.

"Look at me, Cami," Kate said gently but firmly.

Still sobbing, Cami looked up.

"Stop crying," Kate said. "You need to get hold of yourself and look at what we found." She led Cami to a chair, eased her into it, and took the one next to it. When Cami's hysteria finally subsided, Kate nodded to Gunnar.

"Look at this," he said.

Cami scowled. "It looks like a tape recorder."

"It is," said Kate. "For mini tapes. Gunnar found it under Braxton's desk."

"I don't understand. What does this mean?" When neither of them answered, Cami said, "You think Braxton recorded conversations of people who met with him here! No. He wouldn't do that. I know he was ambitious and sometimes ruthless, but he wouldn't stoop to this."

"Do you think Rosita knows anything about it?" asked Kate.

"Rosita." Cami looked perplexed. "Where is she? Suddenly, I'm concerned about her."

"Why?" Gunnar asked. "Because she's not here and doesn't answer her phone? She could be anywhere—shopping, visiting a friend, anything."

"I don't think she has many friends, and what family she has left lives in Mexico. Her job has been her life for years. Anyway, she said she'd meet us here."

Surprised that Cami was that intuitive about Rosita, Gunnar said, "What do you suggest?"

"I'll try her cell phone, and if she doesn't answer, we need to go to her house. I know her number; occasionally I need to get hold of her that way." She dialed the number. Gunnar could tell that there was no answer.

"Let's go," Cami said. "We'll listen to the tape later." Without waiting for a response, she slipped the tiny recorder into her purse and marched out of her husband's office without a backward glance.

Chapter Sixty-Three

"So, you see, Debra, it's not hard at all," Durant told his sister. An hour earlier she had surprised and elated him by saying she was finally willing—and eager—for him to talk with her about his commitment to Jesus.

"I see a peace in you that I envy and…and want," she'd told him.

Hardly able to contain his joy, he explained, as he had many times in the past, how Aunt Kate counseled him at a time he was experiencing some very *un*peaceful moments with his father, living under a cloud of constant criticism that was causing him to actually despise Braxton. This in turn piled a burden of guilt on him. Step by step, Kate showed Durant that his feelings, though natural, were indeed sinful.

But there was a solution.

"An ABC solution," she told him with a wry smile that said she knew he was thinking that kind of logical presentation fit right in with her commonsense mindset.

Opening her Bible and pointing out certain verses[1], she went on to explain:

A—Acknowledge his sin, specifically in his attitude toward his father;

B—Believe that God loved him enough to send Jesus to die for his sin and that His death and resurrection were payment for them;

C—Confess his sins to God and call on Jesus in faith.

---

[1] See appendix for verses.

Kate's words and God's Word touched seventeen-year-old Durant. Without reservation, he gave his heart fully and completely to Jesus Christ.

Now, two years later, Debra was listening thoughtfully, commenting little as he presented Kate's outline. "See, Debra, it's not hard at all. Do you..." He hesitated. The moment was so important. He didn't want to say the wrong thing. "Do you think you're ready to make that decision?"

"I'm not sure. I think so."

"Would you like me to pray with you?"

Her eyes imploring him, she nodded.

Durant bowed his head. "Dear Father," he began. "Thank You for—"

"Debra." A voice broke into the moment.

Not now! Not now of all times! Please, God. Not now.

He had no choice but to lift his head. Before he could look to see who it was, Debra cried out, "Frank!"

Chapter Sixty-Four

Durant sprang to his feet and faced Frank Giovanni. Durant's hands balled into fists at his sides. Anger at Frank melded with frustration of the timing of his visit. *Right when Debra might've been about to accept Christ!*

"What are you doing here?" he demanded, somewhat belligerently.

Frank's tone matched Durant's. "What do you think, Dodo? I came to see your sister."

"Well you can just lea—"

"It's okay, Durant." Debra's voice came surprisingly strong from her bed. "He can stay for a few minutes."

"You gotta be kidding! You actually want to see this jerk?"

"What do you say, Debra?" Frank asked. "Can we have a few minutes—alone?"

"Alone?" Durant heard his voice rise. "You think I'm leaving you here with her alone?"

"Yes," Debra said firmly.

Durant couldn't believe his ears. "No way!"

"Yes way. I want you to go downstairs and get me a Diet Coke and let me talk with Frank."

"No!"

"Yes. And I don't want you hanging around outside. Frank and I have a few things to talk about."

"I can't do that."

"Don't worry, Durant." Frank gave Durant a lazy grin. "I'm not going to harm your sister. I just need to talk with her." He looked toward the bed. "Debra?"

Debra gave Durant a long, level look. He knew that look. It said it would do him no good to argue. "You need to give us a few minutes, Durant."

Frank shot Debra a look of gratitude.

"Go, Durant," she said.

"I don't like this."

"Go."

Reluctantly, Durant left, but he paused long enough to hear Debra say, "No need to get comfortable, Frank. What I have to say won't take long."

Durant grinned. His sister knew how to take care of herself.

Chapter Sixty-Five

Cami rang Rosita's bell for the third time. The building's stylized Spanish architecture suited Rosita's Mexican heritage as well as her efficient personality, she thought.

She couldn't explain the anxiety she felt about Rosita. *What am I doing here? Why should I even care about a woman who's been in love with my husband for years?* Then she thought wryly, *Most people think I'm unaware of that, but how could I have missed it?*

Interrupting her musing, Gunnar reached past her and rang the bell a fourth time.

After waiting another minute, Cami said, "She's not here."

"Cami, that's not strange." Gunnar's tone showed his exasperation. "Why should Rosita not be here? Why should she be waiting around for you to show up?"

"I'm beginning to agree with Cami," said Kate. "Something's not right. Cami, what about getting Rosita's key from the condo manager?"

"Good idea." With the same purposefulness she'd shown at Braxton's office, Cami now headed for the manager's office.

The manager, a stylish fifty-something woman named Luisa Arroyo, expressed sympathy over Braxton's death and readily gave Rosita's key to Cami. "Technically, I should go with you," she said, "but I'm waiting for an important call. Since you're, uh, her employer's wife."

Cami knew Luisa was about to say, "Since you're *Mrs. Braxton Carrington.*"

Luisa continued, "I'm sure it's okay to let you go in. Please let me know if anything is wrong with Ms. DeLuca."

Back at Rosita's condo, Cami hesitated, suddenly wondering about the wisdom of what they were about to do.

"Here, let me," said Gunnar, gently taking the key from her.

Inside, a sense of emptiness met them. The living room, as well as the dining room to one side and the kitchen, visible beyond that, were all painfully tidy. Surveying the room, the only thing Cami saw that seemed out of place was a tiny piece of black ribbon peeking out from behind a cushion on the couch.

"It's so *neat*," Cami said.

"Like somebody cleaned it up before going away for a long time," Kate said.

"Or for moving," said Gunnar. He strode away from them into the nearest bedroom where he went straight to the walk-in closet.

Only a few items of clothing hung on the racks—two or three bright-colored blouses, a full Mexican-style skirt, and a couple of pairs of stretch pants. One worn sneaker lay on the floor like an abandoned puppy.

Cami bent over and picked up the sneaker. Holding it, she said, "I can't see Rosita in sneakers." She touched a red blouse emblazoned with brilliant yellow flowers, "Or wearing this."

"From what little I've seen and what you've told me, neither can I," said Kate, pulling out a dresser drawer. "It's empty." She pulled out another drawer. "This one, too."

"Hmmm," said Gunnar, who stood before the wooden file cabinet against one wall of the bedroom. He pulled out the top drawer. Empty. He opened the bottom drawer.

"Come look!" He beckoned to the women.

The three stared at a shoebox full of mini tapes, stacked three-deep. On top lay a small recorder.

Cami's first reaction was one of relief. "Braxton *wasn't* taping his visitors." Then realization flooded over her. "It was Rosita!" Suddenly she was angry. She picked up the recorder and one of the tapes at random. It was labeled with a date six months earlier. Sitting on the side of the bed, she inserted the tape and started to push "Play."

Kate's words stopped her. "Cami, maybe you shouldn't do this. You might—"

"Might not like what I'll hear? So what? Do you think I've liked everything I've heard for the past twenty-two years?"

"It's not only that," said Gunnar. "We should take these tapes to the police. They wouldn't like us tampering with evidence."

But Cami was beyond reason. Ignoring Kate, she started the tape. She could see Kate and Gunnar exchange worried looks, but she didn't care.

The first words they heard were from Braxton. The sound of her husband's voice was like a hammer to Cami's chest, but she steeled herself and listened to Braxton and a lawyer discussing some shady business practices of a well-known San Diego businessman.

Soon she fast-forwarded to the voice of that same businessman begging Braxton not to go to the authorities. She fast-forwarded again. This time they heard Braxton berating Victor for incompetence. Seeing the looks of embarrassment on her friends' faces, she moved to the next one.

Cami heard her son's pleading voice: "But, Dad, I *have* worked hard this semester. My grades are *good*."

"Your sister has a 4.1 grade point average," Braxton pointed out.

"When will you realize I am not my sister?"

"Oh, I realize that all right. And I realize the reason you're not making all A's is you're spending too much time with that *religious* group you're obsessed with."

"Dad! The opposite is true. The people in that group actually encourage me to—"

Cami stopped the tape and stared at the small recorder. Beside her, she could almost tangibly feel her friend's compassion and love.

"I'm so glad you're here," Cami whispered. "Will you and Gunnar pray for me?"

"You know we have been doing that all along, and we'll keep on."

"I think she means right now," Gunnar put in.

Cami nodded.

Gunnar knelt by Cami. In his strong, confident voice, He asked the Lord to comfort Cami and her children and give them His strength.

The prayer was short, but by the end Cami felt some of the tenseness melt away. "Thank you," she told Gunnar. "That helps." She stood up. "We'd better go to the Coronado police station. I'll give Detective

Lopez the recorder and the tapes and let him know Rosita's gone. He can take it from there." For the first time, a thought hit her. "Do you think *Rosita* was the one?"

"As you said," Gunnar answered, "we'll let Lopez take it from there. And not jump to conclusions." He helped Cami to her feet. "Let's go."

As Gunnar and Kate moved to leave, Cami noticed the strip of black ribbon peeking from beneath the couch cushion. She lifted the cushion. One more tape. The strip of recording cellophane had been pulled almost all the way out and lay puddled around the case. Cami quickly gathered it up and stuffed it in her purse.

"Yes, let's go," she said.

Chapter Sixty-Six

Durant resisted the urge to kick the soda machine and utter a word he hadn't used in a long time. Instead, he hit the Diet Coke button again, then jiggled the coin-return lever up and down several times. Nothing.

"I think the Diet Coke's out," a voice said behind him. He turned to see a small white- haired woman dressed in a coral-colored hospital volunteer uniform. Her nametag identified her as Melba Townsend.

"Must be." Durant let out a sigh of frustration. "I guess my sister will have to drink regular Coke instead." He started to punch that button.

"Or maybe it needs a good kick."

"Oh, no. That's okay."

Before Durant could finish his protestation, Mrs. Townsend had pushed in next to him and swung back one small, sneaker-clad foot. The machine shook with a force that belied the woman's small stature. In a moment, a Diet Coke clattered its way down.

Durant stared in amazement at the woman and the machine. "Wow! Thanks, Mrs., uh...." He peered at her name-tag again.

"Townsend," she said. "I've been a volunteer here quite some time now. Ever since my husband passed away three years ago. He was sick with something or other, some long medical name I can't even remember. When he died, I didn't know what to do with myself. Then my daughter said I ought to—"

"I'm sure she was right." Durant sensed that if he didn't interrupt the little lady, she'd go on for several minutes. But he didn't want to be rude, so he gave her a smile as he said, "If you'll excuse me, I'd better get this to my sister before she starts getting antsy."

"Your sister's here? Oh, she must be that Debra Carrington. And you're her twin brother! I was shocked to hear about her accident, and coming so close after your father's death, too. And your poor mother. Why she must be—"

"She's holding up." Then Durant felt he had to add, "God is giving her strength."

"Oh, I know all about that. When poor Elwin died, I don't know what I would have done without—"

Impulsively, Durant bent over and kissed the pale, weathered cheek. "God bless you, Mrs. Townsend. Now I'd really better go."

The little lady beamed and blushed. "Oh, sure. I don't want to hold you up. I declare, I don't know what the world is...."

The rest of Mrs. Townsend's chatter was lost on Durant as he sprinted toward the elevator. The quest for the soda had taken longer than he'd expected, and suddenly he felt an urgency to get back to Debra's room.

He fired up a prayer for Debra as he jabbed the "Up" button several times. When the doors finally slid open, an intern stood there beside a man in a gurney.

"Sorry, you'll have to catch the next one," he said as the door closed.

Durant waited a couple of minutes; then he dashed for the back stairs. Taking the steps two at a time, he reached the top, to find the door there locked. Frustration mounting, he pounded with both fists. In a few seconds, a nurse appeared. He pushed past her and ran down the hall, nearly knocking over an aide with a tray of food. He navigated a couple of turns, feeling like he'd never get there.

"Debra!" he called as he rushed in. Frank was gone. Good. He breathed a sigh of relief. Debra had already gone back to sleep. Frank's visit must have tired her out. He wondered what she had said to him.

Durant sat the drink on the bedside table and started to settle into the recliner. Something stopped him. Debra was so still. Too still.

He shook her. She wasn't breathing.

Frantically, he punched the emergency button, then ran into the hallway.

"Nurse! Someone! Help!"

Chapter Sixty-Seven

Stan Weston hurried past the reception desk at Coronado Hospital, eager to get away as soon as possible.

"Dr. Weston!" the tiny white-haired woman in a volunteer's uniform called out. She carried a mug filled with some steaming liquid.

Not now, he thought. He recognized her. Nice lady, but a busy-body who talked nonstop. "Mrs. Townsend," he said, understanding the importance people attached to their names. Her blue eyes lit up. Trying to relax and not seem overly anxious to leave, he pasted on a smile and asked, "How are you today?"

"I'm fine, thank you." She paused only a second before hurrying on. "Isn't it just terrible about Braxton Carrington? Dying like that at his own party? And now his daughter's been hurt, too. I don't know how that sweet Cami Carrington is holding up."

"Yes, it is terrible, Mrs. Townsend. Terrible." Stan made a slight move to continue on his way.

"You were at that party, weren't you? You must have seen him die. It must have been awful."

Stan sensed the woman's eagerness to glean a tidbit of gossip to pass on to the other volunteers.

"Yes, I was there," he told her, putting on an expression he hoped looked properly mournful and hid his delight that his wife's lover was dead. "And yes, it was really awful."

"Have you been up to see Debra Carrington? I know you're a friend of the family and all."

Friend of the family? A mental picture of the photo of Erika and Braxton at the door of an inn blinked on and off. *How little you know, little Mrs. Townsend.*

"No. I've been to check on a patient."

"Oh. Poor thing." Mrs. Townsend didn't even try to hide her disappointment—or her sudden lack of interest in Stan now that he was clearly not a source of information.

"Well, I see you're in a hurry. I'll let you go. Have a good day." She hurried off.

So did Stan.

Chapter Sixty-Eight

"Aaghh!" little Mrs. Townsend screamed.

As she had rounded the corner, she collided with another woman. Mrs. Townsend's cup flew out of her hand, splashing scalding coffee onto the thigh of her white pants. Her face contorting in pain, she looked up, expecting the woman to stop. Instead, she fled out a side door. Mrs. Townsend barely had time to take in a shapely figure, a tight green pants outfit, and a mass of flaming red hair. It was enough to recognize her.

Another volunteer rushed up. "Mrs. Townsend! What happened?"

Almost in tears from pain, Mrs. Townsend welcomed the sight of her helper. "Oh, Mrs. Giovanni!"

"Here, let me help you." Terese Giovanni led Mrs. Townsend to a nearby chair. With a towel she was carrying she began to dab at the hot coffee seeping through the older woman's pants leg. "What happened?" she repeated.

"That woman—" Mrs. Townsend nodded toward the exit. "She ran into me. Then she ran off. Didn't even say I'm sorry."

"Do you know who it was?" Terese asked absently while she kept dabbing at the coffee. "We need to get you out of these pants and put some ointment on your leg."

"Sure, I know who she was. It was that nice Dr. Weston's flibberty-gibbet of a wife."

Terese's head shot up.

"Don't know what a nice man like him sees in the likes of her," Mrs. Townsend went on. "Pretty, but no class, if you know what I

251

mean. And not a bit of manners." She groaned again. "I saw him, you know."

"Him?"

"Her husband. Dr. Weston. Not two minutes before that woman ran into me. It was exactly two thirty-seven. I had just looked at my watch. I could tell he was in a hurry, too, but he took the time to stop and talk to me."

"That was nice," said Terese. "Do you have some other pants with you?"

"No. I never needed extra ones before."

"Well, let me get you something for your leg. Then you should go on home."

"I would, but I don't drive anymore," Mrs. Townsend admitted somewhat reluctantly, "and my daughter's not coming for me for two more hours."

"Can you call her?"

Mrs. Townsend averted her eyes. "She doesn't like me to call her when she's showing property. She's in real estate, you know."

"I'll drive you home. You live here on the island, don't you?"

"Yes. On Seventh Street. And all I have to get is my purse."

"Where is it? I'll get it for you."

"In the left bottom drawer of the volunteer desk. I can get it myself."

"Okay. I'll be back in a jiff."

***

Both of the Westons leaving the hospital in a hurry, Terese thought as she waited for a nurse who had gone to fetch some ointment. *Wonder what's up.*

She thought of a certain afternoon a couple of weeks ago. Feeling the stress of Dominic's increasingly fervent focus on the upcoming mayoral election, Terese had needed to get away for a few hours.

She had hoped she could take a drive with her son Frank, the light of her life. Despite his selfishness and the escapades she and Dominic had hushed up with money from Terese's private inherited income, he was affectionate and considerate toward her. He was far more sensitive toward her medical problems than Dominic was and until recently rarely refused her requests for his companionship. But that day he was busy. Lately she felt he was keeping something from her.

Terese drove up the coast to a quiet inn tucked away on a side street in the quaint seaside village of Cardiff by the Sea. There she found a window seat in the inn's cozy dining room. She had decided on the crab salad when a couple entered the room and were ushered to the farthest, darkest corner. She had no trouble recognizing Erika Weston, despite the scarf covering most of her red hair. Hanging onto the arm of Braxton Carrington, she gazed adoringly into his eyes. Curious, Terese lingered over her lunch to see what they'd do next. Within half an hour, the two left the restaurant area and headed for the stairs.

Terese had not told Dominic what she'd seen. She knew he'd use it against Braxton Carrington; and much as she disliked him and wanted Dominic to become mayor of Coronado, she hated the idea of that kind of dirty politics. Besides, it could backfire and possibly be harmful to Frankie.

Now, as the nurse approached with the ointment, Terese smiled, thinking how she rarely used that childhood pet name anymore.

I'd do anything for that boy, she thought fondly. Her thoughts drifted back to Mrs. Townsend's observations about Erika and Stan.

I wonder if Stan Weston finally caught on to his wife's activities. Maybe that has something to do with Erika running off and not stopping to help Mrs. Townsend. Another thought occurred to Terese. *Now that the police suspect that Braxton was murdered, they may be interested in knowing about him and Erika. Maybe I should call them.*

The nurse returned with the ointment, and Terese thanked her. She reached into her pocket for her cell phone, then hesitated. *No. I'll leave it be unless they question me about it.*

Chapter Sixty-Nine

"Were you looking for something, Erika?" His low words oozing with sarcasm and scorn, Stan Weston slipped in front of his wife as she approached her car, which was parked in a slot on the narrow street in front of Coronado Hospital.

Erika tried to back away, but Stan stood his ground. "I asked you a question, *Dear*."

He could almost see the wheels turning in Erika's head as she sought to come up with a good reply. In the end, she only tossed back her red hair and tilted her chin. "What do you mean?"

Stan let out a mirthless chuckle. "Didn't think I saw you plundering through my attaché case, did you?" He knew Erika was aware he often left his attaché case in the doctor's lounge while he was conferring with a patient. He had done so today.

When he returned from checking on a rhinoplasty patient, he first thought the lounge was empty. Then he saw Erika frantically rifling through the case. Her back was to him and she was so intent on her task that she didn't hear him come in. His first instinct had been to rush in and confront her. But another doctor approached at that moment. So he left quietly and rushed out to wait in an unobtrusive spot near her car.

Now, abandoning her pretense of ignorance, Erika narrowed her green eyes. "Where are they? I looked for them all over the house."

Stan hated himself for the way her exotic beauty appealed to him even now when she was referring to photographs of herself with another man. But God help him—if there was a God—he wouldn't let her see.

To cover his feelings he sneered as he said, "Don't worry. They're in a safe place. You'll never find them, so save yourself the trouble of looking."

Erika's defiance melted. "Destroy them, Stan. Please, destroy them."

Stan's lip curled. "Why would I do that? I spent a lot of money to get them."

"I'm sure you did. Having me spied on, like a—"

"Like the cheap hussy you are."

Stan was surprised at how the old-fashioned term seemed to stun Erika. Face pale, she whispered, "Whatever you think of me—and you have every right to—you've got to get rid of those photographs."

Stan knew he couldn't let himself be moved by her seeming contrition. Instead he baited her with a sneering, "Maybe I want to look at them now and then."

Erika dismissed the suggestion with a wave of her hand. "I know you're not that perverse. Don't you see? If anyone gets hold of those pictures, they can embarrass both of us. Maybe worse."

"Why would anyone—besides you—even bother to look for them?"

"You haven't heard the rumors?"

"What rumors?"

"That the police think Braxton Carrington was murdered."

"Murdered!"

"It's supposed to be kinda hush-hush, but it's already going around the hospital. I'm surprised you haven't heard."

"You're making this up!"

"Why would I do that? Now do you understand? You've got to destroy those photos. And pay that detective whatever it takes to erase them from his camera or computer or whatever and to keep quiet. If the police find out about them—"

"—they might think you killed Carrington because he dumped you."

"No. I was thinking they'd suspect *you* killed him out of jealousy."

Stan turned from her and strode away. He had to get rid of those photographs. More importantly, he had to call Lucas Richards.

***

Trembling with fear and unaccustomed feelings of shame, Erika Weston threw her car into reverse and whipped out of the parking slot.

Cheap hussy. Cheap hussy. Stan's calling her that had been like a slap in the face. *Cheap hussy.*

She pulled at her hair, as if doing so would pull the words out of her mind.

Cheap. Cheap. Cheap.
Hussy. Hussy. Hussy.
Cheap.

Chapter Seventy

Kate shifted in the passenger seat of Cami's dark blue BMW convertible as Cami maneuvered around the sweeping curve of the Coronado Bridge. With the top down, Kate's hair blew across her face and tickled her cheeks. Lifting her hair from her nape, she drank in the sparkling bay far below, its azure waters dotted with white—white sails, white gulls swooping across white-capped ripples, and the white wake of a speed boat skimming the water. Beyond she could see a strip of island beach surrounded by lush green grass sprinkled with palms. For a few moments all the tension of the past few days faded, and Kate's spirit lifted and soared as though on the wings of the gulls. No wonder people moved to San Diego from every other part of the country.

The thrilling moment passed as Kate realized Cami had not said more than a dozen words since leaving Rosita's condo. Kate's heart ached for her friend. She noticed that Gunnar, in the back seat, had been silent, too, which was unusual for him. He was definitely not a man of few words. She tried to catch his eye. He was fast asleep.

A wave of tenderness touched her, and she felt the tug of a small smile.

The time difference and lack of sleep have finally caught up with him.

Not for the first time, Kate mentally enumerated the shocks to Cami's system in less than forty-eight hours: she had lost a husband, probably to murder, then nearly lost a daughter, due to an attack. Now her husband's administrative assistant was missing under seemingly questionable circumstances, leaving behind audiotapes that could be embarrassing to a lot of people, including the Carringtons.

I hope that's all, Lord. Surely You won't let anything else go wrong for Cami.

Cami's phone rang.

"Kate, will you get that for me? Look in the side pocket of my purse."

Kate fished out the phone and answered it, identifying herself.

"Oh, no!" she cried a few seconds later.

"What is it?" Dread edged Cami's voice.

Gunnar stirred and asked sleepily, "What's happening?"

"Cami." Kate hardly knew how to go on.

"What *is* it, Kate? Tell me!" The car swerved slightly. Cami got it under control barely in time to miss an oncoming vehicle.

"It was the hospital."

"On no! Debra!"

"They want you to get there right away."

Chapter Seventy-One

Cami's body shook with sobs. Kate eased nearer to her on the waiting area's small couch. In an operating room nearby, several medics worked to save Debra's life. Kate wanted to offer some words of comfort but knew that none would help at the moment. Instead, she prayed, asking God to guide the doctors—supernaturally if necessary—and help them bring Debra through this latest crisis. And she asked Him to give Cami and Durant His strength and more trust than they'd ever had in Him.

Durant. Kate had been so concerned about Cami from the moment they'd received that alarming phone call that she had not given him much thought. Cami had immediately pushed the gas pedal to the floor. She took the last stretch of the bridge at alarming speed. Clutching her armrest and praying—and grateful for the light traffic—Kate tried not to think of the great drop to the water below.

Now she looked for Durant and saw him standing near the wall with Gunnar and Victor, their heads bowed as Gunnar rested one arm on Durant. Dear, dear Gunnar. Durant could have no better human comforter at the moment. Kate was surprised, though, to see Victor seemingly joining the other two in prayer.

And where was Ashley? Oh yes. Victor had told Cami he'd tried to reach his wife but she wasn't at her office and wasn't answering her phone.

Kate checked her watch. They received the call about Debra an hour ago, though it seemed much longer. What had happened to

Debra? Why had she gone into a coma? No one seemed to know what the doctors were trying to treat her for.

The three men raised their heads and exchanged a few words. It looked like Durant was asking Gunnar a serious question. Gunnar seemed to consider it for a few seconds. He gave Cami a long look and nodded slowly to Durant. Victor added his nod of agreement. The three of them approached Cami and Kate.

Durant touched his mother's trembling back and spoke softly. "Mom?"

Cami took a deep shuddering breath that stopped the sobs and looked up into Durant's eyes. Tears had made paths in her foundation, and mascara lay smudged beneath her blue eyes. She patted the seat on the other side of her. Durant sat down but didn't speak right away.

"What is it, Durant?"

"I wasn't sure if I should mention this. But I've talked it over with Gunnar and—"

Gunnar spoke up. "Cami, Durant has a suspicion that we think you should know about."

Seeing the added alarm on Cami's already distressed expression, Kate asked, "Now? Can't this wait?"

Cami took another deep breath. "I know you're concerned, Kate, but I know you've been praying for me, and I believe the Lord is giving me strength to face whatever needs to be faced. I'm Debra's mother. I need to know everything I can. What is your suspicion, Durant?"

Gunnar nodded. Durant rested his elbows on his knees and held his fists tight to his face.

In a this-is-your-mother-telling-you-what-to-do tone, Cami said, "Go on, Durant."

His words spewed out now. "When I came in and saw Debra, her face looked just like Dad's did when he collapsed."

Cami gasped and clutched at her blouse. She searched Durant's eyes. "Just tell me what you think."

"I think Dad's autopsy is going to show he was poisoned, and I think—I suspect, at least—that the same poison may have been used on Debra."

Cami's face twisted in what Kate knew must be the same horror and denial she herself felt. "It can't be," she whispered.

At that moment, Dr. Feldman, the family physician, emerged from the operating area, slipping his mask off his mouth so that it hung around his neck. His eyes were stern, his mouth tight.

Cami, Kate, and Durant jumped to their feet. Gunnar and Victor faced the doctor. He came directly to Cami. With a weary smile, he said, "Debra is going to be okay."

Cami's eyes lit up with joy and relief. "Oh thank God, thank God!"

Now the doctor looked doubtful, as though he didn't know whether or not to go on.

"Go ahead, Dr. Feldman," Cami said. "Tell me what was wrong with Debra. I can take it. In fact, I think I already know."

"Mrs. Carrington, we pumped your daughter's stomach. She was poisoned. If your son had gotten to her a couple of minutes later, she would be dead now."

Chapter Seventy-Two

"Mom, I'm so sorry. I'm so sorry." Durant moaned, as he'd done over and over for the past half hour. "I should never have left Debra alone with Frank Giovanni."

Cami could hardly bear the guilt and despair on her son's face and in his voice. Meanwhile, Kate, Gunnar, and Victor sat at the table in the center of the hospital's boardroom and talked quietly as they all waited for Detective Lopez. Cami remained standing, watching Durant prowl the room and listening to his intermittent apologies.

"Please, Durant, don't keep blaming yourself. Thank the Lord that He nudged you to get to Debra's room. That's the second time in two days you've saved your sister's life." Hearing a knock, she said, "It must be the detective." She let him in and said, "Thank you for coming so quickly."

"Of course, Mrs. Carrington." Cami was glad that though the detective's tone was laced with compassion, it was intense and businesslike.

Lopez pulled the door almost to and looked around at the group. "I don't want to seem insensitive, but under the circumstances, I feel we need to move quickly." He took a seat. "Durant, tell me what happened."

Durant banged his fist on the table. "What happened is Frank Giovanni poisoned my sister."

"Durant, you don't know that for sure," said Cami.

"Tell me what you do know for sure," said Lopez.

He took notes as Durant told about Frank's coming to Debra's room, about Debra's insistence on visiting with him alone for a few minutes and sending her brother for a soda. He spat out his exasperation about taking longer than he'd meant to because of the problem with the soda machine and how the elderly hospital volunteer had given it a quick kick.

"And then—" He stopped and began to shake his head back and forth.

"Then?" Lopez prompted.

"I had a sudden urge to check on Debra. I can't describe how strong it was. I got to her room as fast as I could. I knew something was wrong. I knew it. I ran in and there she was. At first I thought she was asleep. Then I saw that she wasn't—" Durant's voice broke. "She wasn't breathing!" He took a breath and steadied himself. "I screamed for help, and you know the rest."

Lopez considered Durant's words only briefly. Then he got out his cell phone. Seconds later he said, "We need an APB on Frank Giovanni."

For the second time in two days, someone lurked near the almost-closed door, heard Detective Lopez's words, then rushed away.

Chapter Seventy-Three

Detective Lopez rang the bell at Dominic Giovanni's home. As he waited he looked back at the topiary bushes formed into squares and triangles. He looked upward at the roof that sloped sharply to one side so that the house had two stories on the taller side and only one on the other. Long, narrow windows were set at odd angles. On each side of the door, stained-glass squares sported a geometric pattern. Only the multi-colored flowers edging the walkway softened the stark, modern look.

Lopez did not live on Coronado. Couldn't afford to. His modest home was in Imperial Beach, the town at the other end of the causeway that connected Coronado with the mainland. But having worked at Coronado PD for the past twenty years, he had gained a deep affection for the island village and its people, a mostly wealthy bunch with a fiercely down-home loyalty. He hated the changes Giovanni envisioned, changes that were certain to spoil a great deal of the historical as well as charmingly romantic ambiance.

With Braxton Carrington dead, Lopez felt sure that Giovanni would now be elected mayor, simply because he was a more charismatic figure than the only other potential candidate, Dan Clark. But if it turned out that Giovanni's son Frank was involved in Debra Carrington's near-fatal poisoning, that would be a different story.

When the door opened, Lopez was surprised to see Terese Giovanni. He had expected a servant. From long habit, Lopez automatically and quickly summed up her appearance. She had dark, short, softly waved hair, smooth olive complexion, and a tiny mole over her lip. Crow's feet fanned around her placid hazel eyes. She was a tall woman, slender and attractive in a soft, maternal kind of way. She wore well-cut black pants, topped by a short-sleeved shell in several shades of gray and black and a chunky ebony and crystal necklace with matching earrings.

More than appearance, however, Lopez was always interested in mood, especially in how a person reacted to the appearance of a police detective. Without seeming to, he eyed Terese carefully as he flashed his badge and introduced himself. It was hard to miss how her face went pale.

"Detective?" she asked, her expression worried, her tone somewhat defensive.

"Yes, Mrs. Giovanni. May I come in, please?"

She hesitated only a second before responding graciously, "Yes, do come in."

"Thank you," he said, noticing the way she played with the ring on her right hand—a large black pearl surrounded by diamonds. He felt a stab of compassion. In a few moments he would be questioning her and her husband about Frank. Everyone knew how dedicated she was to her only son.

Terese led Lopez through a marble-floored foyer with a huge Picasso landscape on one wall beneath a ceiling that soared on one side along with the roofline.

Cold, Lopez thought. The room didn't seem to reflect the woman's character but fit perfectly with the changes Giovanni planned for the island.

"My husband is in the sitting room." Terese led him into a room off the foyer.

Taking in a room whose modern cream-colored furnishings were softened by several floral arrangements from Terese's award-winning garden, Lopez thought, *Now, this is more like what I expected.* He smiled inwardly as he thought of how his artsy wife had taught him to recognize certain famous artists. Before he knew her, he couldn't have recognized the Picasso in the foyer or identified the lily pond painting over the unframed, mantleless fireplace as a Monet.

Dominic Giovanni sat in a large chair that had angular lines but thick, comfortable looking cushions. A scowl flicked over his face when Terese introduced Lopez. Almost immediately the scowl disappeared.

As Dominic arose, Lopez took in the attire that was as flashy as his wife's was conservative—a Hawaiian style shirt in reds and oranges, a shell necklace, jeans, and Birkenstocks. Barely taller than his wife, with thinning black hair above a classic Italian face, the man exuded confidence and energy. His full lips spread in a hearty smile that revealed none of the worry his wife had shown.

His voice was slightly croaky when he boomed, "Come in, come in, Detective. Make yourself comfortable. Drink? No, no, of course not. Not while you're on duty." He laughed as though he'd made a clever joke.

Lopez took the chair that matched Giovanni's, while Terese sat stiffly on the couch, her back not touching the rose and teal pillows piled behind her. "I'm sure you've heard about the attempts on Carrington's daughter."

"Sure. Sure, we have," Giovanni's loud words cracked a little. He cleared his throat. "Sorry. I'm getting over a cold." He cleared his throat again. "Carrington's daughter, um, Deidre? Danielle?"

Giovanni's pretending not to know the name of his opponent's daughter didn't fool Lopez for a nanosecond.

"Debra," said Terese. "How is she, Detective? We heard what a close call she had."

"Her brother got to her just in time. A couple more minutes would have been too late."

"Thank God," Terese breathed.

"Yes, yes, we're glad she's going to be okay," said Giovanni, his tone lacking sincerity to Lopez's ears. "We're both busy men. So why don't we get right to the point?"

"Suits me. I'd like to speak with your son Frank."

"You're out of luck. We don't know where he is."

Lopez frowned. "You don't know? I find that hard to believe."

"What Dom means, Detective," said Terese, "is that we don't know *exactly* where Frank is."

"Hmmm," was Lopez's only comment. He bent his head over his notepad and scribbled a word or two, deliberately drawing out the silence. He often used this method to cause his interviewees to wonder what he was up to. Many times they blurted out useful information.

When he raised his head, he saw wariness in Dominic's face and extreme agitation in his wife's.

"I think you'd better explain, Mrs. Giovanni."

"What my wife means...."

"I'd like to hear your wife tell me what she means."

Giovanni's face darkened and his jaw tightened.

Twisting her ring back and forth, Terese said, "Well, you see, Frank said he was going on a little road trip. He didn't say where."

"He's done this before?"

"Yes, Detective," Giovanni spoke up. "Our son has a sense of adventure and sometimes takes off on his own—when his work at my office is caught up of course."

"Of course," said Lopez wryly, deliberately bating Giovanni.

The other man made a visible effort to control himself. "As I was saying, sometimes he takes a spur-of-the-moment trip and stays gone a few days."

"Without telling you his destination?"

"Sometimes. Anything wrong with that? He's an adult. Twenty-four years old. Doesn't have to report every move to Mommy and Daddy."

Lopez suspected that statement was a sarcastic reference to the tight rein Braxton Carrington had kept on his twins. "And where does he go on these spur-of-the-moment jaunts? I assume he occasionally tells you where he's been."

"Oh, yes!" said Terese. "He always tells me about his little trips and usually even brings me a gift. Like this ring." She held out her right hand.

Lopez was no jewelry expert, but he knew this was no Wal-Mart bargain.

"He bought it for me in San Francisco," Terese continued. "And once he brought me some emerald earrings from Las Vegas." Despite her description of her son's costly gifts, her face twisted in distress.

Professionally, but somewhat regretfully, Lopez put aside another twinge of compassion for Terese and continued his interview. "Mr. and Mrs. Giovanni, your son was the last person known to be seen with Debra Carrington before she was poisoned. And it seems the two of them and Braxton Carrington had a fight a few days ago. I hear Frank was pretty upset that Debra broke up with him after that."

"Oh, no. That can't be true," said Terese. "I'm sure he wasn't even serious about her."

"The point is, Mrs. Giovanni, we've got to find your son and question him. I need a description of his car and the license plate number, as well as his cell phone number."

"Of course, of course," said Giovanni, irritating Lopez with his constant repeating of his opening phrases. The earlier belligerence had disappeared from his face. "Terese keeps a note of all the family license numbers in this phonebook." He picked up a tooled leather binder, flipped it open, and handed it to Lopez.

Lopez wrote down the information.

"Detective," Terese began, clearly reluctant to say her next words.

"Yes?"

"Frank didn't—"

Giovanni let out an exasperated blasphemy. "Spit it out, Terese. The detective doesn't have all day."

"Frank didn't take his phone with him. I found it in his room. He must have forgotten it."

I bet he did. "Mrs. Giovanni, if you know where your son is, you need to tell me. If he's innocent, running away will only make him look guilty."

"I resent your implications, Detective," said a red-faced Giovanni. "Anyway, Frank may not have been the last one to be with Debra."

Surprised, Lopez asked, "What do you mean?"

"Tell him, Terese."

"Do I have to?"

"Terese, our son may be arrested for a horrible crime he didn't commit!"

Terese stood and stepped to the large multi-paned window that looked onto an exquisite flowerbed. Lopez sensed that it was best not to force her. Yet.

After several seconds of silence, during which Terese stared out the window, seeming not to see the exquisite flower garden outside, Giovanni jumped to his feet. "Tell him, Terese!"

Terese pivoted around. "Both Stan and Erika Weston were at the hospital about the time of Debra's poisoning."

"So?" What could she be getting at? After all, Stan Weston had doctor's privileges at Coronado Hospital. It wouldn't be strange for his wife to meet him there.

Terese sat on the couch again, suddenly eager to talk. "Several weeks ago, I saw Erika Weston and Braxton Carrington having lunch at the Seashell Inn in Cardiff by the Sea."

She let the picture sink in. Lopez had no difficulty imagining Carrington with the provocative, curvaceous Erika. Over the years, he'd heard whispers about Carrington's possible extra-marital activities but the man had been discreet, so the rumors always petered out.

"I'm sure they didn't see me," Terese continued. "They were… well, they didn't talk much—just stared into each other's eyes. They ate quickly and went upstairs, where the guest rooms are. They had their arms around each other."

"Why didn't you tell the police this before now?" Lopez asked coldly.

Giovanni, voice tight, said, "My wife didn't even tell me until yesterday. She was afraid of what I might do with that kind of information. Maybe use it against Carrington in the mayoral campaign."

"Would you have?" Lopez asked.

"To be honest, maybe. Why not? At any rate, she's told you now. I have a feeling that Carrington, with the election a few months away, dropped Mrs. Weston. She'd have been a definite liability to him."

"You're guessing, Dom," said Terese. "That's another reason I didn't mention it before."

"Sure, sure. But if I'm right, she would've had an excellent motive for killing Carrington."

"And if Dr. Weston found out about the affair, so would he," said Terese. "And both of them were at the party."

Lopez was silent for a few moments while he took notes. Actually, he wasn't writing much, mostly scribbling and gathering his thoughts. Finally, he looked up and said, "You've made some good points. I can see how both the Westons could have a motive for getting rid of Carrington. But I don't see how that connects with his daughter."

"Don't you see?" said Terese, almost pleadingly. "He—or she—could be so eaten up with anger and jealousy and resentment they went crazy and lashed out at anyone related to Braxton. I see a lot of that kind of consuming emotion in my volunteer work at the hospital. I work mostly in the psychiatric ward, you know."

Lopez snapped his notebook shut and put it away. Directing his comments to Terese, he spoke gently. "As I said, you've made some good points, and I will definitely look into them. But for the moment, your son is still the last person actually seen with Debra Carrington. It's imperative that we find him. It won't help him at all if you protect him."

"I resent that, Lopez. I resent that," said Giovanni.

"Resent away," said Lopez. "Resent away."

Chapter Seventy-Four

"Mom, thank you sooooo much for getting me released from the hospital!" Debra stretched languidly and patted her mother's knee.

Mother and daughter sat side by side in matching recliners in the den. Kate, Durant, and Gunnar lounged nearby.

Kate knew that Debra's blithe tone and relaxed demeanor were forced, hiding the anguish she'd displayed earlier over her father's death. It also hid the fury she'd shown over Frank's visit and the ensuing implications. Kate smiled at the girl's dramatic way of expressing herself now. It reminded her of the way Cami used to dash into their dorm room full of eager, exaggerated descriptions of her newest outfit.

It was absolutely made *for me, Kate! I just* had *to buy it.*

Or her latest blind date.

You should have seeeeen *him, Kate! His ears stood straight out from the sides of his head! And the way he kept chomping his popcorn during the movie, I didn't hear a single word!*

Debra was like her mother in another way. Behind the girl's outward breezy demeanor dwelt superior intelligence; and even at her young age, she possessed a business savvy that Braxton must have wished for in his son. Debra, however, was more assertive than Cami. More her own person. She'd have confronted a husband's misdeeds more than Cami ever had.

Kate loved Cami's children almost as if they were the ones she herself had never borne. It broke her heart that bright, clever Debra had so little interest in a real relationship with the Lord. She seemed to treat the matter as beyond unimportant—more like a non-issue. She believed in God, belonged to a church. Lived a good life. What more did she need?

Interrupting her musing, Kate noted that Cami didn't return Debra's smile. "I couldn't let you stay there another hour after you got over the stomach pumping. I needed you to be here at home. With me. Safe." Her face contorted in a mixture of sorrow and anger.

"Oh, Mom. I'm so sorry. I didn't mean to be flip. I guess it's my stupid way of dealing with all that's happened in the past couple of days."

Edie, the maid, came in at that moment and spoke to Cami. "That detective is here, Mrs. Carrington." Her mouth tightened in disapproval. "Wants to talk to Miss Debra."

"Let him in, Edie," said Debra before her mother could answer.

Cami looked at her with concern. "Are you sure, Honey?"

"Definitely."

Cami nodded to Edie, and a few seconds later Detective Lopez entered the room. After preliminary greetings and settling into a chair, he spoke to Debra. "I hate to bother you, Miss Carrington, but it's urgent that I talk with you about this matter."

"I feel bad that I was so out of it when you tried to question me at the hospital. But I feel fine now. I'd like to get this over with. And please, call me Debra."

"Good. And I'll have a few questions for you, too, Mr. Carrington."

"Durant."

"Durant it is. First you, Miss... Debra."

Debra's lighthearted pose disappeared. Her face darkened. "There's not much to tell. Frank showed up. I asked Durant to leave us alone for a few minutes."

"Bad idea!" said Durant. "I can't believe I went along with such a dumb—"

"Durant," said Cami. "Let Debra talk."

"Go on, Debra," said Lopez.

"Well, like I said, I asked Durant to leave. Then Frank started acting all sorry about Dad and about me getting attacked and all. Ha! As if I'd believe a word he said. I got madder and madder 'til finally I blew up. I told him what I thought of him—in language I don't want to repeat in front of my mother—and I told him to leave."

"And then?"

"Duh," said Durant. "Then the guy slipped poison into her water glass and left!"

"Durant! That's enough," said Cami.

"Did you see Frank touch your glass?" asked Lopez.

"I don't remember." Debra stopped. "Wait. Yes, he did. While I was chewing him out, he was sitting there looking all dog-faced and moving things around on my bedside table."

"Moving things around? How?"

"You know. Moving them back and forth, kind of like to have something to do instead of listen to me."

"I'm sure you're fingerprinting the glass," said Gunnar.

"We are," said Lopez wryly.

"But a person wouldn't have to actually touch the glass to drop poison in, would they?" Kate asked.

"Besides," Gunnar put in, "several people probably touched that glass—the nurse who brought it in, somebody in the kitchen, Debra, Frank, and who know who else."

"Right," said Lopez. "But we still need Debra to tell us all she can. What happened next, Debra?"

"I told him to leave."

"How long would you say he was in the room?"

"No more than five or six minutes." Debra's mouth curved down in disdain. "It didn't take me long to say what I wanted to. Durant hadn't come back yet, so I got up and went to the bathroom, and when I got back I took a sip of water."

"Why just a sip?"

"Because I knew Durant was bringing me a soda—and because in a couple of seconds I started feeling funny." She paused. "And that's all I remember."

"What about you, Durant?" asked Lopez. "Do you have anything to add to what you told me at the hospital?"

"No. Like I said, I had trouble with the soda machine. Then I got a feeling I ought to get to Debra right away. You may think this sounds pious, Detective, but I really believe God gave me that feeling."

"I don't think that sounds pious at all, Durant. That feeling, as you put it, no matter where it came from, probably saved your sister's life—that and the fact she ingested so little of the poisoned water. How long would you say it was between the time you left the room and the time you returned?"

"Eight to ten minutes at the most. Maybe less."

"So, Frank was there five or six minutes. Then Debra went to the bathroom. For how long, Debra?"

Debra didn't blush or flinch. "About two minutes."

"Hmmm. She came out and had a sip of water. You, Durant, must have come in almost immediately afterward. It's a good thing you paid attention to that feeling you got."

"Look, Detective," said Durant. "I'm sorry for how I acted."

"No apologies necessary."

"It makes me so mad to think Frank Giovanni nearly killed my sister and I almost let it happen."

Lopez stood. "That'll do it for now. Again, my apologies for having to bother you. I'll let myself out."

For a minute or two after Lopez left, no one spoke. Kate felt that everyone was, like herself, mulling over the brief interview. Then Debra rose from her recliner. "I'm exhausted. I'm going up to my room."

"I'll come with you," said Cami.

"That's okay, Mom, I'll be fine." She bent over and kissed Cami on the cheek. "Thank you again for getting me out of that hospital. I'm so glad I'm here where we're all together." She smiled weakly at Durant.

"We'll get through this with the Lord's help," said Durant.

Debra's smile froze; her face hardened. She seemed about to speak, but after a darting glance around the room, she clamped her lips shut. She turned away from her brother, whose expression bounced from surprise to hurt to regret, all in the space of a heartbeat, and left the room.

What in the world? Kate wondered. Why was Durant surprised at Debra's attitude about God? It was certainly nothing new. Well, maybe it was. It actually seemed worse than before. *Something's happened, and I'm going to find out what.*

Rather than comment on her children's little exchange, Cami rose and said, "I thought of something. We never took those tapes to the police. I'm going to listen to them now." She had already told Durant and Debra about them.

Protests tumbled on top of each other from around the room: "Mom! No!" "Do you think that's wise, Cami?" "The police won't like that."

Kate spoke up. "At least let me and Gunnar go buy a couple of extra recorders, Cami. We can help you get through them faster."

"Good idea," said Cami. "We'll get started as soon as you return."

Another chorus of protests followed Cami's newest suggestion.

She looked from face to face. "I appreciate everyone's concern," she said. "But this is something I have to do. I've lived in a fairy tale too long—always expecting to be rescued by the handsome prince. Well, the handsome prince is gone, and the fairy godmother has skipped town."

"But God hasn't, Mom," said Durant tenderly.

"No, He hasn't."

Chapter Seventy-Five

Debra heard Durant's knock but didn't respond. She knew why he was here. She'd hoped she wouldn't have to face him right away yet knew the hope was in vain. Curled up in the corner of her lime green love seat that faced the open oceanfront window, she had waited for the rhythm of the waves to relax her. That too had been in vain.

When the knock came again, she sighed heavily and called out. "Come in, Durant."

He came in and strode straight to her. "What's up?"

Debra let out another heavy sigh. "Sit down, Durant."

Durant perched himself at the end of Debra's bed. For several seconds their eyes locked. During those few seconds, Debra felt that familiar, inexplicable bond to her twin and hated how she was about to hurt him.

At last he spoke. "What happened down there?"

Hoping to gain a brief respite, Debra said, "Down where?"

"Quit stalling. You know I'm talking about how you acted when I mentioned God."

"I think your exact words were, 'We'll get through this with the Lord's help.'"

"Right. So?"

"And you gave me this, this look. Like you and I had some kind of agreement."

Durant stood and began pacing. "I guess I thought we did."

"You mean because of our conversation at the hospital."

"Yes. We were about to pray together when Frank Giovanni came in."

"Think, Durant. *You* were about to pray."

"Yeah. But it seemed to me like you were thinking seriously about giving your life to Christ."

Debra's reply came out in a whisper as she momentarily relived the moment. "I was."

Durant halted mid-step. "What happened?"

The brief, longing memory evaporated, leaving anger in its wake. "Are you serious?" Debra sprang to her feet. Immediately a rush of dizziness hit her. "Oh!" she said, groping for the chair.

Durant caught her and eased her down. "I'm sorry. I shouldn't have brought this up now. I'll go."

Debra leaned back and closed her eyes. "No, don't go. I'd rather go ahead and talk."

Durant perched against the end of the bed. "Okay. But only if you feel like it."

Weak, but still trembling with anger, Debra snapped her eyes open. "First our father is murdered, then I'm assaulted on the beach, then somebody tries to poison me. And now you have the nerve to say the Lord will help us through this!"

"But Debra, He will!"

"Oh yeah? Then He'd better wake up from His nap."

"Debra!"

"Sorry. That's how I feel."

"If He hadn't given me the feeling something was wrong with you, you'd be dead!"

"Like Dad already is."

Seeing the pain that dropped over Durant's face, she softened her voice. "Anyway, you had that *feeling* from the moment Frank walked in."

"Not like down at the soda machine. It was so strong I knew I *had* to get to you. Nothing could have held me back."

"Please, let's not argue, Durant. Can't you accept the fact I don't believe the way you do?"

Voice flat, Durant said, "No, I can't." After a short silence, he asked, "Does this mean you don't believe in God?"

Debra thought for a few seconds, wanting to give him an honest answer. "No, it doesn't mean that. It means I don't see Him having the personal interest in me that you claim."

Durant pushed away from the bed and stared down at Debra. Surprising her, he smiled. "I'd better let you get some rest."

When Durant had gone, it seemed to Debra as if a ray of hope left with him.

***

Durant's smile disappeared as he left the room. *I thought I'd reached her when we talked in the hospital, Lord. Please show me what to do next. Or what not to do or say. Please, please, save my sister.*

Chapter Seventy-Six

"There are so many of them." Cami looked in dismay at the box of tiny tapes from Rosita's condo. They were stacked on the floor in Cami's personal home office next to the antique roll-top desk that had been reconfigured for a computer and four-in-one printer.

Kate shook her head. "She really had some kind of obsession, didn't she?"

"Poor thing," said Cami.

"You're very generous-hearted, Cami," said Gunnar, "to feel sorry for a woman who was obsessed with your husband."

"But her obsession was hopeless, and she knew it," Cami told him. Seeing his look of doubt, she went on, "For all his faults and straying—which I was more aware of than most people thought—Braxton loved me. *Me.*" She stopped, unable to continue.

"What do you say we get busy?" Kate picked up one tape and looked at the label. "They're all dated."

"That's how Rosita would do it, all right," said Cami. "Her efficiency is one thing that made her so valuable to Braxton."

"Do you think Victor will keep her on with Carrington Investments?" Gunnar asked.

"More to the point," Kate put in, "do you want him to? That is, assuming she isn't the one who murdered Braxton."

"I don't know. That's beyond my ability to consider right now. Anyway, first she's got to show up."

"As Kate pointed out," Gunnar said, "Rosita may have murdered Braxton, then flew the coop."

Cami frowned. "I don't think so. I mean, why? After all these years, why would she suddenly become so dissatisfied she'd want to kill him? He was her life." She surveyed the tapes again and groaned. "Where do we begin?"

"Why not start with the most recent ones?" Kate held up one tape. "This one is for June of this year."

Cami picked up another tape. "This one is for August, this month. Let's go back and start with May, June, and July."

A few minutes later the three had separated—Kate and Gunnar taking handfuls of tapes and small recorders to their rooms, and Cami remaining in her office.

***

An hour later, Kate entered Cami's office as Cami was removing her last tape from the recorder.

"Find anything?" Cami asked.

"Not a thing. At least, not anything helpful. Braxton held various things over several people's heads, and I've listed those. But nothing seems major. Who knows what the police will think?"

"Ditto," said Gunnar, entering with his box.

Cami stretched, took a deep breath, and let it out slowly. "Okay. Let's go to July."

Chapter Seventy-Seven

Forty-five minutes later, Kate and Gunnar burst into Cami's office. With a sudden sense of dread, Cami said, "You found something." She stopped the tape she was listening to.

"Gunnar did," said Kate.

Gunnar's face was grim as he laid his recorder on the desk. Kate took the one extra chair in the office, while Gunnar remained standing. He leaned over and pushed "Play".

"*Come in, come in.*" Braxton's voice sounded mockingly hearty. "*Have a seat.*"

"*No, thank you. I'll stand.*" This time the accent was distinctly English.

"That's Ashley," said Cami. "Probably there to discuss the party."

Gunnar put a finger to his lips.

"*Suit yourself,*" Braxton told Ashley. "*Although I think you'll wish you were sitting.*" After a pause he said, "*There, that's better.*"

"*What is this all about Braxton? I'm quite busy, as you know. I still have a lot to sort out for your party.*"

"*Yes, you're a busy girl, aren't you, Ashley?*" Braxton's tone suggested an amused smile. "*Always have been, haven't you?*"

"*What do you mean?*"

"*As I told you earlier, someone* rang me up *this morning—after I'd put out a few feelers of my own.*"

"*You mean you've been checking on me.*"

"*Spying? Oh no. Doing a little background check that I should have done long ago.*"

287

"Background check?" Cami broke in.

Gunnar nodded.

"B-background check?" Ashley was clearly distressed.

"A few weeks ago I heard you say something about your first husband."

"I remember that. I explained at the time that I was making a joke. I was simply referring to Victor as my first, and only, husband."

"You didn't convince me," said Braxton. "That's why I got in touch with one of the managers at the Carrington Investments London branch. It didn't take him long to come up with this."

"What can it be?" Kate spoke in a hushed whisper above the sound of rustling paper.

After nearly a minute of silence, Braxton said, "Afraid to read it out loud, Ashley? Afraid to read the copy of your marriage certificate? Your marriage to one Reese Jones, originally from Swansea, Wales?"

"Ashley married before?" Cami's mouth fell open in disbelief.

"What's the big deal?" Ashley asked. "Lots of people get divorced. I suppose I should have told Victor, but that was such a terribly painful part of my life I didn't want to talk about it." She took a deep breath. "I'll tell him now. Actually, it will be a relief."

"When you tell him," said Braxton, his voice suddenly hard, "you may want to avoid using the word divorce. *Here, look at this."*

The sound of paper rattling again met the ears of the three listeners. Cami leaned forward, her body stiff, her blue eyes wide.

"So, you couldn't find a record of my divorce." Ashley spoke dismissively. "That's probably due to some clerical error."

"I considered that and even gave you the benefit of the doubt."

"I bet."

"You underrate my kindness, Ashley, Luv." Braxton seemed to be enjoying taunting Ashley with the British endearment. "Anyway, my man

in London did a little more digging and found your Reese Jones living back in his native city."

"There must be a dozen Reese Joneses in Swansea."

"Which is why it took my man several weeks to find the one living in a church-sponsored mission, having originally gone there to get off a six-month drug and alcohol binge that began after his wife—one Ashley Langtry Jones—left him without benefit of divorce."

Cami pushed the "Stop" button. "I don't want to hear anymore," she whispered.

"You have to," said Kate.

"It's almost over." Gunnar gently moved Cami's hand back to the "Play" button.

"So what do you plan to do?" Ashley asked, her tone resigned. "You obviously haven't told Victor yet."

"Nothing."

"Nothing?"

"Nothing. At least not until after this party—which, by the way, I appreciate your generous offer to put on at your own expense."

"No way!"

"Yes, Luv," said Braxton, taunting Ashley again. "Now don't protest. No need to remind me that I can afford any number of such galas. But I really don't think I should let you get off deceiving my brother Scot-free. Or should I make that English-free?"

"I get it," said Ashley. "You don't want the adverse publicity this would get you. That mayoral election is so important to you that you're willing to let your brother unwittingly commit polygamy. But what about afterwards? It's three months before the actual election."

"Haven't decided yet. But you can breathe easy for the time being. And now, I have an important appointment." The sound of Braxton slapping his hands down on his desk and rising from his chair filled the tape. "I'll see you out."

Ashley's next words came out breathless and provocative. "Perhaps you and I can come to some arrangement, Braxton. Victor is terribly naïve, as you've discovered."

"Don't humiliate yourself, Ashley. It's, as you Brits would say, most unbecoming."

"You're a vile man, Braxton Carrington."

"Tch, tch. Do I hear the pot calling the kettle black?"

"You'll get your party—the best this island has ever seen. The best my money can buy. But you'll be sorry. Sorrier than you can imagine. You won't get away with this."

The sound of Braxton chuckling nearly covered Ashley's stomping steps and the slam of the door.

"That's it," said Gunnar as he stopped the tape.

Cami felt as if all the blood had drained from her face—and that something important had drained from her soul. She squeezed her temples with her fingertips. Her voice stony, she said, "My husband, my own husband, the father of my children, the man I loved for more than twenty-two years and thought I knew! How could he be so...." She paused, realizing Kate and Gunnar, like she, were probably filling in the blank with the word Ashley had used: *vile*. They'd probably also noticed that Cami had not said she couldn't believe what she'd heard.

But you do believe it. The thought surprised but didn't amaze her. She put that thought on hold and went on, "And Ashley. I've never liked her much, and she's made no secret of her dislike for me; but surely she wouldn't actually kill."

"She might, Cami," said Kate softly. "And she was sitting near Braxton at the head table. It wouldn't have been difficult to drop something into his glass."

"Are there anymore tapes?" asked Gunnar. "That was the last of mine."

"There's a little left on this August one," said Cami. "I'll go ahead and play it."

Chapter Seventy-Eight

For the second time in the past few minutes, a female voice sounded from a tape. Cami assumed Braxton had put his phone on conference call.

"Braxton?" The voice was husky and provocative—and tentative sounding.

"I've heard that voice," said Cami.

"Why are you calling me here?" Braxton was abrupt, cold. *"I thought we agreed you'd never call me at my office."*

"I wouldn't if you'd answer your phone." A clear note of pleading filled the woman's words.

"I'd think you'd get some kind of hint from that fact."

"Erika!" Cami said the name along with Braxton's recorded voice.

"How can you do this, Braxton? To me? To us?"

"There was never any us—at least not in the way you're implying— except in your vivid imagination."

"No! You were going to leave Cami and I was going to divorce Stan so that we could get married."

Cami stared at the tape recorder in horror.

"I never said any such thing. You shouldn't have to search your memory too deeply to recall that you were always the one to suggest those things. I never would have suggested them because I never would have done them. I love my wife and do not plan to leave her—ever."

Cami found little comfort in her husband's words.

"How can you say you love your wife when what you and I have is so wonderful?"

"Had. What we had was exciting and memorable, but—"

"Memorable!"

"But it's over. I thought I made that plain at the restaurant. You'd do well to accept that fact and move on with your life with Stan."

Erika's tone turned bitter. "It's all because of that election. You don't want word of our little memorable affair to get out and spoil your chances. How do you know I won't spill the beans myself?"

"And risk losing all Stan has provided for you? I don't think so. And don't blame it on the election. I was going to end our little fling soon anyway."

Erika drew in a sharp breath. "Our little fling? That's what you call it?"

"Look, Erika, this conversation is at an end."

After a few seconds of silence, Erika responded in a hard tone that matched Braxton's. "See you at the party, Braxton."

"That wouldn't be wise."

"Wise schmize. Nobody treats Erika Weston like this and gets away with it."

"Are you threatening me?"

"Take it any way you wanta, honey."

The sound of a phone slamming down ended the recorded conversation and the tape.

***

Cami jumped to her feet, seized the tape recorder and raised her arm to throw it.

Gunnar caught her wrist and snatched at the recorder. Cami resisted him, but he easily overpowered her. Holding her wrist, he said quietly, "You might damage the tape if you throw it."

Reluctantly Cami relinquished the little machine.

"I went ahead and listened to the August batch," she said. "There are dozens of earlier ones, but I don't think we need to bother with them."

"The police have to hear these two conversations immediately," said Gunnar. "The one with Erika adds at least two more suspects."

"Two?" asked Cami.

"Erika," said Gunnar, "and her husband—what's his name?"

"Stan," Cami supplied. "Dr. Stan Weston. But he's not on the tape."

"No, but what if he found out about Erika and Braxton?"

"I see what you mean."

"I'll call Detective Lopez," said Kate.

"No!" A deep, burning fury began to swell up in Cami—against Ashley, against Erika, and even Erika's husband Stan, but most of all against Braxton, the man she loved and had been faithful to and tried to provide a pleasant home life for. Yes, more than anyone, Braxton was the brunt of her fury.

"He was my husband," she said firmly. "I'll call the detective. And I won't rest until I know who killed Braxton."

Chapter Seventy-Nine

Cami lay on her back, still and stiff in the king-sized bed she had shared with Braxton. Maybe it hadn't been such a good idea to sleep here tonight after all. Kate had urged her to use the second twin bed in her room, but after two nights in a recliner at the hospital, Cami wanted nothing more than to sleep in her own bed. She was so exhausted from the events of the past few days that she retired early. It was only nine o'clock.

Now the silence in the space beside her kept her awake. Braxton hadn't been a snorer, but he'd often make little noises in his sleep: soft grunts, little explosions of breath. Cami sometimes tried to imagine what was going on in his mind. Was he hassling with his stockbroker? Was he giving a competitor a piece of his mind? Sometimes she'd ask him the next morning, but he always claimed he didn't remember.

Now the little strangely comforting sounds were silenced. Forever. Cami felt a certain disloyalty to herself for missing them. She should be holding onto the anger she'd felt after hearing the tapes, not wishing her heartless, cheating husband were lying next to her. Confusion churned in her brain and heart and even her stomach.

Trying to put aside memories of Braxton, she thought of how Detective Lopez had been unhappy with her and Kate and Gunnar for listening to the tapes before turning them over to him. "Withholding evidence," he'd called it.

"But we didn't know they were evidence until we listened to them," Cami told him.

That didn't mollify him, but at least he didn't press charges. Immediately, he put out his second APB in as many days: this time on one Rosita DeLuca.

Later, Cami consulted with Kate about the advisability of telling the twins what was on the tapes. The mother in her wanted to shield her children, even if only for a little while.

"They'll find out soon enough," Kate said. "It's better if it comes from their mother. Besides, Jesus said, 'you shall know the truth, and the truth shall set you free.'"

"But I thought He was talking about the truth about Himself—about salvation through Him."

"He was, but it seems to me the principle applies here. It could be that both your children need to know the full truth about their father—Durant so he can free himself of the expectations Braxton's put on him, and Debra...."

"Debra so she can understand what her idol was really like. She's the one I'm most concerned about. What will this do to her?"

"Eventually, the truth will set her free as well."

So Cami told her children and was surprised it was Durant who had the most trouble accepting what he heard. That's when Cami realized Debra had pretty well understood her father all along. Durant, it seemed, had clung to threads of hope about Braxton's integrity—threads now raveled to bits.

As she processed these thoughts, Cami prayed, *Please protect my babies, Lord.* She gripped the sheet in the empty space beside her. *Please don't let them be destroyed by all this.* She lay motionless for a few moments, then went on, *And please help* me. *I'm not even sure how I want You to help me. I only know I can't handle it without You. If only there were something I could* do. *I feel so helpless.*

The ringing of her bedside phone broke through her thoughts. She picked it up. "Hello."

"Cami, it's Victor. Are you all right?"

Sudden thoughts of Ashley's deception brought on a stab of pity in Cami. She knew Victor and Ashley's so-called marriage had always been volatile. She dreaded the explosion that would surely occur when he learned the truth. He'd have to know soon, but Cami would leave that to Detective Lopez.

"I'm okay, Victor," she said, answering his question.

"You don't sound okay."

"Well maybe okay is an exaggeration. Mainly I'm tired." *And confused and wondering if your wife killed my husband.*

"I hope it's not too late to call, but I thought you'd want to know everything is set for the funeral tomorrow. As you know, as soon as the autopsy results were in, the police released the body for cremation. I wanted to know if there's anything you need."

"I appreciate your concern, Victor. I'm okay. Thank you so much for taking care of everything for me. I know this has been hard for you, too."

Without commenting on Cami's last statement, Victor said he was more than glad to help, sounding as though he truly meant it.

As Cami hung up the phone, she caught sight of the small powder-blue Bible she kept by her side of the bed. It was old, a high school graduation gift from her parents twenty-four years ago. The embossed monogram in the right corner read "Camilla Leigh Stewart." Picking it up reverently, she felt a little ashamed that it was almost as new looking as when she first received it. She took hold of the silky navy blue ribbon peeking from the bottom. The Bible opened to the fourth chapter of Philippians. Cami began to read the Apostle Paul's words to the Christians in the city of Philippi: "Therefore, my beloved and longed-for brethren, my joy and crown, so stand fast in the Lord, beloved."

Stand fast in the Lord. So simple a statement. So definite. Why does it seem so hard to do?

A few verses later, she read, "Rejoice in the Lord always. Again I will say, rejoice!"

Rejoice always? All the time? Cami remembered hearing somewhere that Paul was in prison when he wrote those words, yet he was able find joy even there. Well, she was not Paul.

"Be anxious for nothing…"

For nothing? Don't worry about anything? Impossible.

"…but in everything by prayer and supplication with thanksgiving, let your requests be made known to God…"

Cami's first thought that there wasn't much to feel thankful for was cut short by gratitude that twice Durant had been on hand to rescue Debra, who was now alive and safe. And that Kate was here. What a rock she had been. Gunnar, too. And there was Victor taking care of the funeral arrangements. *Thank You for reminding me, Lord.*

"…and the peace of God, which surpasses all understanding, will guard your hearts and minds through Christ Jesus."

The peace of God. Cami lifted her eyes upward. *How I want that, Lord.* She bowed her head and waited quietly. She half expected some mystical aura or bright lights to go off in her head. Instead, a gentle calmness stole over her that seemed like a good start toward the peace she sought. She raised her eyes again and whispered, *Thank You, Lord.*

Chapter Eighty

On the den couch, Kate snuggled into the curve of Gunnar's big arm draped about her shoulder. It felt so good. So right. There had been little time to think about her own situation in the past few days, but Kate was almost sure that tomorrow afternoon, sometime after Braxton's funeral service, she would call the RV company and cancel the sale of the motorhome she'd chosen. Fortunately, she hadn't put any money down on it.

These few days spent so much in Gunnar's company had brought her closer and closer to a definite conclusion concerning their relationship. If only she could get past that last inkling of doubt.

Gunnar tightened his hold. "I wish you weren't heading up to Oregon before returning to Boston," he said, brushing her hair with his lips.

"Me, too, but I'm committed to teaching that month-long Poly-Sci class at Portland U. They scheduled me three months ago."

"Will you fly straight home from there?"

"No. I've already got reservations to fly back to San Diego. I'd planned to come back and pick up the motorhome, you know. Besides, I'd like to see Cami again for a day or two before heading home."

Gunnar made an impatient noise. "At least we have a few days here before I go back on Saturday."

"Well, we'll have to make the most of that time. Cami may need me some, but her parents are coming in tomorrow in time for the service, so she'll have them. Maybe we should spend a day at the zoo."

"Ahh. San Diego's world famous zoo."

"And another day we can go to—"

Gunnar's phone broke into her sentence. He ignored it, instead tipping Kate's chin up with one finger and kissing her.

The phone rang again. He grinned and kissed her again, and again after the third ring and the fourth. Finally the ringing stopped.

"Mmm," said Kate. "Wonder who's calling you at ten p.m. Whoever it is is probably calling from Boston. It's one a.m. there. Maybe you should have answered it. It could be an emergency."

"Too busy." Gunnar kissed Kate.

The ringing began again, prompting him to lower his face toward hers. "Hey, I like this."

Kate laughed and pushed him away. "Answer the phone, Gunnar."

With a mock growl, he read the name on the tiny monitor. He rolled his eyes as he answered the call. "Hey there."

The sultry voice on the other end was loud enough for Kate to hear clearly. "Hey there, yourself, Tiger."

Tiger? Kate stiffened.

"What's up?" Gunnar asked his caller. "You're burning the candle pretty late."

"Well, you know what they call me."

"Night owl Natalie."

Kate's eyes widened and she inched away from Gunnar, who seemed not to notice.

"So, what's going on? This is a late time to call, even for you."

"Oh, I knew it was three hours earlier there. Besides, I wanted to make sure you haven't forgotten about Friday night."

Friday night? Kate moved a little further from Gunnar.

Gunnar, looking embarrassed, stood and moved a few steps away.

Kate could no longer make out Natalie's words, but the flirty tone was unmistakable. And she had no trouble hearing Gunnar say, "No, you're not interrupting anything."

Not interrupting anything! Calling during a romantic moment isn't interrupting anything?

She heard Gunnar let out a groan. "You mean that shindig is *this* Friday night? I was thinking it was next week"... "Yes, you could say I've been a little distracted." He looked toward Kate and started to grin, then raised his eyes in surprise. He listened to a few more breathy words and groaned again, "That's right, I know it's a big deal, but they don't need me there." … "Come on, Natalie. I know I promised, but you'll have a dozen escorts to choose from, and I think my career can survive my missing this hoopla."

The conversation went on for several minutes, during which time Kate felt herself growing angrier and angrier. The upshot of it was that Hub Digital Corporation's tenth anniversary celebration would be a huge gala at the CEO's estate in the suburbs—an event Gunnar had never bothered to mention to Kate, clearly because he had promised to escort Natalie. Apparently, too, it wouldn't be good for Gunnar's career to miss the event.

At last, Gunnar said, "You're right. I should be there. I'll change my reservation and leave here on Thursday."

Kate could hardly believe her ears. He was leaving two days early?

Gunnar was concluding his call. "I'll call you when I get in town."

By the time Gunnar put away the phone, Kate felt like her blood was literally boiling. Gunnar's face told her he knew how she was feeling.

"Um," he said, scratching the back of his head. "I guess you heard that."

"I did."

"I can see you're upset, but I can explain."

Kate simply glowered at him.

"You see, there's this big, important celebration."

"For Hub Digital's tenth anniversary. If it's so important, why have I never heard a word about it? No, don't answer that. How could you tell me about it when you were planning to take *Night Owl Natalie?*"

"Well, yes, I had promised her." Gunnar dropped to the couch and slouched against the back, his long legs stretched out before him, his fingers laced behind his head. "You see, Natalie and I have a kind of complicated background."

Knowing and not caring that she sounded sarcastic, Kate said, "This should be interesting."

Without looking in Kate's direction, Gunnar said, "You know about Brita. I've told you how crazy with grief I was when she died."

A touch of sympathy touched Kate's anger. She of all people knew about "crazy with grief," but she was too angry to give in to sympathetic feelings.

"And I told you how I went through almost a year of rebellion against God." He stopped.

"Go on."

"What I didn't tell you is that during that time, I, well I took comfort—or tried to take comfort, at least—with a woman."

Kate felt as though Gunnar had plunged a dagger into her heart. "And the woman?" she forced herself to ask, knowing the answer.

"Natalie. She had gone through a bad patch herself, a broken engagement, and we were both vulnerable."

"But you were still back in Minnesota at that time."

"Yes. Anyway, after almost exactly a year, the Lord got hold of me again, and I came to my senses and broke off with Natalie—fortunately before it went too far. Then I got the offer from Hub Digital and knew it was God's way of getting me away from Minnesota and its temptations."

"But she followed you."

"Not exactly. She happened to get a similar offer."

"Gunnar! Surely you're not that naïve. She *followed* you there. She's still in love with you."

"She never was in love with me. I was a convenient outlet for her. And I'm ashamed to say it was the same with me. You could say we used each other."

"But you still see her."

"Sort of."

"Sort of? How can you sort of see somebody?"

"A few weeks ago, she began asking me some spiritual questions, and we began meeting now and then to discuss the Bible."

"Oh, that old ploy."

"Kate."

"Yet you never thought it important to tell me all this." Suddenly a thought occurred to Kate. "How old is she?"

Gunnar cleared his throat. "Thirty-five. I know what you're thinking. That's eleven years younger than me."

"Ever married?"

"No. One reason her engagement fell apart is she was more interested in a career than a husband and home."

"Pretty?"

Gunnar looked as if he didn't want to answer that one. He cleared his throat again. "She's attractive." He looked at Kate now and sat up straight. "Kate, Natalie means nothing to me. It's you I love."

How she wanted to believe him. How she wanted to simply forget the conversation and confessions she'd heard and snuggle back into his arms the way they'd been a few minutes earlier.

She couldn't do it. "Why didn't you tell me all this before, Gunnar?"

"I should have. But I was embarrassed. I looked at you and saw someone pure and good and deeply committed to the Lord, and I couldn't bring myself to tell you about the one period when my life wasn't an open book."

"But the Lord forgave you for all that, Gunnar."

"Yes He did." Blowing out his lips, Gunnar slumped in his seat.

"But you couldn't be sure I would."

"No," Gunnar answered simply.

That hurt Kate as much as anything that had transpired in the past few minutes. She had always had to fight being judgmental. Apparently she hadn't fought it hard enough. But that didn't change the fact that he'd not been open with her.

"Back to Natalie," she said. "You said you had a complicated relationship. What did you mean?"

"Well, as you now know, she came to Boston."

"How long ago?"

"Four months."

"That's two months after you and I met."

"When she got there, she needed some help settling in—finding an apartment, learning her way around town, things like that."

"And there was big, nice guy Gunnar ready and willing to help."

"Things had changed between us. She seems to be more aware of our age difference than she was before and kind of looks up to me like a big brother. We kid around the same way I do with my sisters."

Kate didn't know whether Gunnar was the most naïve man on earth or the best actor. "Do you plan to keep on being Big Brother?"

"No. I'd already planned to start backing off from being with her and help her find some woman to discuss spiritual questions with."

"That's a good idea. But you still plan to escort her to the party this weekend?"

"Yes. I made a promise to her, and I really should attend anyway. Besides, it will be a good time to set some things straight."

"Such as."

"Such as how much I love you. She knows all about you, by the way."

Kate sat silently for a few moments, the anger that had boiled up in her having settled down to a deep ache. She rose, and he jumped up to join her.

"I don't know what to say, Gunnar. I need to think and pray about all this. I'm finally ready and able to put my feelings for Joel in the past when I learn this."

"Kate, please." He reached for her.

She stepped back. "We'll talk tomorrow." With heavy steps, she climbed the stairs to her room.

Chapter Eighty-One

Cami was dreaming. Somehow she knew she was dreaming. At first, one image bounced on top of another with faces and names mixed up or switched. One moment Kate seemed to be Durant and Durant became Ashley, while Gunnar somehow looked like Erika. The next moment a stranger—a short, ugly man—tried to kiss her, but when she slapped his misshapen cheek, the face became Braxton's.

At last the jumbled images faded and segued into one that was all too real. Cami saw herself at the Oceanfront Ballroom of the Hotel del Coronado the night of Braxton's party. Every detail was as sharp as in real life, from the tiniest etching in the ice sculpture crown, to the pattern in the carpet, to the dark storm clouds beyond the huge windows that looked out toward the ocean. She could almost feel the diamond and sapphire necklace against her throat and the silky fabric of her silvery blue dress.

And she could see people as clearly as though they were standing by her bedside. There was Kate, smiling and supportive, her shining dark hair swinging against her cheek when she moved her head, surprisingly stylish in an emerald green and navy pants outfit. Nearby, Durant and Debra engaged in a seemingly serious conversation. Across the room were Victor and Ashley, faces tense, apparently having another of their arguments. Near them stood Rosita, wearing a dark dress that differed little from the conservative suits she wore to the office. On the other side of the room, Stanley Weston glowered at Erika in her slinky bronze-colored pants, sashaying toward the laughing group that surrounded Braxton.

Braxton. There was Braxton. Tall, dark-haired, blue-eyed, achingly handsome. Exuding charm with every word, every quirk of his eyebrow, every tilt of his head.

Cami saw herself drifting toward him, drawn to him, loving him, wanting to be near him, to touch him, despite the doubts and fears that had so recently assailed her and the argument they'd had before the party.

Suddenly, Cami was seated at Braxton's side at the head table. A waiter placed fresh flutes of pink champagne at their places. A TV cameraman trained his lens on the head table. The guests looked their way expectantly as Victor, on the other side of Braxton, introduced his brother as the "next mayor of Coronado."

Braxton stood, made a few remarks, and commented on the streak of lightning that lit up the moonless sky beyond the oceanfront windows. Smiling down at Cami, he reached for his flute of champagne and took a sip. In her dream, Cami felt a swelling of pride and a determination to seek God's help for their marriage more diligently.

But something was wrong. Braxton frowned; his face twisted as if in pain. He dropped his glass and clutched the tuxedo fabric over his heart with both hands. One hand let go and reached out toward Cami. He called her name.

Astonished guests gasped, a crash of thunder shook the room, and the lights went out. A moment later, as quickly as they'd gone off, the lights again flooded the room.

In her dream Cami felt the scream that rose from her throat and melded with those coming from the guests all around the room.

Beside her, Braxton lay motionless across the table. The rosy champagne in his toasting glass trickled across the snowy white cloth like pale blood.

***

Cami awoke screaming and sobbing and crying out again and again, "No! No! No!"

"Cami! Cami! What's wrong?" Kate's voice broke through Cami's wails. Cami gripped Kate's arm, digging her nails into the flesh.

Kate sat beside her, helped her sit up, and held her, tenderly whispering, "There, there," and "Lord, help her, comfort her," until the screams stopped and the sobs subsided into pitiful hiccups.

At last, spent and exhausted, Cami lay back and stared at the ceiling, not bothering to wipe away the tears that still streamed down her cheeks.

"That was a bad one," Kate stated.

Cami covered her face with her hands. "I don't think I can stand it, Kate. I can't go on. I can't comfort my children when I'm a major basket case myself. I can't face my parents' pity. I can't bear the thought of the funeral. I can't do it!"

"No, you can't."

Surprised Kate hadn't said of course you *can*, Cami uncovered her face.

"*You* can't. But with the Lord's help you can do anything. Remember Philippians 4:13?"

Cami's answer came out in an awed whisper. "'I can do all things through Christ who strengthens me.'" She hiccupped one last time. "Kate, I was reading and meditating on those very words before I went to sleep."

Kate simply smiled and nodded.

The two longtime friends relaxed in a companionable silence. Cami was grateful that she didn't need to talk about her feelings anymore right now and that Kate understood them without words. After a few minutes, Cami sat up again and said, "Thanks, dear friend. I'm all right now. You can go back to bed."

"Are you sure you're okay? It's already 6:30; I usually get up about this time anyway."

"I'm fine. Really, I am." Cami pushed back the covers and swung her feet over the bed and slid them into her slippers. "I'm getting up, too. There's a lot to do. Mom and Dad get here about ten."

"Nine fifty-five, as I recall," Kate teased, her eyes twinkling.

For a moment, Cami stared at Kate, then both burst into laughter. They laughed and laughed and laughed, holding their sides and finally flinging themselves backward on the bed.

"Okay," Kate said at last, jumping up. "I'm getting out of here and getting myself dressed. Gunnar will probably be down for breakfast soon, and I'd like to get a bite before he comes down."

For the first time, Cami noticed a shadow in Kate's eyes. "Trouble in Paradise?"

Kate gave her a wry smile. "Funny you should put it that way. That's exactly what Gunnar said back in Boston when I said something about possible problems between you and Braxton."

"Well?" When Kate didn't reply right away, Cami asked, "Or would you rather not talk about it?"

"Not yet. For now, let's say you're right—there's trouble in Paradise."

"Oh, Kate."

"Not to worry." Kate rose. "You and I will have a long talk about it soon." As she started to leave, she gave Cami a look of concern. "Do you think TV reporters will cover Braxton's funeral?"

"I hope not. I've had my fill of them. I can still see the cameraman moving in on us when Braxton collapsed. And when they reported it on TV, I couldn't bear to watch." Cami shivered.

"That was awful. I hope you don't have to go through that tomorrow."

"Me, too. At least there won't be much to report. It's only a funeral."

Chapter Eighty-Two

The funeral at lovely, old gray-stone Christ Church was dignified and somber, the music outstanding, the majestic sanctuary
packed to capacity. Most of the people at Braxton's party had turned
out, plus many other locals, including the Giovannis. These were
matched in number by dignitaries from the City of San Diego and
the State of California. Cami's parents arrived in plenty of time, but
neither of her brothers had been able to get away. A reception followed
immediately afterward in the church, and guests spoke glowingly of
Reverend Fitzgerald's eulogy. He presented Braxton Carrington as a
man of vision and energy, a man who had taken his family business to
international heights, a man of dedication to family and to his beloved
island of Coronado, a man who had donated large sums of money to
the church. Tactfully, he didn't mention that Braxton only occasionally
attended services.

On the way home, Durant told Cami, "I asked Reverend Fitzgerald
for a DVD of the service, Mom."

"Thank you for doing that." She sat silently for a few minutes as the
mortuary limousine drove them to the house, her mind going over the
events of the past few days.

Kate interrupted her musings. "I've been thinking, Cami. Durant's
mention of the DVD made me wonder if the TV station would give us
a copy of the film of the party."

"I guess they would. But so what?"

"There might be something on the film that would give us a clue
about Braxton's murderer."

Excitement stirred in Cami. "You're right! I'll call the station when we get home. I know one of the anchormen, Brian Kepple."

Fifteen minutes later, Cami had charmed Brian Kepple into having a copy of the film delivered to her house, although he emphasized that doing so was "highly irregular."

"I thought of something, Kate," Cami said when she hung up the phone.

"What's that?"

"Before I fell asleep last night, I asked the Lord to show me some specific action I could take. It may sound mystical—and I'm no mystic—but I believe this is the answer He's given me."

"I believe so, too," Kate agreed.

***

All the pastor said about Braxton was true, Kate thought, rinsing out a teacup in the Carrington mansion kitchen. *Even the part about dedication to family. In his own way, Braxton cared for them. But what about dedication to God? What about spiritual heights?*

She was not surprised that Reverend Fitzgerald hadn't mentioned those things. He struck Kate as having too much integrity to offer false praise, even for the sake of a grieving family and loved ones. Still, the thought saddened Kate. She ached for Cami and her children, especially Durant, unable to think of husband and father now at home with God. Kate shuddered.

"Cold?" Gunnar's deep voice interrupted her musings. "Here. Let me warm you up." He pulled her to him and enfolded her with his arms. She wrapped her arms around his waist and, despite herself, responded eagerly, then laid her head on his broad chest, her hair barely touching his chin. He lowered his head and kissed her gently but deeply.

"Where is Cami?" Gunnar asked, still holding Kate.

"She's on the patio with her parents and the twins," Kate said, giving Gunnar a squeeze as she pulled away.

"Good. They need some time together. The Stewarts are great people. I'm glad they've offered to stay with Cami for a while."

"Me, too. There's only one problem."

"What can be the problem? They're retired, in good health, free and able to be away from home."

"It's for those very reasons they've been able to get really involved in missions work through their church in North Carolina." Kate picked up a dish towel and began drying the cup she had rinsed. She was glad the maid was occupied in another part of the house. She needed these little everyday activities.

"Right," Gunnar replied. "I know they just returned from Peru." Gunnar took the cup from her and set it in an open cupboard.

"And they had planned another mission trip, beginning almost immediately."

"Had?" He closed the cupboard.

"Yes. They've already told Cami they're canceling that trip."

"Too bad. But it's probably the right thing. Their daughter needs them."

As Gunnar paused before going on, the front doorbell rang. Kate heard Edie answer it and say a few words.

"What about you?" Gunnar asked, a slight edge to his voice. "How much longer are you staying?"

"My class at Portland U begins next week, you know. I'll stay until then."

"I see." The slight edge sharpened.

Kate searched his face. Dreading the answer, she asked, "And you?"

"I have an early flight tomorrow. I need to get back to work."

And the party and Natalie, Kate thought.

"Besides, it seems that I've outstayed my welcome."

"Gunnar! You know that Cami's been glad and even grateful to have you here."

"I wasn't talking about Cami." He looked down into her face. "Kate, surely we can work this out."

"I hope so—with all my heart."

"Kate! It's here," Cami said, coming into the kitchen. "Oh." She stopped abruptly. "Sorry to interrupt." She started to leave.

"It's all right," said Gunnar. "You're not interrupting anything at all." He gave Kate a sad smile and left.

"I'm sorry, Kate," Cami said when Gunnar was out of hearing range. "This could have waited."

With a wry look and a shrug, Kate pointed to the package in Cami's hand. "The TV film of the party?"

"Yes, but we don't have to watch it right now. You should go to Gunnar."

"Yes, we do. And Gunnar and I can talk later."

"Are you sure?"

Kate could see that Cami was torn between concern for her and eagerness to get started.

"I'm sure. But what about your parents?"

"They're completely exhausted—with traveling here, then heading almost immediately to the funeral. They've gone upstairs for a nap. We'll get the twins to watch it with us. They might see something important."

Suddenly Kate was as eager as Cami. "Where do we set it up?"

"On the big screen in the den."

Big screen? Kate thought. *How about theater sized?*

"Okay, then. Let's hit it."

Chapter Eighty-Three

$\mathcal{Sp}$

All of a sudden, the idea of watching the DVD of Braxton's party was unthinkable to Cami.

Come on, girl, she commanded herself, *get your act together. This is a good idea.* She exchanged glances with her friend, whose sympathetic smile said she understood Cami's feelings. Trying to bolster her courage, Cami told herself, *It can't be any worse than this morning's dream.*

Holding the remote control, she looked around. The twins occupied chairs on either side of the room, rather than sitting side by side; and she noted a definite coolness between them. A somewhat subdued Gunnar had also joined the group but sat far away from Kate. Briefly she mentally likened the dynamics in the room to the storm that had hit the island the night of Braxton's death.

Don't get fanciful, she chided herself. She knew she'd sift through it all later, but right now there was a job to be done. She pointed the remote toward the TV.

Durant touched her arm, stopping her. "Mom, let's ask the Lord's guidance before we begin."

Ashamed that she had not thought of it herself and wondering when her little boy had turned into a godly man, Cami said, "Why don't you do it for us?"

Durant's prayer was short—"Lord, please show us anything You think we should see. Amen."—but it helped. Cami pressed "Play".

The television segment had lasted less than a minute, but the full footage ran about half an hour. The images on the screen captured the

313

festive mood of the party and revealed what an excellent job Ashley had done—as she'd defiantly promised Braxton she would.

Only the knowledge of what was to come kept Cami from enjoying the shots of freshly cut flowers, intricate ice sculptures, and elegant centerpieces. The photographer had caught these but used most of his footage on the guests milling about the room. It seemed that he'd done cameo shots of nearly every guest: family members, influential locals, important government officials, officers and spouses from North Island Naval Air Station. The array of the women's designer outfits, the men's tuxedos, and sharp naval uniforms outshone even Ashley's efforts.

About halfway through, Debra spoke up. "I've had enough. I'm going to my room." She started to rise.

"No, please, Debra," said Cami, who was handling the viewing better than she'd thought she would. "This is difficult for all of us, but the video may show us something that will help us find out who killed your father."

Killed. Cami wondered if the day would come when that word wouldn't conjure up awful pictures in her mind.

"Okay, Mom, you're right," said Debra. She dropped back into her chair and leaned forward to watch more intently.

At last, the dreaded moments arrived. Every person in the den tensed up when the scene shifted to the head table. There was the waiter pouring the fatal pink champagne, Braxton taking a sip then clasping his chest, the lights going out. Soon there was the chaos following the moment the lights came back on revealing Braxton lying across the table. The screen went blank.

The room was silent. Breathing seemed to be stilled. Cami was sure they all felt as she did—sickened, grief stricken, reluctant to be the first to speak.

After nearly a minute, Debra broke the silence. She spoke briskly, as if to cover her emotions. "Run that last part again, Mom."

"The last part?" *I can't bear to watch that again.* She cast a pleading look at Debra.

"Come on, Mom. You're the one who insisted on this."

"She's right, Cami," said Kate. "Let's begin again at the part where the meal is over and we see the head table."

"I'd like to see that again, too," Gunnar put in.

"All right." Cami handed the remote to Durant. "You do it, please." Angry with herself for her moment of weakness, she balled her hands into fists on her lap as the picture flickered on again.

I can do all things through Christ, who strengthens me. The unexpected thought was so real that Cami looked around quickly to make sure no one in the room had spoken the words. She relaxed and gave her attention to the screen.

There it was again—a shot of the guests nearest the head table looking eagerly in that direction. There was the waiter pouring the champagne. There was Victor standing to introduce Braxton.

"Stop!" Kate commanded.

Durant hit the remote.

"Back up to the waiter."

"Durant rewound the film a short way and stopped it at the waiter.

"Look at him," Kate said.

All eyes were focused on the slim, sandy-haired, mustached waiter, his head bent over the glass, the champagne bottle in his left hand.

"What is it, Aunt Kate?"

"Durant, does this TV have the capability to zoom in on a specific area?"

"This TV does everything, Aunt Kate." A note of pride touched his voice.

"Then zero in on the waiter's face."

In seconds, the face filled most of the screen. It was a slender, very fair, almost effeminate face surrounded by thick, light brown hair combed in a kind of Ken doll style. The head was slightly bent, so not all the features were clear, and thick Coke-bottle lens glasses with wide dark frames practically hid the eyes. A full mustache covered most of the upper lip.

"Don't you see it?" Kate asked.

"Oh, my!" Cami exclaimed. "His mustache is crooked."

"You're right," Durant and Gunnar said at the same time.

Debra looked more closely. "Yes! I knew there was something odd about him."

"I thought so, too, but I wasn't sure what," said Kate. "You can hardly see it because of the angle of his head."

Everyone was silent again for a few moments. Finally, Gunnar expressed the thought Cami knew was on all their minds. "So, what does this mean?"

"It means that waiter was there in disguise," Cami said. She could hardly process the thought. "But why?"

"I think the why is obvious, Cami," said Kate, her voice loaded with sympathy. "The question is *Who*?"

"Let's back it up some more," said Durant.

"You mean, find more shots of the waiter?" asked Gunnar.

"Yeah." Durant started at the beginning, then fast-forwarded to every scene with a waiter.

A few minutes later, the head table scene appeared again, and Durant stopped the DVD. He frowned deeply. "He wasn't there. Or at least, the cameraman didn't photograph him until the end."

"Durant, humor me and back it up once more," said Kate.

"How far?"

"To any scene with a waiter."

Durant obeyed. "There. How about this one?"

"Hmmm. Good. Back up to another waiter."

"What are you looking for, Kate?" asked Gunnar as Durant played the scene again.

"Maybe nothing. No, wait!" She pointed at the waiter now on the screen. "Look at his shirt."

Cami leaned forward. "What about it? It's white with a black jacket and bowtie."

"Go forward to the next waiter shot, Durant." When another waiter's image filled the screen and Durant stopped the action, Kate said, "What do you see now?"

"Same thing, Aunt Kate," said Debra. "What are you looking for?"

"Now go back to our boy at the head table."

"I'd hardly call him a boy," said Cami. "Not with those deep lines in his forehead and cheeks."

Again, the crooked-mustached waiter appeared on the screen.

"I see it, Kate," Cami said in awe. "His shirt is different from the others. It has pleats. And look at his jacket. The collar is much wider than the other waiters'."

"And that hair," said Debra. "That's gotta be a wig. The face is really pale, too, probably from light-colored makeup."

Cami looked at Durant. "Looks like the Lord answered your prayer," she said. "Now we need to call Detective Lopez. I'm sure he's already seen the film, and maybe he's already noticed the things we saw."

"Or maybe not, Mom," said Durant. "I'll call him right now."

"I'll do it," said Debra. "I don't know who that waiter is, but he's obviously the man who killed our father." As she reached for the phone, it rang.

After saying a few words to the caller, she handed it to Cami. "For you, Mom. Reverend Fitzgerald."

"I think I'll take it to another room," Cami said, taking the portable receiver. A few moments later she took a seat at the glass-topped table in the sunroom. She pushed aside the thought that this was the very table she had set so carefully to celebrate her and Braxton's anniversary a few days ago. Or was it eons?

"Hello, Reverend," she said.

"How are you, Dear, and your children?"

"You know the saying—'as well as can be expected.' Thank you so much for the lovely eulogy for Braxton."

"You're more than welcome. And you know you and the twins are in my prayers."

"Thank you. That helps a lot, and it's wonderful that my parents are here. I'm truly trying to trust the Lord."

"I have full confidence in His help for you." Reverend Fitzgerald paused. "I had a particular reason to call you. It could have waited, but I took this as an opportunity to go ahead and check on you."

"Yes?"

"Durant requested a video of the service, and I wanted you to know it's ready. You can pick it up any time, or I'll drop it by your house."

For a moment the thought of watching Braxton's funeral service gave Cami the chills.

But I don't have to watch it now, she thought. *And I would love a good excuse to get out of here for a few minutes.*

"You know," she told the minister, "I think I'll come and get it right now, if that's all right."

"Wonderful. Pop into my office, and I'll have it ready for you."

"Great. I have to go out and pick up a prescription anyway."

"Fine. I'll be waiting for you."

Cami dashed up the stairs to freshen her makeup and get her purse before returning the telephone to the den. She fumbled with the purse, dropping it to the carpet. Several items fell from the outside pocket, a few rolling under the bed. As Cami gathered them up, she saw that one was a long, thin piece of black ribbon spilling from a small plastic case.

The tape I found under a sofa cushion at Rosita's condo. That means there's more to hear. I can't do it. I can't listen to anymore. She was relieved to remember that she should take the tape to Detective Lopez. Maybe doing so would make up for not taking the others to him before listening to them.

Cami left the bedroom and went to her office, where she found a heavy, cream-colored envelope. She slipped the tape into it and put it in her purse. When she entered the den, Debra eyed Cami's purse and car keys.

"Mom, where are you going?"

Cami explained about the call from Reverend Fitzgerald and her intent to stop by the pharmacy on the way to the church. "Did you call Detective Lopez?" she asked Debra.

"Yes, he's coming over to discuss what we saw. You should be here, too." Debra's words held unmistakable reproach. "He said he'd be here within an hour."

"I'll be back by then," Cami assured Debra. "By the way, I found another tape. I'll drop it off at the police station. Maybe Detective Lopez will have time to look at it before coming here."

Chapter Eighty-Four

Kate noticed that Debra was a bit miffed about her mother's dashing out. "I think she really needed to get away for a little while," Kate said. "She won't be gone long. I'm sure she wants to be here when the detective arrives."

"That's right, Debra," said Gunnar, coming up behind Kate and placing his hands on her forearms.

Kate allowed herself to lean back toward him, hating to admit how comforted she felt by his strength. She looked toward Durant. "While we're waiting, would you humor me one more time?"

"Anything you want, Aunt Kate."

"Would you play that part with the disguised waiter again?"

"Again?"

Kate smiled and moved away from Gunnar. "You said 'anything.'"

Shaking his head, Durant complied. Soon, for what seemed like the umpteenth time, Kate was looking at the zoomed-in face of the waiter.

The telephone rang, and again Debra answered it.

Kate noticed how the young woman's face darkened soon after she greeted the caller.

"Mrs. Giovanni," she said stiffly. She paused while Terese said a few more words. "No. My mother isn't here. She's headed down to the church to pick up a video of Dad's funeral." … "Yes, I'll tell Mom you called." Debra hung up without saying goodbye.

"I could almost see icicles around your words," said Gunnar.

"I know. I was rude, wasn't I? I don't have anything against Mrs. Giovanni; she's a nice lady. She can't help it that she's married to a jerk and the mother of another one."

"What could she want with Mom?" asked Durant.

"Probably wants to say some words in defense of her little darling. Look. Let's forget about her and go back to the DVD."

"What are you looking for, Kate?" asked Gunnar as Durant paused the picture so that the waiter's face filled the TV screen.

"I'm not sure. I feel like we've missed something. If nothing else, we can be prepared to be explicit when we talk to Lopez. Debra, is there paper and a pen handy?"

"There's some right here." Debra opened the table that the phone rested on and got out a small pad of paper and a pen for Kate.

Kate sat down and, pen poised over paper, said, "Okay, what have we got so far?"

"The crooked mustache," said Debra. "And the wig."

"The thick glasses are probably a disguise, too," Gunnar put in.

Kate wrote the observations onto the small pad.

"The shirt and jacket are different from the other waiters," said Durant.

"Right," said Kate, still writing. "And don't forget the pale complexion." She stopped and looked at the screen.

Debra drew in a sharp breath.

"What is it?" Durant asked.

Debra simply stared at the image on the screen as if she'd never seen it before. "I know who it is," she said.

The room erupted in a chorus of "Who?" and "You know?" and "Tell us!"

Debra's eyes grew large and she brought both hands to her mouth, seeming unable to speak again.

"Debra, tell us," said Kate.

Debra brought her hands down and said in a hoarse whisper, "It's Frank."

Chapter Eighty-Five

ঔ৶

Lopez strode across the front walk of the Coronado Police Department, struck anew by the attractive low, white stucco building set in a lush lawn with palms and semitropical flora. It looked nothing like any other police station he'd ever seen.

At his personal mail cubby, he retrieved two manila envelopes and took them to his utilitarian office. The first was letter-sized and thick. The other was smaller and had the CPD logo and address in the left corner. It contained something small and hard. Apparently someone had dropped off the item at the desk and the receptionist had placed it in an envelope.

Lopez set down the Starbucks vanilla bean frappuccino he'd picked up on the way to the station, settled himself comfortably in a swivel chair, and looked at his watch. Not due at the Carrington home for another twenty-five minutes. Time to check these items out. He reached for the larger envelope addressed "For Detective Carlos Lopez ONLY" and pulled out a sheet of paper with an obviously hurriedly handwritten note from Lucas Richards, a private detective Lopez knew and highly respected.

Carlos, Sorry I missed you. Would prefer to give you enclosed photos in person. Current assignment in emergency mode. Couldn't wait for you to return. Ordinarily wouldn't break client confidentiality, but urgent you view pix ASAP. Weston has originals. Good luck. Lucas

Having heard Erika's conversation with Braxton on tape, Lopez wasn't amazed when he saw the photos of Braxton Carrington and Erika Weston in compromising circumstances. He looked at them one by one, glad that Lucas had meticulously noted the dates and locales. He leaned forward, elbows on the desk, hands together at his mouth, fingertips tapping. Clearly, Richards felt the Westons should be on the list of suspects in Carrington's murder. He was right. They already were.

Setting aside the other envelope for the moment, Lopez got out the small notepad he always carried and a legal-sized yellow pad. Across the top he'd written "BRAXTON CARRINGTON" along with the date, locale, and circumstances of Braxton's murder. Most of the rest of the page was divided into three columns, with a heading for each: Suspect, Possible Motive, Possible Alibi. He surveyed what he'd written so far after interviewing each subject, questioning dozens of other people, and searching various records.

A couple of lines below the murder suspect list, he had drawn a horizontal line. In the middle of the page he had written "DEBRA CARRINGTON," along with brief summaries of the circumstances of her attack on the beach and her attempted poisoning. So far this "list" contained only one name, Frank Giovanni.

Lopez thought of Terese Giovanni's suggestion that both Stan and Erika Weston could have motives for Braxton's murder as well as Debra's poisoning. How had she put it? That one of them could be so eaten up with anger and jealousy they went crazy and lashed out at anyone related to Braxton. It seemed a bit farfetched to Lopez, but he'd long ago learned that in real life nothing was too farfetched when it came to human reasoning.

That line of thought led him back to Ashley Carrington and the fact that she *hadn't* gone to the hospital when everyone learned that Debra's life was in danger. Or had she? He berated himself for not thinking to question her about that. He added her name to the list, now more and more convinced that the two incidents were linked.

This was giving him a headache. Lopez put the list aside and picked up the smaller envelope. On the back, the receptionist had written "From Cami Carrington." Puzzled, he tore open the flap. Inside was another envelope of heavy, cream-colored, high-quality paper. He opened it to find a tiny audio tape with the ribbon partially pulled out. Immediately, he punched in an inter-department number.

"Lopez here," he told the young woman who answered. "Get me a miniature tape recorder."

While he waited, he carefully rewound the ribbon, hoping it hadn't been ruined. Within a couple of minutes he was listening to a conversation between Braxton Carrington and his brother Victor in which Braxton refused to give Victor money to cover a gambling debt. He also heard Braxton's call to "Vicky Boy," nailing the gambler to the wall and saying he'd pay $20,000. He wondered if Victor knew about that second call. He stopped the tape and added a notation next to Victor's name on the suspect list: *Resentment against Braxton for not lending $.*

The next part had a few gaps where the ribbon was tweaked. It was clear enough, though, for Lopez to hear Braxton telling his visitor that he was going to replace his longtime administrative assistant Rosita DeLuca with pretty young Scarlett Starling. Again Lopez pressed "Stop". Beside Rosita's name he wrote, *Jealousy. About to be axed.* Before listening to more, he made stars beside the names of the Westons and Rosita. After musing a few seconds, he put two stars beside Ashley Carrington's name.

Chapter Eighty-Six

"Frank?" asked Durant, pointing to the screen. "How do you get Frank out of that?"

"Look." Debra's finger shook as she touched a tiny spot next to the waiter's mustache. "It's a little mole. I used to tease him about it. I told him it was wasted on a man, that I wanted it. He said it embarrassed him and he wished his mom had had a daughter to pass her mole on to."

"He's done a good bit of theater work, hasn't he?" asked Durant.

"Yes. His mother made him take acting lessons."

"Hmmpf. I can imagine Giovanni's reaction to that."

"He wasn't too happy, but Mrs. Giovanni insisted. I think it was one of those cases where parents relive their youth through their kids. I guess she did a bit of acting in college."

"Back to Frank," said Gunnar. "It sounds like it would be easy for him to impersonate a waiter. That's one more bit of evidence we can offer Lopez."

"We keep focusing on the waiter's face," said Kate. "Durant, zoom in on his hands. If he used light makeup, his hands would be darker than his face."

Now the thumb and wrist of the waiter's left hand, holding the champagne bottle, filled the screen. The skin on the hand was noticeably darker than that on the face.

"Well, that cinches it," said Durant.

Chapter Eighty-Seven

Cami's stops at the pharmacy and the police station took longer than she'd expected, but now she had her prescription and was pulling into a parking spot near the lovely old church where Carringtons had worshipped since the church was established in 1894. As she got out of her car, she took a moment to admire the weathered gray stone, the sharply pitched roof, and the stained-glass windows. At the black wrought-iron fence that ran beside the church, she entered a gate and took the stone pathway leading through an enchanting memorial garden and to the pastor's private entrance.

Suddenly Reverend Fitzgerald dashed out, straightening his clerical collar as he ran in her direction.

"Oh, there you are, Cami! I'm so sorry, but I've got to run down to the hospital. They called me about a bad accident and want me to come and talk with the family."

"Oh, I'm so sorry. I can come back later."

"No, no. You go on in. The door's open, and I left the DVD on my desk. My secretary's already gone home, so if you'll flip off the light in my office and turn the lock on the outside door as you leave, I'd appreciate it. And, oh yes, please lock the one that comes in from the other side. Now, I really do need to run."

Cami entered the pastor's roomy but simple office, seemingly the only lighted room in the building. She shivered. Strange how a house of God could feel so worshipful when filled with people and so creepy when you were alone.

The DVD lay on the desk, as promised. Cami leaned over to pick it up, wondering if she would ever watch it. As she was straightening, she heard a noise. She spun around and stopped short. There in the inside doorway that led to the church offices stood Terese Giovanni.

She held a gun.

Chapter Eighty-Eight

Lopez started the tape again. If he'd been surprised by the part about Rosita, he was utterly amazed by what he heard next. The segment began abruptly with Braxton speaking.

"Terese! What are you doing here? I was expecting Dom."

In an expressionless tone, Terese Giovanni said, "Dominic is sick. I heard your message commanding him to come see you and decided to come in his place."

"I see."

"No, you don't."

"Does Dom know you're here?"

"I didn't see any reason to bother him when I can handle this myself."

Lopez shivered at the eerie calmness in Terese's voice.

"How can you handle something when you don't know what it is?" Braxton asked her. *"My business is with your husband, Terese. You need to go back home. You don't seem well to me."*

"DON'T SAY THAT! DON'T EVER SAY THAT!"

Lopez nearly jumped out of his chair at the sudden screeching words.

"Here, let me help you sit down," said Braxton. *"Come on now. Calm yourself."*

"Calm myself? You're telling me to calm myself when you're trying to ruin me and my husband and my Frankie? Don't touch me. Get your hands off me!"

"Okay. Okay. But tell me what you're talking about."

"I'm talking about you planning to spread lies about Frankie. He's a good boy. All those things that happened in Washington—none of them were his fault." Braxton tried to interrupt, but Terese, her calm demeanor completely gone, kept raving. *"If you think I'm going to let you and that cheap daughter of yours ruin my Frankie—"*

"Watch what you say about my daughter."

"Like you're going to watch what you do to my son? He came home last night with a bruised and bloody face from where you attacked him."

"And I'd do it again."

"And you spewed out lies about him."

"I have proof of everything I said, and more."

Terese seemed not to hear Braxton's statement. *"And he told me how that Debra—"* Terese spat out the name like it was a nasty word. *"—believed your lies and how you're planning to print them in the* Coronado Eagle.*"*

"Terese. Calm down. I'm not going to pass Frank's escapades on to the Eagle. *Not unless he ignores my instructions to leave my daughter alone. Completely. If I ever hear of him coming near her, I'll call every newspaper in the state."*

Suddenly Terese began to sob uncontrollably.

"I think you should let me call Dominic."

Terese's sobbing stopped abruptly and the eerily calm tone returned. "Don't tell me what I should do. The doctors tell me that all the time. They don't know anything."

Several seconds of total silence followed, and when she spoke next, Terese sounded completely normal. "I'm leaving, but I won't rest until you and your precious daughter—have paid for what you've done."

Lopez didn't wait to hear anymore. Pulling out his car keys, he ran out of the station to his car and sped to the Carrington home.

Chapter Eighty-Nine

Kate picked up the remote and adjusted the zoomed-in picture so that the waiter's other hand, holding a flute half-filled with sparkling pink liquid, appeared.

Debra let out a scream. "Look! Look!" She scrambled to the screen and pointed to the waiter's finger. "Zoom it in more, Aunt Kate."

When Kate did so, a distinctive ring appeared. Several diamonds encircled a large black pearl.

"I've seen that ring before. I know I have," said Debra. She squeezed her eyes shut tight in concentration.

"Think, Debra," said Durant. "Where have you seen the ring?"

Debra's eyes snapped open, now filled with terror. "On the beach. The night I was attacked. All I've been able to remember is seeing a flash of something bright. It was the ring! Frank's mother wears one like that all the time. Terese Giovanni is the one who attacked me!"

Durant jumped up. "That means she's the one who killed Dad, too!"

"Mom!" Debra exclaimed. "I told Terese where Mom is!"

Chapter Ninety

"Terese! What are you doing here?"

Terese moved forward a little, and Cami noticed a strange light in her eyes not at all like the gentle expression she usually wore. The woman's lip curled, and she punched the gun forward.

"Well, if it isn't Mrs. Perfect. The perfect wife with the perfect husband and the perfect children and the perfect figure and face."

Terese stepped forward a little more.

"What are you talking about?" *Lord, help me!*

"You know perfectly well what I'm talking about—you with your little scheme to get your husband in as mayor of Coronado."

"Scheme? What scheme?"

Terese went on as though she hadn't heard the question, and Cami found herself sending up more prayers for help.

"You thought Braxton could beat out Dom, didn't you? Him with all his charm and connections. And that stuck-up daughter of yours. She thought she could toss my son aside like a piece of garbage."

Terese took another step forward. Cami backed into the desk.

Her heart pounding against her chest, Cami forced her voice to sound steady. "Calm down, Terese. You're distraught, I know. But we can talk about this."

The light in Terese's eyes had gone from strange to mad, even maniacal. "There's nothing to talk about, you holier-than-thou prude. I took care of your husband."

Terese killed Braxton? Horrified, Cami could hardly wrap her mind around the possibility. "But how? You weren't at the party."

"I was disguised as a waiter. I used to be quite the actress, you know. Anyway, twice I nearly got your daughter."

"You did that, too?" Was there no end to this woman's madness? "We thought it was Frank."

Her son's name seemed to distress Terese even more. "My Frankie. Everybody is always picking on my Frankie. Nobody will give him a chance. And now the police think he's the one who poisoned your perfect daughter, and he's gone." Her face crumpled. "Frankie is gone. I had to make him leave so they wouldn't arrest him. But he wouldn't tell me where he was going."

"Does he know what you did?"

The distress became indignation. "Certainly not. Even if I'd told him, he wouldn't believe me. Stop trying to distract me! Nothing you say will make me forget—it's your turn to die!"

Cami's mind scrambled for words. She'd never felt so frightened.

Keep her talking, Cami.

You have to help me!

Think of what you have in common.

Cami knew what she needed to say.

"Terese, I'm a mother too. I know I'd be distraught if my Durant were gone. Let me help you. Together you and I can find Frank and bring him back to you. We can do it, I know we can. Come on, let me help you."

For a moment Terese faltered and hope flickered in her eyes. Then, just as suddenly, the madness was back. "You help me? Why would you help me? They'd send me back to the crazy house and fill me up again with medicines I don't need." She waved the gun.

Keep her talking, Cami.

"How did you know I'd be here, Terese? I didn't tell anybody but my family where I was going."

"Maybe you shouldn't have told them. I called the house for you, and your fine Debra told me you were headed here." Terese's face darkened. "She was very rude to me."

"But how could you be sure I'd be here alone? Pastor Fitzgerald was supposed to meet me, but—"

"But he got called away to the hospital to pray with someone who'd had a bad accident."

"How did you kn—" Cami caught her breath. "You made the call!"

Terese let out an evil laugh. "Pretty clever, huh? And I knew the rest of the church staff was taking the afternoon off. And the door was even left unlocked for me."

"Yes, Terese, that was *really* clever of you, Cami said, hoping to placate the mad woman. "*Everyone* is going to say how clever you were." Feeling a burst of courage—and certain of its Source—Cami took a step toward Terese. "Please, let me help you."

"Don't come any closer." Terese steadied the gun. Her finger tightened on the trigger. Cami steeled herself for the shot.

"Mom! Stop!" Frank Giovanni's voice boomed out.

Terese spun around to face her son. The gun dropped from her hand. "Frankie! Frankie! You're here!"

A look of desolation and love crossed the young man's face as he took his mother into his arms. "I've been looking all over the island for you, Mom. Finally, I saw your car in front of the church." He stroked her hair and spoke gently, as though to a child. "You forgot your meds again, didn't you? Don't worry, though. I'll get them for you. I'll take care of you."

"Yes, yes." Terese seemed almost happy now. "My Frankie always takes care of me."

At that moment Detective Lopez, accompanied by three policemen, appeared at the door.

"Are you okay, Mrs. Carrington?"

A shaken Cami nodded her head.

Lopez, with his usual mix of compassion and law enforcement efficiency, now spoke to Frank. "I'm sorry. But I'm going to have to arrest your mother for the murder of Braxton Carrington and the attempted murders of his wife and daughter."

Thursday, August 21

Chapter Ninety-One

Kate's head rested just under Gunnar's chin as they stood in an embrace near the security checkpoint line at San Diego's Lindbergh Field airport. She had driven him there in Cami's car and stayed with him as long as possible. Now his plane would begin boarding in a few minutes.

"I should go," he said.

"Yes." She didn't move away, and he pulled her closer.

"You're flying to Oregon next week?"

"Yes."

They released each other and walked to the back of the security line, hand in hand.

"You know," he said, "strange as it may seem, I feel a certain relief that you know about Natalie. It's as if the Lord freed me when I told you. Will you pray for me, that I'll have the right words when I talk with her?"

Kate gave him a mischievous grin. "My main prayer is that when you get done Natalie will want another escort for the party."

"I hate leaving this way, Kate," Gunnar told her. "I came with such high hopes."

"My hopes were high, too," she said. They released hands, but she pulled him back and reached up to touch his face, stroking it so that her fingertips could memorize the feel. Then she stood on tiptoe and kissed him. "And they still are," she whispered. Without looking back, she hurried away before she begged him to stay.

***

Cami strolled with her children on the beach across the street from their home.

By unspoken consent, they stopped and faced the ocean, letting its ever-constant ebb and flow roll over their bare feet. Debra inhaled deeply and threw out her arms. "Oh, how I love this. The look. The sound. The feel. It's what I miss most when we're at Pepperdine."

Cami smiled at her precious daughter and said, "You've been like that since you were a toddler."

"Mom," said Durant, "are you sure you want us to go back to school Monday?"

"Definitely. You've only got two weeks left; then it will be time to get ready to go to Edinburgh. I'm sorry you had to drop your Israel trip, Durant, but I feel sure the Lord will give you another opportunity." She didn't add that maybe the Lord would also give Durant more opportunities in Edinburgh to lead Debra to Him.

Cami knew that a couple of days ago, Debra's memory of the night of her attack on this very beach had returned. She'd remembered calling out to God for help just before she lost consciousness. Kate had pointed out that He indeed helped her—twice bringing Durant to her aid in time to save her life. Still, the independent young woman resisted Him.

"Um, Mom." Durant stopped and gave Debra a pleading look.

"What is it?" Cami asked. "Is something wrong?"

Debra answered, "We've decided not to go to Edinburgh."

Cami looked down at water swirling over her toes for a few moments. She raised her head and looked from one twin to the other. "I've been expecting this," she said. "So I'm ready for you."

As one, the twins gave each other an "I don't know what she's talking about, do you?" look.

"This is something I want you to do," Cami went on. "It meant a lot to your father, and despite everything, I believe you both want to honor his memory. Please do this—go to Edinburgh, study hard, soak up the culture." She wrinkled her nose. "Just don't come back with a brrrrrogue."

When Durant started to protest, Cami shook her head. "Let me finish. I'll have my bad days, I know; but Mama and Daddy are going to stay for as long as I need them. You know what spiritual giants they are. With their help and, most of all, with the Lord's, I'll be okay."

Durant nodded, and Debra said, "Yes, Mom, I believe you will."

***

Cami had not told the twins or anyone else about the conversation she'd had with her parents earlier that morning. She was about to join them in the sunroom for breakfast when she heard her father say, "Too bad it came up right now, Lucinda, but it's a no-brainer. We will not leave our daughter alone at a time like this. She's never needed us more."

"Absolutely," Cami's mother replied with complete assurance. "I'm glad we can be here for her."

Cami entered the sunroom. "Too bad what came up right now, Daddy?"

Clearly startled by her untimely appearance, the Stewarts' faces took on looks of consternation.

"You two look like I caught you with your hands in the cookie jar," said Cami. "Too bad what came up right now?"

"Well," said her father. "We got a call a little while ago from a man who's leading a mission trip to Cabo San Lucas. That's at the southernmost tip of Baja California in Mexico, you know."

"I know." Cami suppressed a grin. She hadn't lived this close to Mexico for twenty-two years without knowing where Cabo San Lucas was. "Did he want your advice about something?"

"No," Cami's mother replied. "The man who's been in charge of a Southern Baptist mission down there has taken seriously ill, and they want Charles here to come down and run the mission—for several months. They didn't know our daughter was recently widowed and that we were planning to be here with you. Naturally, we said no."

Cami slipped into a chair across the table from them and looked from one to the other. What wonderful parents they were, and what outstanding examples they had set for her and her brothers. Her own spiritual shortcomings were no fault of theirs. She saw in their faces the longing they were trying so valiantly to hide.

"When do they want you?" she asked them.

"In about ten days," said Lucinda. "But we aren't going."

Cami knew what she must do. Forcing her voice not to quaver, she said, "You are going."

It wasn't easy, but at last she convinced her parents that she truly wanted them to go to Mexico. Now, if she could only convince herself.

Chapter Ninety-Two
Five Weeks Later

The two friends sipped mocha lattes at a small table near the luggage carousel at Lindbergh Field. Kate had just returned from teaching a month-long Political Science class at Portland University.

"I can't believe I was here only a few weeks ago," said Kate, taking in the scurrying passengers in the spacious airport. "What different circumstances."

"What do you hear from Gunnar?" asked Cami.

"He had a long talk with Natalie. Turns out she had no real interest in spiritual things after all."

"Surprise, surprise."

"Yeah, sure. Anyway, Natalie opted out of the anniversary party and on the next Monday asked for a transfer to a branch in Canada. She's already left Boston."

"And yet, you're not ready to go back?"

"Not for a while. I feel like I'm back to square one—needing time to think over my relationship with Gunnar."

"Have you forgiven him for the fling with Natalie?"

"That was the easier part. That happened before I met him. Besides, it was never a full-blown affair. The hard part is getting past his keeping it from me. Even worse, he deceived me about her being in Boston."

"But you will, Kate, get past it, I mean."

"Meantime," Kate said, becoming excited, "tomorrow you and I head out to the RV lot and pick up that motorhome before they think

I've changed my mind again and sell it to somebody else. Then it's you and me off on our adventure."

"You can't imagine how grateful I was when you called and asked me to join you for a few weeks, Kate. I knew it was the right thing to send the twins to Edinburgh and my folks to Mexico, but I truly didn't know how I was going to handle being alone in that big house."

"And I had begun to wonder why I thought I wanted to travel alone, so I'm excited to have company while the Lord helps me get my head on straight about Gunnar."

"And I'm trusting Him to help me get straight about a lot of things." Cami patted Kate's hand. "What a friend you are, Kate. A gift from God if ever there was one. But are you really *sure* you want me tagging along?"

Kate let out an exaggerated puff of exasperation. "Cami, I'm not only sure. I can hardly wait." With a twinkle, she went on, "It'll be like our days back at Compton College."

Kate stopped. She looked at Cami. Cami looked at Kate.

Cami had a mental image of the ultra-serious-minded student Kate had been. Kate could suddenly almost hear Cami's endless discussions about her beaus.

They burst out laughing and said together, "Let's hope not!"

Epilogue
Five Weeks Earlier

Coronado, Home of Victor and Ashley Carrington

"You really played me for a fool, didn't you, Ashley?" Victor Carrington, arms folded over his chest, leaned against the fireplace in the master bedroom. Coolly, steadily, he eyed his supposed wife. After his initial surprise, embarrassment, and anger upon learning about Ashley's deceit, the only emotion he now felt was a kind of disembodied pity for the woman cowering in a chair before him.

Ashley's dark head was bent, and she repeatedly wrung her perfectly manicured hands. When she looked up, the hazel eyes were swollen. Her question came out in a pleading whisper. "What do you plan to do, Victor?"

"That's the same question you asked my brother. My answer is the same as his: nothing."

"You mean you and I can—"

"You and I? Where do you get that, Ashley? There never was any you and I. Only two people living together."

Ashley rose and came to face him. "We can change that. I can get a divorce and we can get married legally."

"You'd like that, wouldn't you?"

"What do you mean? Sure, I'd like it."

"I bet you would. Do you think I don't know that from the moment you realized I was not much more than a puppet vice president in Carrington Investments, you wished it was Braxton you'd married instead of me? You were always jealous of Cami for being the president's wife. You always thought you were better suited for the position."

Ashley's chin came up, and Victor recognized some of the fire he was used to seeing in her. "Well, it's true." She moved closer, placed her hands on his chest and looked up at him. "Now that you're taking over as president, I can stand by your side and be a real asset—much more than Cami ever was for Braxton."

He shoved her back into the chair.

"It's no good, Ashley. We never had a real marriage—even if it had been legal. I don't see any future for us." He stopped for a moment and gazed at her dispassionately. "I have arranged to take a suite at the Del for this next week. When I return, I expect to find you and all your belongings gone."

To her credit, Ashley rose and left the room with dignity.

Watching her leave, Victor felt strangely elated. Yes, he regretted that his marriage had been nothing but a sham, and he truly grieved the death of his brother. But now, out from Braxton's shadow, he felt a sense of purpose that was new and invigorating. Though he was more in tune to day-to-day affairs of the company than Braxton had ever realized, he recognized that taking over Carrington Investments would be a major challenge. Some trepidation accompanied his excitement.

He smiled and thought of Cami Carrington. He knew that she would suggest that he turn to God for help.

Who knows? he thought. *Maybe I'll talk to Cami about that one of these days.*

***

Coronado Cays, Home of Dr. Stan Weston and wife Erika

When Erika Weston entered the master bedroom, her husband Stan, as Victor Carrington had done earlier, stood by a fireplace. Despite the warm August day, flames licked over the artificial logs. Erika watched Stan for a few moments, her eyes fixed on the letter-sized manila envelope he held. The dejection she saw in his bent head wrenched at her heart.

The past few days had been among some of the most difficult and eye-opening in her life. First there had been Stan learning about her affair with Braxton. Then came the shock of Braxton's death and Erika's certainty that Stan had killed him. The worst part, though, had been that day in the hospital parking lot when Stan called her a cheap hussy. It wasn't the first time she'd been called an unflattering name; her parents had done a good job of that. But somehow that day it hit home and ate at her until she could stand it no longer.

In her two years of marriage to Stan, Erika had felt a kind of affection for him but had looked elsewhere for real love and excitement. Now she saw all that as empty and shameful.

She crossed the thick carpet to her husband's side. Without touching him, she asked quietly, "What are you doing?"

Still staring into the fire, he held out the envelope. "I'm about to burn these."

"The photographs of me and—"

"Don't say his name! I never want to hear his name again."

"Neither do I," said Erika. "I wish I could wipe his name and face and everything about him from my memory—and not only because he rejected me in the end."

Stan didn't look away from the fire.

"I thought you killed him, you know," she said quietly.

Stan let out a mirthless chuckle. "And I thought you did."

"Stan, is there any hope for us? Can you ever forgive me for what I did?"

"I'm the one who needs forgiveness, Erika. I'm the one who thought I could buy the affections of a beautiful young woman and make her happy." He looked at her again. "But I want you to know that I truly loved you from the moment I saw you modeling that ridiculous orange outfit in the restaurant in Boston."

"Loved?"

"And I didn't want to lose you. I was *desperate* not to lose you. That's why I had the detective follow you and take these pictures. I don't know what I thought I'd do with them. But somehow, in my twisted thinking, I thought I could use them to bring you back to me." He opened the envelope, pulled out one photo, face down, and held it near the fire.

"Loved," Erika said again. "You *loved* me?"

"I still love you, Erika. Despite everything, I love you."

"Stan, I can't say I love you the way a wife should, but I do care for you, and I want more than anything for us to try again. If you say no, I'll leave quietly and go back to Boston."

"Do you mean that? You really want to try again, that is?"

"I mean it. I've never meant anything more."

Stan looked at her as if he were afraid to believe her words.

"Here," she said, taking the envelope from him. "Let me help you."

She tossed the envelope into the flames. He threw in the one photo he held. Together they watched them flare up, curl at the edges, and turn to ashes.

***

Coronado, Home of Dominic, Terese, and Frank Giovanni

Frank Giovanni, hands stuffed deep in his shorts pockets, gazed at the Monet lily-pad lithograph above the mantel-less fireplace. He remembered the day he had given it to his mother. He'd bought it during one of his many spur-of-the-moment trips, that one to Giverny, France, where Claude Monet painted the original. Terese's face had lit up when she saw it, and she'd immediately hung it in place of the iron scrollwork that had been there.

Frank heard his father enter the room, sink into a chair, and snap open the newspaper. Frank turned, hands still in pockets, to study Dominic's glowering face. Frank had always had a convoluted relationship with his parents. He loved his mother deeply, so deeply that many people considered him a "mama's boy." But his love was marred by pity for her bipolar condition and a lack of respect for Terese's weak character. On the other hand, he shared and even admired his father's ambitious nature and cold willingness to do whatever it took to obtain his goals.

After a few seconds, Dominic looked up. "Something on your mind, Frank?"

Well, yeah. My mom's in jail, and the man she killed was the father of a girl I had really started to like. That's all.

346

Frank kept these thoughts to himself and sat in the chair opposite Dominic. He leaned forward, his forearms resting on his knees. "What's going to happen to Mom?"

Frank was used to seeing cold expressions on his father's face, but not like this. The man's eyes were icy with disdain and something bordering on hatred for his own wife and the mother of his child. He shrugged. "She'll be tried for murder."

"And two counts of attempted murder," Frank added.

"And they'll find her innocent by reason of insanity."

"Insanity?"

"Yes. We've got a good lawyer. He'll convince the jury that Terese was temporarily insane because of not taking her meds."

"So, what will happen to her?"

"A few years in a hospital, with psychotherapy and physiotherapy and whatever other therapy they can throw at her. Then they'll declare her well—like they've done before—and let her out." Dominic's mouth turned down and his nostrils flared. He stood up and flung the newspaper to the floor. He began to pace back and forth before the fireplace.

"What is it?" asked Frank, sensing that something more than his mother's fate had angered Dominic.

Dominic kicked a hassock, sending it rolling across the room to crash into a wall. "Why did she have to do this *now*? I was going to have a hard enough time defeating Braxton Carrington in the election. Now, with a wife up for murder one and—" He gave Frank a meaningful look.

"—and certain unpleasant facts about your son possibly coming to light," Frank added, rising to face his father. "Between the two of us, Mom and I messed it up royally for you, didn't we, Dad?"

Dominic ran his fingers through the front of his hair. "I'm sorry. I didn't mean it that way."

"Sure you did. It's all about you, isn't it? It always has been."

"And you?" asked Dominic with a sneer. "You're altruism personified?"

Deflated, Frank sank back to the chair. "Hardly. You taught me well."

The room was silent for a few moments. "But I do love Mom," Frank continued, "and I plan to stand by her. But when this trial is over, I'm outta here." He rose again and strode toward the door. As he left the room, he heard his father mumbling, having apparently forgotten about him.

"Dan Clark will have a clear field now," Dominic muttered between clenched teeth. "After all my work, and Braxton's too, that colorless, personality-minus dud has beat us both out."

***

Somewhere in Mexico

Rosita Rivera munched on a shrimp taco hot from the fire of a street vendor's grill. Next to the taco stand was a kiosk crammed with newspapers, gossip sheets, and cheap novellas featuring lurid covers, mostly in Spanish. She pushed back her long, thick black hair, free from the bun she had worn at Carrington Investments for so many years, and eyed the newsstand's offerings until she found what she was looking for.

There it was. One copy of the *San Diego Union Tribune*. And only two days old. The headline seemed to scream aloud to her:

Opponent's wife murders Coronado billionaire Braxton Carrington.

Terese? Terese Giovanni killed him? Rosita could barely fathom the idea. She picked up the paper and gave the vendor a few pesos. Back at the taco stand, she settled herself on a nearby wooden stool. For several minutes she devoured the lead story, which continued to a double-page spread inside.

She separated the article from the rest of the paper, which she folded carefully and dropped on top of an overflowing trash barrel. She tucked the article into her oversized purse and disappeared into the crowded streets of the town.

Appendix

Dear Reader,

How we hope you enjoyed reading *Storm over Coronado* as much as we enjoyed writing it. We aimed at a story that would entertain while inspiring you to walk closer with our Lord.

In chapter fifty-four, Durant presented the "ABCs of Salvation" to his sister Debra. You'll find it below. Mostly, we have not quoted the verses indicated. One reason is that this form is great to paste in the front or back cover of your Bible. Another is that it's good to let the person you're sharing the Gospel with see the verses in their natural context.

Perhaps the Lord will allow you to lead someone to a saving knowledge of Jesus Christ by using this "plan." Perhaps you yourself will come to that wonderful knowledge. In either case, we'd love to hear about it.

God bless you every one!

Donna and Peggy

ABCs of God's Plan of Salvation

(All Scriptures are taken from the New King James Version
of the Holy Bible)

Acknowledge Sin.

- Romans 3:23 – <u>All</u> have sinned.
- Romans 6:23a – The wages of (payment for) sin is death.
- Psalm 32:5 – I <u>acknowledged</u> my sin to You,
  And my iniquity I have not hidden.

- Jeremiah 14:20 – "We <u>acknowledge</u>, O LORD, our wickedness...."

Believe Two Things.

1. <u>God loves you</u>.
   - John 3:16 – Put your own name into this verse.
   - Romans 6:23b – (See Romans 6:23a, above) "...but the <u>gift</u> of God is eternal life in Jesus Christ our Lord."

2. <u>Jesus can save you</u>."
   - John 14:6 – He is the only way to salvation.
   - Acts 16:31 – Anyone who believes on Christ will be saved.
   - John 1:12 – Whoever receives Christ as Savior becomes a child of God.

Call on Jesus in Repentance.

- Luke 13:3 – Repent or perish.
- Romans 10:13 – Whoever calls on Him is saved.

In Book Two of the PICS (Partners in Crime Solving) series, Kate and Cami head to Albuquerque, New Mexico, where murder, illegal imports, and kidnapping face them as the city plans for its annual Hot Air Balloon Festival. The book begins…

MURDER IN THE AIR

PROLOGUE

"*Any trouble with that shipment?" The caller, pressing a cell phone to one ear, clearly anticipated a positive report.*

"None at all," came the expected reply.

"What about the border crossing?"

"Clear sailing. Our Border Patrol man saw to that."

The caller let out a satisfied chuckle. "Should have, for what we pay him."

"There's just one thing."

Alertness snapped into the caller's voice. "What's that?"

"Somebody's got suspicious."

The caller let out a curse. "How'd that happen? You assured me everything was under control."

"It is—or will be soon."

"Who is it?"

"Nobody important. Just an old Indian church janitor here in Albuquerque. Guy named Kanuka."

"Take care of it."

"I'm on it."

"No traces."

"Never are."

"Make it look like an accident."

"Good as done."

Breinigsville, PA USA
10 September 2010
245126BV00001B/2/P